BEHIND THE SCREEN

BEHIND THE SCREEN

HACKING HOLLYWOOD

A Novel

Mark Stone

iUniverse, Inc.

New York Lincoln Shanghai

BEHIND THE SCREEN
HACKING HOLLYWOOD

Copyright © 2007 by Mark Stone

iUniverse books may be ordered through booksellers or by contacting:

iUniverse
2021 Pine Lake Road, Suite 100
Lincoln, NE 68512
www.iuniverse.com
1-800-Authors (1-800-288-4677)

Because of the dynamic nature of the Internet, any Web addresses or links contained in this book may have changed since publication and may no longer be valid.

This is a work of fiction. All of the characters, names, incidents, organizations, and dialogue in this novel are either the products of the author's imagination or are used fictitiously.

ISBN: 978-0-595-46166-0 (pbk)
ISBN: 978-0-595-70164-3 (cloth)
ISBN: 978-0-595-90467-9 (ebk)

Printed in the United States of America

In Memory of Betty and Dave

Acknowledgments

This novel was mostly written at Blenz Sandalwood Coffee Shop in Kelowna, BC. Many thanks to the wonderful staff there! Much appreciation to Ken and Sue Scott, Judy Beauregard, Patricia and Dena Fiddler, Natasha Bylo, Doug Striefler, Shirley Tam, JP Ouellett, Arlena de Bruin, Davina Huey, Mike Johnson, Tam Katzin, Shani Friedman, and Barry, Shirley and Archie Stone. Big thanks to Jennifer Fuller of Atomic55 for the great cover design.

A very special thank-you to my wife Reena for all of her love and support. She is the greatest source of inspiration for me and I couldn't have written this novel without her support and understanding. I cannot ever thank her enough.

PROLOGUE

───────▼───────

His hands fumbled about the buttons of her top. His tongue was in her ear now; he breathed heavily in hopes that his hot breath would melt her into submission. That point where the line between 'no' and 'yes' is crossed and there is no turning back.

Then again, what did he have to worry about? He was the hottest thing going. Who was this girl to say no to him? She was just like anyone else lately—unable to resist him. This should be easy.

This wasn't named Bad Boy Drive *for nothing, he thought. Nicholson, Beatty and Brando knew what they were talking about. The lights of Los Angeles were brighter than a sunny day in the snow, and appeared to be as clear as ever. The Capitol Records building stood out prominently in front of the downtown skyline. He had experienced this view from Mulholland Drive several times, but never in the company of such a hot woman.*

They had left the party arm in arm and seized a large blanket from the linen closet on the way out. He didn't even know who was throwing the party, and didn't really care. Right now all he cared about was getting it on with this sweet young thing who had been staring at him ever since he arrived at the house.

"I really don't think I can do this," she said, re-fastening a few buttons on her top so that her chest was no longer hanging out of it. "Don't get me wrong, I love being here with you, but I really want to talk a bit and get to know what you're really like!" She felt a few sharp blades of grass dig into her elbow as she rested her arms past the front of the blanket, admiring this unrivaled view of the city.

"I'm flattered, but seriously sweetie, look at this view. How often in life will you get the opportunity to be with a guy like me in a place like this?" He knew that those

words came across as incredibly arrogant, though it didn't stop him from unbuttoning the buttons on her top again, then deftly moving his hands between her legs.

She moaned and allowed his hand to slip between her skin and the soft fabric of her underwear. She couldn't stand it anymore. She was here, with him, *and he was right: How often would this opportunity present itself to a girl like her? May as well give in to the moment. And how could she turn down this guy who has the looks of a young Brad Pitt?*

He had heard that kind of moan before. To him it was an unmistakable signal that all systems were go. He smiled at her and went in for the kill.

CHAPTER 1

▼

The desert sun had a way of beating down on you with its powerful rays, holding on to you and never letting go. It is addictive. It is one of the main reasons why locals remain in Palm Springs, and why tourists keep coming back.

In the middle of December, it was shining brilliantly as Jonathan Davis arrived at work. John, thirty-four years old, is a recovering gambling addict. He has not gambled at all in over a year. His evenings as an overly active participant at the card tables of Morongo Casino in Cabazon are behind him. He is proud of himself, but is heavily in debt. He has somehow been able to conceal his past addiction from his colleagues at DesertFinancial.

As usual, John began his daily routine of checking the firewall and intrusion detection logs. If there were to be a cyber-attack from the outside world, the logs would be the best place to look.

"Ya know, I'm starting to wonder whether these logs are ever going to reveal anything fun!" John said.

"It's not really about *fun* though—this is the way it is. Welcome to the life of a security analyst," Dan pointed out.

Dan Thompson is John's supervisor. Dan was instrumental in hiring John, seeking him out from a job bulletin posting for Certified Information System Security Professionals. Both were certified CISSP, each having suffered through the six-hour certification examination. They often commiserated over the experience that never failed to leave the exam participant feeling like he or she were just run over by an eighteen-wheeler. With spiked tires.

"I know, I know. I was just hoping that there'd be more to it than just reading logs. Do you know how hard it is on the eyes?"

"That's why you're the one doing this shit. See these glasses? My eyes don't work the same as yours, Mr. Security Baby," Dan said rather sarcastically, making reference for the tenth time this week that John, at thirty-four, was the youngest in the security department.

The security department was made up of four people: John and Dan, the technical guys, along with two administrative staff, Jill and Marilyn. In the two months that John had been working there, John, Dan and Jill formed a pretty strong bond. Marilyn was simply biding her time until retirement and didn't socialize much.

John's two-month tenure of professional boredom ended abruptly with an email from Barbara Stevens.

From: Stevens, Barbara
To: Davis, John
Subject: confidential

Hey John,

I was wondering if I could meet with you sometime. There is a serious issue here that I hope you can help me with. I work in the insurance department on the 3rd floor, and I got your name from a co-worker. I trust what I tell you will be kept confidential.

Barb

John was ecstatic. After months of reading logs, it seemed like he was finally going to get the chance to do something *interesting*! Secretly, he wondered what this Barb looked like. Before he even had the chance to reply, a shadow appeared over his computer screen and there was a woman lurking over his shoulder.

"Are you John?" the woman said.

"That would be me. May I help you?" John replied.

"Yeah, I'm Barb, I just sent you an email."

"Wow, you're fast! This must be pretty important. How did you find me by the way? And how did you get into this area?" John asked. Non-IT staff was not supposed to have access to the Information Technology area.

"I have my ways. Let's just say I know a lot of people here in IT," Barb bragged.

"Well, we'll save that discussion for later, but what can I help you with? That email sounded pretty serious. Tell me all about your problems," John said, in his best Sigmund Freud imitation.

"Come with me," Barb blurted out quickly, as she dragged John by the arm and led him down the hall.

Dan looked at the two of them leaving the security area with a quizzical look. John couldn't help noting that Dan likely felt partially rejected, wondering why Barb didn't come to *him* first. Dan knew of Barb and her reputation, but never really had the chance to personally substantiate any of the rumors.

Barb led John to an empty meeting room. John sat down in one of the mega-comfy chairs and Barb quickly shut the door, then joined him across the meeting table.

John's adrenaline was surging through his body. Who is this woman and why is she so bold? The curiosity was killing him.

"So, you dragged me in here, it must be really important!" John started.

"It is. We're being spied on. Our manager's a bitch and hates us all," Barb snarled.

John was now noticing that Barb was actually an attractive woman, in a cougarish sort of way. He was trying to peg her age—probably about forty-two, he thought.

"Start from the beginning. Why do you say your manager is a bitch and what makes you think she is spying on you?" John asserted, in the most professional tone he could muster.

Barb explained how her manager, Paula, was an untrusting person who liked to micromanage every aspect of their department's work. Paula was under intense pressure from the department's VP to make sure things got done at any cost. This particular VP did not care about his employees. Barb, along with three of her friends that worked with her, were being scrutinized from Paula because, according to Barb, Paula was jealous that the *Four Musketeers* were prettier than she was.

"She's just a fat, jealous, micromanaging cow!" Barb exclaimed.

"You sure aren't one to mince words," John said.

"I call 'em as I see 'em. Anyway, John, the main thing I wanted to get out of this meeting is to find out if Paula has the ability, or even the authority, to go into our emails."

"Well, our information security policy states that a manager does not have the right to go into their employees email accounts without the consent of either Human Resources, or us in Information Security," John stated in his most professional security-sounding voice. "What makes you think she's read one of your emails?"

Barb paused briefly. Her eyes lingered around the room as if she was contemplating how to best answer the question. John looked her up and down.

"Tara sent me an email yesterday bitching about Paula's attitude lately, and how she was thinking of asking for a transfer out of the department. This morning Paula called me into her office and asked if I knew anything about Tara wanting to leave us. I found it way more than a coincidence."

"It certainly sounds fishy. I'm still not sure what I can do to help you from this point. I've told you what the rules are, and if in fact she read Tara's email then she would be in violation of our policy. I don't think we would be able to tell you whether she did or not though," John said, clearly feeling like the consummate professional now.

"I just wanted to make you aware of it. If there's anything you can do at all or anything you find out, please let me know, John," Barb said, again emphasizing John's name, in a very soft, feminine voice.

John assured Barb he would do so.

John returned to his desk. As soon as he got back to the security area, Dan was itching to find out what the meeting was all about. John gave Dan the recap and asked if this was a normal thing. Dan explained that Barb has somewhat of a reputation as being a troublemaker, but has also heard that Paula could not really be trusted. John wondered whether DesertFinancial was really no different than any other company in that there's always going to be issues like this. His first few months had him believe that maybe this job was the exception to the rule.

"So what should we do, Dan?"

"Let's go for a walk and we'll talk about it."

John and Dan went for a stroll down Tahquitz. Winter was only a week away, but the desert was in the middle of a warm spell. Contrary to what some believe, the Coachella Valley can get quite chilly in December and January. John recalls once in 1990 eating dinner at the Seven Lakes Country Club with his family around this same time of year, when several people jumped up and cheered at the sight of snowflakes. Many at the dining room that evening had never even seen snow before.

John grew up with snow though, as the first fifteen years of his life were spent in Winnipeg, Manitoba, Canada. Winnipeg was one of the coldest large cities (of 700,000+ population) in North America. Nice summers, but brutal winters. John will never miss the winters there, but in the summer when the desert is one hundred and ten degrees everyday he sometimes wishes he were back there.

"So is there anything we can do for Barb?" John asked.

"I think we're going to have to rely on our superior judgment here, John. With a situation like this, it doesn't hurt to take a look inside Paula's email and see if we find any evidence of her knowing. We can't do it without HR's permission though, so when we get back to work I'll call Laura and give her the lowdown. She's well aware of Paula's reputation."

John was somewhat taken aback by Dan's response. What about employee privacy? Aren't we supposed to be protecting it, and not violating it? He was excited about the opportunity to read someone's email but still felt rather uncomfortable.

"Cool. Working here has sure become interesting. I can't thank you enough for hiring me. Nice to finally have a manager that sees me as both an employee and a friend," John gushed slightly; worrying he came across as too touchy-feely for this man-to-man walk they were on.

"No problem, John. Don't get too far ahead of yourself though. Can't forget who's the boss ... ahahahaha."

Dan laughed his hearty laugh. There was seriousness to his tone, but enough of a friendly vibe that told John that Dan was a good guy. They continued to walk up Tahquitz to Highway 111 and then turned back.

John couldn't believe how Palm Springs had changed since moving here almost twenty years ago. Back in the 80's, the place seemed like more of a large town than an actual city. Sometime in the late 90's John could sense a shift in the area's overall essence. Many people are unaware that Palm Springs, along with the eight surrounding cities, is one of the fastest growing areas in the country. In each decade since the 80's, population has essentially doubled. Living in the Coachella Valley for some reason seemed more hip now than ever before. It was difficult to describe to an outsider, but many younger residents could discern the same thing. Bring on more *young* people, most thought.

Dan stopped at the corner store for some cigarettes and lit up. John had never smoked a day in his life and wondered what the deal was with smoking. Since starting with the company, he would joke with Dan about being a lifetime smoker, and Dan would just shrug it off.

As soon as they entered their area, Jill told them that Dan's presence was requested in Patrick's office—*stat*. Patrick was the *Grand Fromage* of IT, the Big Cheese, the Head Honcho, the *Boss*. It was a running joke that each time Patrick came looking for Dan, Dan would be off on a coffee or lunch break. John chuckled to himself—this never seems to get old.

Patrick Bowman was the one who ultimately hired John, in a twilight zone-like interview where Patrick did all the talking and John barely got to utter a single word. John was surprised when he got the job.

Dan didn't return until the end of the day so John would have to wait for his first attempt at espionage.

*   *   *   *

John got in bright and early the next day. Traffic was really light as many were taking time off for Christmas. This was his eighteenth Christmas in the desert, yet he still couldn't believe that green was so predominant here, as opposed to the white that blanketed most of the country. Somehow Palm Springs was able to maintain its lush green landscape year round, despite experiencing such low amounts of rainfall. John never quite understood that logic.

As soon as he sat down at his desk Dan filled him in on the update from Laura in HR. "Laura's given us the green light. Yee-hah. Time to do some diggin'. Seems that there have been several official complaints about Paula, and HR is concerned. Let's sit at my desk and we'll fire up her email."

John couldn't contain his excitement. He didn't know Paula, but the thought of being able to read someone else's email was pretty damn cool to him. Still, he was able to maintain his professionalism and was ready to partake. Dan fired up his Outlook and chose File, Open, Other … and typed in Paula's name. Exchange Administrators with special rights were able to open anyone's mailbox. John knew that this special 'Exchange Admins' group on the network was a very powerful thing: only he, Dan and Jill had that access. John felt a sense of power he hadn't experienced in some time. It didn't beat the thrill of pulling a full house from the river card, but it was pretty damn close.

"What do we got here, Johnny … do you see a smoking gun?" Dan asked.

John took control of the mouse and scrolled down the email messages in the Inbox folder and quickly glanced through all the subject headings. All business related, with nothing jumping out at him as being overly suspicious. He clicked beside the plus sign beside the Inbox to reveal several other folders, most notable of which was one titled "stuff". John opened the "stuff" folder, and then he and Dan looked through the subject headings. Most of these emails appeared to be from her husband, and as they glanced through the subjects, the titles became increasingly hostile. It was obvious that whatever was in those emails, it wasn't good. Paula's marriage was in trouble.

"I think we've seen enough," Dan said. "It's obvious she's having issues at home but there's nothing I can see that points to what we were looking for."

"Too bad," John replied with a bit of a laugh. He instantly regretted making light of things, but was relieved by Dan's friendly smile when his gaze met John's.

"What should we do now?" John wanted to know.

"Not really a whole hell of a lot we *can* do. Either Barb's just trying to cause more trouble or I dunno what the—really, we did our part so I'll just tell Laura in HR that we couldn't find anything."

"Alright. Sounds good, Dan. So quick question though: Do we tell Laura anything about what we saw, as in Paula's home life?" John wondered.

"We *could*, but there's really no point. Just leave it," Dan asserted.

John returned to his desk. The rest of the day couldn't really live up to the way it began. Lots of password resets, assigning network rights, recovering deleted files. Pretty routine stuff. His boredom was relieved just after three thirty when he received another email from Barb.

From: Stevens, Barb
To: Davis, John
Subject: Well ...?

Hey John,

What did ya find out? This is really important to us in our group. Tara is having a really hard time. She was crying earlier today and she is sure that Paula is up to something. Let me know if there's anything you came up with. Hey Paula: if you're reading this, STOP SNOOPING.

John quickly replied and told Barb that there was nothing they could find, and expressed his sympathy for Tara and that he wished he was able to help them.

*   *   *   *

The next day he returned to work and upon opening his Outlook, yet another new email from Barb:

From: Stevens, Barb
To: Davis, John
Subject: re: Well ...?

Thanks for your reply. Really sucks that you didn't find anything. Pardon my Bulgarian but Paula is a fucking bitch. Seriously John. I was wondering if we could chat a bit more about this.... What are you doing for coffee this afternoon?

John read and reread the email. He was curious. Instinctively he asked himself whether Barb was trying to get to 'know him better' or whether her motives were strictly professional. Plus, he would have to have a chat with her with regards to her use of language in a corporate email. It was also apparent that Barb didn't really care about being spied on if she's willing to email her suspicions to him. In his view, Barb was likely just grasping at straws with the spying thing; there was probably a much more logical explanation.

He looked over his shoulder to make sure nobody from his group could see his computer screen. He decided that she may in fact be slightly interested in him, but her intentions were likely a mix of personal and professional. Either way, he would suggest that they meet at the coffee shop across the street. In an attempt to not appear at all desperate, he waited an hour before sending the reply.

*   *   *   *

They both arrived at the coffee shop at the same time and each took a seat at an undersized table. John's heart was beating fast, and he was feeling inexplicably uncomfortable.

"So now that you have me outside of work, what's up? I can't imagine you being any more *frank* away from the building, but is there anything you haven't told me?" John asked.

"Nah, there's really nothing you don't know. I just thought we could chat. I think I could give you the whole story, from day one. At least you'll really know where we're coming from with Paula."

"So tell me about your group. There are four of you, right? I know there's you, Tara—"

"Andrea and Chloe. They're awesome!" Barb interrupted.

Barb told him all about their group and how Paula came to be jealous of them. John wanted to share what he knew about Paula's home life but swore to himself he would never, ever, in the course of his professional career, reveal anyone's personal secrets. He listened intently as Barb explained her group's work history. They eventually diverted their conversations towards movies, TV, music and ultimately, personal lives.

Barb revealed that she was divorced, and John shared his story about almost getting married but having his engagement break off at the last minute. He found Barb easy to talk to, but his instincts told him that there was something a little *off* about her.

John didn't get much time to reveal much about himself, other than a few subtle hints at the fact that he used to be a big-time poker player. Barb seemed to be too wrapped up in herself to allow him more than a few words in edgewise.

Half an hour had passed awful quickly. Employees at DesertFinancial were allowed two fifteen-minute coffee breaks, and an hour at lunch. John wondered whether Dan would be upset with his extra long coffee break. He also neglected to inform Dan whom he was meeting. Not that it was any of Dan's business, but for some reason he still felt guilty.

✳   ✳   ✳   ✳

John returned to his desk and tried to avoid eye contact with Dan. He sat there, reading his email, checking service requests, and all the while worrying about whether Dan would chew him out about the supersized coffee break. Nada.

Awesome, John thought, maybe he didn't notice.

Later that day before it was time to leave, John approached Jill and asked her about the unofficial word on coffee breaks there.

"So hey, Jeeeel, can I ask you somethin'? What's the deal with coffee breaks here? Does anybody care if you take a long break? Does Dan care?" John asked, referring to Jill as Jeeeel, stretching the 'ee' sound, mimicking the way their co-worker Marilyn pronounces Jill's name.

"Dan? We're talking about *our* Dan here, right? Are you kidding? Dan couldn't care less how long you take for your break. Have you ever timed some of *his* breaks? Better yet, have you ever timed the technical support group's breaks? Watch for them next time. You'd be amazed what people get away with here. Don't worry about it. As long as you get your work done Dan won't say anything. I think we're pretty good about it here in our group, but other departments definitely have their abusers," Jill explained.

"Whew, that's a relief and a half. I kind of thought that the support boys sure took their sweet time at coffee; maybe like they were in a group meeting or something. I dunno," John said, peering over Jill's cubicle wall to ensure nobody from the tech support group was within earshot.

"Group meeting, my ass. Hey, they get their work done, and they're all good guys, but c'mon ... it's pretty bad when the whole company can't reach anyone there during their extended coffee time. But what can you do, right?" Jill said, shrugging her shoulders.

John spent the next twenty minutes at Jill's desk getting more of the low-down on office politics. He really respected Jill; thought of her like a big sister. Jill was forty-six, and had been with the company for fifteen years. She knew the ins and outs of the corporate culture, and served as John's primary source of information about who's who and who does what, even who's doing what to whom. He enjoyed his late afternoon chats with Jill.

*   *   *   *

That evening, John thought about his coffee break with Barb. He was somewhat intrigued about her, but there was something just, well, 'off' about this woman. There was definitely a slight attraction there, but he wasn't completely feeling it. He tried to imagine what it would be like to sleep with her. He pretty much went through this process with all women that he found attractive. And what guy didn't? John figured. He thought she was probably wild as hell, perhaps an eight out of ten on his potential-sex-o-meter. Still, he was sure that after the eight-rating sex, there was the distinct possibility that she could rate a nine out of ten on his psycho-meter. He reminded himself that any woman that scores higher on his psycho-meter than she does on the potential-sex-o-meter is definitely not worth the trouble. He decided he would rely on this line of thinking in future dealings with her.

CHAPTER 2

▼

The next few weeks were rather uneventful as Christmas holidays really slowed things down. John's mother lived only a few miles away in Rancho Mirage so he was able to visit her frequently. Christmas was certainly no exception. He loved time with his mom; as an only child he always shared a special bond with her.

His parents divorced many years ago, when John was fifteen, and rarely talked. At the time John took it rather hard. He internalized the situation and went through several years of blaming himself for their divorce. Despite their efforts, John's parents were unable to convince him otherwise. It wasn't until he was eighteen, when he met Stacey—his girlfriend throughout most of his college years—that he was able to properly deal with and eventually get over his parents' divorce. Stacey was wise beyond her years and taught John a lot. He still missed her. He frequently thought of calling her but always chickened out. He has resigned himself to the fact that she will forever be the "one who got away."

✳   ✳   ✳   ✳

January. Start of a new year. John felt that this was going to be the *Year of the John*. He wasn't one for New Year's resolutions, but he wanted to resolve, to himself at least, that he was going to make this year something special. His career was finally kicking into gear, and although his social life wasn't quite what he was hoping for, he would make it a point to change that this year.

DesertFinancial had several remote offices in the area, and a few of them were making the switch to wireless networking. John was fascinated with wireless, and spent a lot of his spare time learning about how wireless works. He was no expert by any means, but tried to spend time with Lee Finch, a networking guru who knew everything about anything—even security issues. John wished he had *half* the knowledge Lee had.

It was a Thursday, which always meant the weekly technology round-up meetings. Until now, John had not yet been part of these, as Dan would normally attend on behalf of the Security department. This week's meeting was going to be focusing on the use of wireless at the Palm Desert location. Lee suggested that John attend.

John was hopeful about the meeting. Perhaps this would be a perfect opportunity for him to assert himself as a strong voice for the Security department. His hopes for professional fame were quickly dashed after attending the two hour marathon; complete with all the bickering, bitching, insipid commentary and everything else that seemed to be the norm any time you get multiple departments together, each with their own agenda. John didn't even get a chance to express his opinions. Patrick Bowman, the IT Director, ensured that he was *the* voice for IT and spoke on behalf of everyone, whether they liked it or not.

John was unhappy and disillusioned. He cornered Lee as they walked out of the meeting. "The hell was that all about? Please tell me all the meetings are not like this," John begged.

"Afraid so, my friend. It is what it is. No point trying to change it. I gave up on doing anything about it long ago. I come here, I do my job, I say my piece. I don't let it get to me and I don't stress over it. Come to my desk and we'll talk about our plan for the wireless stuff," Lee said, as he flashed his badge at the card reader outside the IT department door to allow them back into the area.

"I wish I had your resolve, Lee. You da man! Yeah, tell me your master plan for the wireless stuff, this should be good," John said.

John followed Lee to his desk. Lee had a plethora of wireless tools: hacking software, hardened Linux laptop, and multi-functional wireless card, everything one would need. Lee suggested that they go on a covert mission to the Palm Desert branch and see what they could find. Awesome, John thought! More covert ops! Security sure is the field to be in for IT. Fuck programming, man. Yeah, they make good money, but the fun is in security!

John was pumped.

Lee called Dan and the three of them made plans for a *war drive*. They'd rent a van and drive to the Palm Desert branch and do their thing. Everything was set for next week.

✳   ✳   ✳   ✳

War driving day was awesome. They started by calling the director of the Palm Desert branch and told her that they were going to be doing the operation at some time today. She would be the only one at the branch who knew it was going to happen. They headed to the van and brought all their sweet gear. Lee made a wireless antenna from a Pringles can; John figured that was probably their coolest accessory. Upon seeing the can, he got hungry and asked if they could make a coffee and donuts run. They stopped at Krispy Kreme, loaded up on coffee and donuts, and headed out.

Driving down Ramon road they passed by many businesses small and large. John and Lee watched intently as the different wireless networks popped up on the laptop screen. Dan drove the van, and was apparently unhappy that he was unable to partake in the wireless festivities. Lee sensed Dan's unhappiness and without prompting told Dan that he was volunteering to drive back to the office so Dan could have his fun, too. This seemed to placate Dan for the rest of the drive.

"Can you believe all the unsecured wireless networks we're seeing?" John asked incredulously. He had never been on a real war drive before, and had read that most wireless networks did not have encryption on, but seeing it for himself was a special experience.

"I would say at least eight out of ten are not encrypted. No surprise really. You know that when encryption is not on we can read the network traffic with these tools, right John?" Lee asked.

"Yeah I know! I was trying to download the tools for my own laptop last night but they're just not the same on Windows." John wished he were the Linux guru that Lee was, but he was grateful for all the things he was picking up from Lee.

"Don't get me started on Windows, man. Aren't you sick of my pro-Linux rants *yet*?" Lee asked.

"With anyone else—but you always seem to have something new to add each time. I'll say it again Leo, you are *da man*, yo!" John was fascinated with African American culture. This fascination was completely lost on Lee, who, according to John's assessment, was 'whiter than sour cream'.

Dan turned off Ramon and onto Bob Hope Drive. As they approached Gerald Ford Drive, Dan stopped the van. "There's a big office here, guys," Dan said. "Let me climb into the back and let's do a little experiment".

Netstumbler, the program that shows available wireless networks, showed a strong signal coming from the unencrypted network being broadcast out of the office building. The three security geeks looked at each other as Lee fired up Ethereal, a program that captures network traffic and can show the data payloads. Payloads are basically the meat and potatoes of the data, containing the relevant text, and in many cases, even passwords.

Dan spoke up first: "Okay guys, we're going to sniff the traffic for a few minutes and see what we see. I know the manager of this office and before you hit the button, Lee, I'm going to call him and tell him that we're doing a little experiment. We have to keep this legal."

Dan called the manager from his cell and got the go-ahead. "Go, boys!"

Within forty-five seconds, web requests for porn sites were popping up. Ten seconds after that, an email sent from one office employee to his girlfriend flashed across the laptop screen. They didn't even need to read the rest of the email; it started with "hey hun when I get home at lunch my hard cock will work your chocha so good ur gonna purrrrr...." The boys looked at each other in disbelief. "Who talks like this shit?" John asked, somewhat rhetorically. Laughter broke out. Dan closed Ethereal and put an end to their experiment. John was pissed off. He wanted more of this.

They continued their trek to their company's Palm Desert location. Their instructions were to pull as close to the branch without being noticed. Surprisingly, they were able to park about one hundred feet away for twenty minutes before being noticed, even with the Pringles can hanging out the van door. A branch employee approached the van and asked if he could help them with anything. They explained who they were and what they were doing there. Lee confirmed that they were able to capture enough of the encrypted data to attempt cracking the encryption key when they got back to the office. The only other wireless access point they found at the branch must have been a test unit, unencrypted, but no sensitive data was being broadcast. Their work was done.

John loved this. He was so excited about this job and what fun lay ahead. He was pumped. He resolved to do more research into wireless and anything else he could learn to try to catch up to Lee.

CHAPTER 3

▼

Seventeen-year-old Jennifer Billings was running home from school, rushing across the sand swept landscape that spread behind the community where she lived. A senior at Cathedral City High, Jennifer pretty much embodied the typical high school girl. She was fairly popular; she made good grades, and generally enjoyed attending school. Her boyfriend of two years had recently broken off their relationship when grade twelve began, and the sting of that long, hot evening in early September still haunted her.

Over the last few months Jennifer had been turning to MSN chats in order to boost her self-esteem. Chatting online was nothing out of the ordinary for her and all her friends. With the increasing use of webcams enhancing the MSN experience, she and her best friends were getting good mileage out of engaging in video chats with members of the opposite sex. Age was not a criteria they paid much attention to: many of their chat victims' ages were anywhere between fifteen and forty. Jennifer learned at an early age that men, both on and offline, rarely cared about how old a girl was before hitting on her.

She was twelve years old when her parents divorced. Her way of dealing with it was to actively seek out a new group of kids to hang out with. Her grade six friends no longer meant anything to her; it was all about that cool group of teenagers in grade nine and ten.

For three years between ages twelve and fifteen, Jennifer lead a very active social life. She rarely spent time at home, and partied far too much. Life with the wrong crowd consisted of drinking, occasional marijuana use, several shoplifting excursions, as well as the odd break and enter stunt.

Her life changed when a group of friends were killed in a car accident. An excessive amount of alcohol was consumed before getting behind the wheel. The loss of these friends had a profound effect on Jennifer. She swore she would never again be that reckless, and from then on resolved to live a cleaner lifestyle.

As soon as she got home she threw her knapsack on the kitchen table, grabbed a towel from the bathroom and wiped off the sweat/sand combination that accumulated on her face, and whipped out her cell phone to call her friend Cassie.

"Cass, is it time yet? Are you at home or are you still in the car with Assface?" Assface was the moniker that she and Cassie used for Cassie's stepbrother, Mike, who also happened to be in the same grade. Mike's behavior made himself worthy of being their arch nemesis. Making Mike's life in high school a living hell was one of Jen and Cassie's main goals for senior year.

"Yeah, Assface is still driving us home. We're stuck on Ramon, and there's some dumbfuck accident that we can see up ahead. But we should be home like soon, k? Don't log on without me okayee? I think today is a good time for one of our two-fer rooms."

Two-fers were when Jen and Cass would start a video chat together, then randomly invite people to join them. They would flirt like mad and drive the guys wild. They've been perfecting this art of teasing for a few months now, and they prided themselves on being pretty damn good at it. They knew that these guys were just pervs, and certainly not worthy of their time, but the thrill it provided, along with the boost to their fragile teen egos, was too great to give up on.

Jen logged on to MSN with her screen name, *Jennaybobennay*, and opened her male buddy list to see which of the guys were online and available to chat with. Initially nobody worthwhile was online, but within minutes, Shawn, a guy in her math class signed in, and Jen double-clicked on him to start up a chat:

Jennaybobennay:	*hey shawn, wutup?*
JBR_91:	*nada yo, u?*
Jennaybobennay:	*dick all. u gon watch the OC 2nite?*
JBR_91:	*fo shizzle. cant wait. summer summer summer … can you say wet dream?*
Jennaybobennay:	*stfu. jerk. I'm hotter than summer ya know …*
JBR_91:	*hmmm …*
Jennaybobennay:	*what? no comment?*

JBR_91:	*u kno I think ur kinda kewt and all. whaddya want me 2 say?*
Jennaybobennay:	*tell me u luv me. u know u do.*
JBR_91:	*ur such a teez tho jen. the guys talk about u being such a big cocktease. u do know that rite?*
Jennaybobennay:	*u said that last time but I don't know if I beleev u. whatevs.*

This was certainly not news to Jen; she knew that she was regarded as a *cocktease* at school. This was never the case when she was dating Brad, but ever since the big breakup her flirtatiousness with the boys at school was something she just couldn't bring herself to stop. She wasn't stupid—she understood how boys her age think—clearly anyone with a *dumbstick* could be turned on with the slightest flip of the hair, or showing of any skin whatsoever.

Jennifer strolled into the living room and turned on the TV. May as well watch some soaps while waiting for Cassie to call so they could start their fun. At the end of the first hour of soap opera indulgence, Jennifer couldn't help herself from falling into a deep sleep. She hadn't been sleeping well lately. In fact, ever since *parting ways* (Cassie's way of naming the breakup when discussing it, clearly to soften the blow) with Brad she found sleep was difficult to come by. Afternoon naps were quite common for her.

Her mom came home from work and called her name. It took a minute of poking and prodding for Jen to finally be brought out of her sweet slumber.

"Whaaa-aaat? Can't you see I'm trying to slee-eep?" Jen grumbled, wiping the accumulated bit of drool from the side of her mouth with the blanket.

"C'mon sleeping beauty, time to get up. It's almost dinner time—naps are good for you, but sometimes taking these long, deep sleeps in the afternoon aren't helping you when you try to go to bed at night. Get up! I'm making my special pizza tonight. Wanna help with the sauce?" Mom asked.

"Yeah, yeah, just let me wake up and I'll help soon."

Jennifer got up and went to her room. She quickly logged on to MSN to check if anyone cool was online. No luck. It'll have to wait until later, she thought. No big dealio.

Before joining her mom, she stopped by the bathroom and caught a look at herself in the mirror. *You look pretty good*, she told herself. She knew she had beautiful blue eyes, and her recent hair color job mixing some red and blonde into her light brown hair certainly enhanced her self-image. Although she didn't have the same size chest as many of her classmates, she was generally comfortable with her body. In spite of everything, she couldn't help but feeling self-conscious, more so than usual.

She reached beside the mirror, opened the medicine cabinet door and checked over the various bottles of medications that presented themselves before her. Her mother had *quite* the collection of antidepressants, she thought. Until this moment, Jennifer had resisted the urge to see how she herself would react to them. She ran her hands across the bottles, and settled upon the third one from the left. Prozac. Bingo! *How much can it hurt?* She asked herself. If anything, they would just keep her in a good mood all day.

She popped two into her hand, grabbed a cup of water and washed them down.

CHAPTER 4

▼

As John grew more comfortable with his authority and position within the company, he gained enough confidence to send out company-wide emails about new corporate security policies. Antivirus updates, new policies with respect to emails and web surfing, and various other security issues were communiqués that needed to be sent out to everyone. John told Dan that he felt confident enough in his communication skills to be the official spokesman for the security department. John was both thrilled and proud of himself to have attained this position with the company, especially after only being there for eight months now!

John noticed that with every new email sent, many witty replies would come back to him. Most of these email replies came from various women around the office. John loved the attention! He would always try to be as equally clever in his replies to their messages. Email was becoming a huge part of his day. Some nights he would even lose sleep thinking about all of the brilliant things he was going to say in his emails the next day.

The most prominent email banter was coming from Tara, Barb's friend, the one who feared that Paula was spying on her emails. John had seen Tara a few times, sometimes outside of work. He was excited that he was getting all this attention from her all of a sudden—albeit only from email. He found her incredibly attractive: 5'9 (tall, but perfect for John's height of 6'1), athletic yet not too skinny, medium-length light hair, perfectly small breasts and a 'killer booty'. John loved small breasts. When asked why, he could never really explain himself. He wished he knew. Most of his friends loved big chests on women, but John's dream girl was more like Gwen Stefani. Tara didn't look like Gwen Stefani, but she really 'did it' for him.

Their emails started out innocently, and really didn't progress towards anything *sexual*, but they did grow increasingly *personal*. They eventually shared a *lot* about each other. For about two weeks in May, John figured that two hours of each workday was devoted to his emails with Tara. They hadn't even met for coffee yet; it seemed like both of them were getting off on having their relationship based on email. One Friday, Tara revealed to John that she wasn't actually single, and was in fact living with someone! *Living with someone*!!! John was stunned and hurt.

From: Williams, Tara
To: Davis, John
Subject: confession

Ok John, I think it's time I confessed something to you. I've always enjoyed our emails. I look forward to them every day. Actually, I think we've progressed to the point of actually meeting for lunch or something, no? Have I been sending you the wrong signals though? I dunno. We've seen each other a few times like in the hallway, but other than email, do we really know each other? Am I rambling? Of course I am. Stop it, Tara. There I go talking to myself again. K, John, I'm going to come out with it, I'm living with someone. We've been seeing each other for 2 years now, and even though our relationship isn't exactly great right now, like, well, we're still together. I really want to continue this—whatever we have here John—so I thought I should tell you about Randy and I. Let's go for lunch on Monday and we'll talk about it, k? I hope I haven't been leading you on or anything. Don't be mad at me, k? Have a super weekend and we'll meet for lunch on Monday. How about we take a drive to Carl's Jr. on Date Palm? I haven't been there in months and I need my burger fix!

Hoping you're not mad at me …;)

Tarawara

John read, reread, and again reread the email. Could this be really happening? He thought that Tara was going to be 'The One'. *Okay John, you can handle this*, he told himself. He had been on a few dates lately, but nobody that really *did it* for him. John considered himself a picky guy. He loved the company of women, but when it came down to them being a potential for a relationship, he was super picky. He hated himself for being so hung up on looks, but he couldn't do anything about it. Tara had everything he wanted in a woman. Masturbating to her had now become a nightly ritual. Fuckitty fuck *fuck*! This was going to be a shitty weekend.

*   *   *   *

Saturday morning he woke in a pissy mood. He slowly got himself out of bed and pulled the blinds aside in order to look out the window. Despite the sun shining brightly, not a cloud in the sky, and Mt. Jacinto clearly visible in the distance, John couldn't get over Tara's email. Eventually he asked himself why it was getting to him so much. It's not as if he knew this girl that well. Why was he taking it so personally?

He decided it was a perfect day for one of his contemplative drives to LA; excursions that he took often, especially when he felt that he needed time to 'think life over' and just have some good private moments. He threw on a loose fitting pair of Bermuda shorts, a bright white Banana Republic Tee, and jumped in his car. It was only nine a.m. but the temperature was already ninety-three degrees and although he really loved the heat, today he really wasn't in the mood for it. He looked forward to getting out of town and enjoying some cooler weather.

As he started out and made his way to I-10 North towards LA, he flipped the radio to 97.7, deciding he needed some perky top 40 to brighten his mood. He still mourned the recent loss of Power 100.5, which in his mind was probably one of Southern California's hottest top forty stations, one that used to be on the cutting edge of great dance and R&B hits. He couldn't understand their recent switch to adult contemporary. Isn't there enough AC radio here in the desert already? Yuck. Oh well, what can ya do. As was always the case, he was looking forward to approaching the broadcast area of Power 106, LA's hottest hip-hop station.

Passing all the wildly turning windmills that lined the east side of I-10 as he drove out of the desert area, he chuckled to himself thinking how they resembled a field of orphaned airplane propellers on sticks. He was struck with an immediate mood-altering idea: Cabazon shopping detour! John fancied himself as somewhat of a metrosexual, a guy who liked to dress well, keep up on all the latest grooming products, and loved to shop—without being gay. He knew this was *so* against stereotype for an IT guy. He prided himself on this.

Cabazon proved to be a wonderful diversion. The thought of visiting Morongo didn't even enter into his mind, either; perhaps his recovery was going better than he even thought! He appreciated that the temperature there was only seventy-four, so he ended up staying a bit longer than planned. He purchased clothes at both the Banana Republic Factory store and the Oakley Vault store. He felt better already. John didn't consider himself a shopaholic, but couldn't deny the rush he felt when getting new clothes.

John maneuvered through the freeways of LA, stopping for a Fatburger, and promptly headed back towards the desert. John was able to settle in to his inner feelings and made his regular attempts at self-analysis. It really bothered him that Tara's email had such a profound effect on his psyche. "Is my self-esteem such that it would suffer from something as inconsequential as an email like I got yesterday?" he asked himself, aloud. He resolved to approach Tara with an open mind and an open heart on Monday. Perhaps instead of just trying so hard to be the boyfriend, maybe now he would just start with friendship and see where things went from there. John returned home feeling like the drive had served a useful purpose, and his mood was restored.

✳   ✳   ✳   ✳

Sitting at Carl's Junior on Monday with Tara, chomping on his double cheeseburger, John finally gave into his lustful thoughts. He was doing such a great job of suppressing them to this point. For a moment he completely tuned her out and thought of what a great time he would have fondling her breasts with his tongue. He got instantly hard, and stealthily moved the napkin across his lap to literally *hide the salami.* His eyes glanced across the restaurant, casually observing how the patrons seemed to be rushing through their meals, literally swallowing their food instead of chewing it. Doesn't anyone take the time to appreciate even fast food anymore?

"So why do you think he's cheating on you? Did he ever come out and say anything that would lead you to that conclusion?" John asked seriously, enjoying this recent turn of events.

"I just know it. Call it women's intuition, although I don't really believe in that shit. Outside of that, of course there's those telltale hang up calls in the middle of the night. I pick it up and the bitch just hangs up on me. I know it's some bimbo skank that he probably sees when he goes to the bar on his 'guys night out'. Why do men need those anyway?" Tara asked, stuffing five fries in her mouth at once.

"Why do women need *their* 'girls nights out'? Huh?" John bounced back.

"Stop answering my questions with other questions! You've done that three times so far today!" Tara practically shouted.

"Okay, I can't speak for all men, because I'm not really the *guys night out* type, but I know that lots of guys were just brought up that way. They feel like it's their *right* as a heterosexual male. Go out, have some beers, eat like pigs, and look at women—"

"Like pigs," Tara interrupted.

"Hey, not all men are pigs. Some of us are really nice guys. Hint hint, wink wink, nudge nudge."

Tara touched John on the knee. This was the first time she had actually touched him. He loved the rush it gave him, even though it was pretty inconsequential. He just smiled at her and she smiled back.

They continued their discussion about whether her boyfriend could be cheating on her. John offered as much advice and sympathy as he could muster without trying too hard to think about what it would be like to sleep with her.

Tara was tired of discussing her relationship, and quickly changed the subject. "So anyway, enough about me and my shit. What about you? You've never told me about your gambling days. You brought it up in an email once and have never really talked about it since. How did you get hooked? Or do you not want to talk about it?"

John shifted uncomfortably in his seat. He really *didn't* want to talk about it, but he figured he might as well tell her about how it all started.

✳   ✳   ✳   ✳

They were all in the front row of the synagogue waiting for Ian Golden to recite his maftir, *the large torah portion that 13-year-old Jewish boys spent a year in class memorizing before their big day. Ian's Bar Mitzvah was as big as they come; the synagogue was beyond capacity and the big party planned for the country club that night was to be one of the hottest social events for anyone lucky enough to be invited.*

"So how many times do you think he's gonna screw up?" John's best buddy David asked him.

"I don't know. His voice is cracking so much and he's sweating like a pig. I kinda feel bad for him. He's been nervous about it forever. Yesterday in math class he couldn't stop kvetching about being up there in front of everyone," John said.

David turned to John and whoever else was listening and spoke loud enough for his friends to hear, but quiet enough as to not attract the attention of the Rabbi or anyone else on the bima: *"I say we all bet on how many times Ian screws up. We all put in a buck and whoever is closest, takes the pot. Who's in?"*

John looked up at Ian, and at all the other synagogue heavies who were up on the bima with him. Although John and his family were not exactly religious Jews, something about making bets in shul *did not feel right. Plus, John knew that it was his turn to be up there in five weeks, and he was incredibly nervous. How would he feel if his buddies were to bet on him screwing up? Regardless, John couldn't help himself from piping up. "Okay, I'm in, what the hell. C'mon everyone, let's do it. Quick. Before the Rabbi gets us in trouble!"*

Six guys were in. John guessed it right on and collected the six dollars at the huge Bar Mitzvah bash that night.

For the next five years, John, Ian, and David regularly took turns playing host to weekly card nights. Poker, Guts, In-between, Chase the Ace, and other fun games were in order, and often coupled with way too much pizza and Coke. The games increased in popularity with the other boys at school, and along with that popularity came a proliferation of cash required to join in.

*   *   *   *

"I didn't know you were Jewish. So is it true you can't eat bacon or pork, or eat cheeseburgers? What am I saying—you just finished a cheeseburger. What's up with that? What kind of Jew are you, anyway?" Tara asked.

"One who doesn't exactly follow the dietary laws? I wish I could. My family never really kept kosher, although we did go to synagogue often. Once my parents divorced though, I became somewhat disillusioned by religion. Don't get me wrong, I'm a proud Jew, but I just don't practice the rules that often. You'd be surprised how many bad Jews like myself there are. Pretty sad, but that's the way it is. One day soon we can have the *religion* talk," John said, glancing at his watch, "but right now we gotta get back to work." He planted a huge frown on his face to signify how upset he was that their lunch was over.

They agreed that they would keep their friendship as is, and would make it a habit to go for lunch once a week. John was pretty satisfied with how this turned out.

*   *   *   *

Work was getting more and more lively and John found that Dan, and even Patrick Bowman, the big cheese of IT, were trusting him more and more with additional responsibilities.

It was almost the end of June, summer was here, temperatures were scorching, and staff at DesertFinancial were preparing for summer holidays. John really didn't have any plans to take any holidays until the fall, so he was looking forward to a summer filled with time spent on research and development projects to keep him busy. The day before Dan was to take three weeks of holidays, he approached John and asked him if he was interested in taking any training over the summer.

"Johnny Boy, looking forward to being the main man in the security department while I'm away? I'll be out of town but I'll always be reachable on my cell. Summer is pretty quiet around here, so I don't anticipate any big fires for you to put out or anything. What do you think of signing up for some training? SANS is offering some awesome courses in Denver in August, maybe you should look into it. I think it would do you some good to get your intrusion detection skills up," Dan said.

"I'd love to … what's the process to get approved? Is it too late now? I know you're leaving tomorrow!" John wondered.

"Nahh, I'll sign off on my part right away. If you find something you're interested in I would fill in the training requisition form and just get Patrick to approve it. Pretty simple. We're pretty progressive when it comes to training our IT staff. One thing though: once you've taken some training we've paid good money for, you can't quit for a while. Otherwise they'll make ya pay back the cost of the training. Plus if you quit, I'll kill ya myself. Hahahahahaha." Dan laughed his hearty laugh, as only Dan could. His laugh could be heard from miles away.

"Understood. I'd love to take an intrusion detection course. Hopefully it's available and Patrick will approve it. It'll be fun I think. Though I've heard those courses are pretty brutal. My buddy took one last year and told me it was like rewriting that damn CISSP exam all over again!"

Dan found the training requisition form and signed his part. John found the course he wanted, found out it was available then filled out all the information. Patrick approved it the next week. He was all set to go to Denver in late August. John was looking forward to the course. Even more, he was looking forward to getting away; it seemed like he hadn't really been out of Southern California since George Bush Sr. was in office.

CHAPTER 5

▼

John found Denver to be an amazing place. He had never been there, and was intrigued with getting to know the city. He arrived a day early so he could spend the day exploring.

He spent a lot of time walking around and seeing as much as he could see. He couldn't believe how vibrant downtown was. 16th street just seemed to go on forever with great shops, restaurants, and people to watch. This sure was a change from downtown Palm Springs, which was extremely tame in comparison. He instantly took a huge liking to downtown Denver, and placed it on the top of his *best downtowns in America* list. San Diego and Minneapolis had now been displaced.

The SANS course was as hard on the brain as he anticipated. Monday to Saturday, six days, full throttle learning time. Material was presented at break-neck speeds, and one had to be both extremely alert and overly caffeinated in order to keep up. He loved absorbing all this information though, and couldn't wait to put a lot of this newly learned material to use when he returned to work.

After Friday's grueling session, he returned to his hotel to take a nap; he would need the renewed sense of energy to hit the bar with two friends he had met in his class. He looked forward to getting out and having some male-bonding time. John had a few male friends, but really considered himself more like the kind of guy who got along better with women.

They met in the hotel lobby and planned their evening. Dale and Steve were network engineers from Atlanta and it was apparent to John that they were ready to really tie one on tonight. John enjoyed a good beer or two when he went out, but he didn't consider himself to be much of a drinker.

"Ready to go party hard, boys? That course required more brain cells than I've had to use in years. Man that shit is rough. I plan on depleting a few hundred of them there brain cells tonight I tell ya!" Steve said, in his infectious Georgia accent.

"Fuckin A brother. Fuckin B, C and D too, man," Dale added.

John enjoyed the camaraderie, but as the evening went on the Atlanta boys were out-drinking him three to one. They were hanging out at an outdoor bar situated right next to a Cheesecake Factory, which happened to be one of John's favorite restaurants. This bar almost seemed as if it was set up at the last minute—it was certainly a summer thing, very bare-bones, but John could easily see this type of setup working well year-round back in Palm Springs.

The clientele at the outdoor bar was primarily college students. John headed to the bartender and ordered his third beer. This was rare for him; drinking more than two drinks at one outing was almost unheard of. As he approached Dale and Steve, he noticed that they were chatting up two beautiful college girls—a brunette and a redhead.

"Johnnay, Johnnay, get yo ass over here," Steve called out. "This here's Sherry and her friend Brittany. Guys, this is our buddy John from Palm Springs."

"Pleasure to meet you," John said, somewhat sheepishly, as he pegged these girls at about nineteen, probably first year college students, likely sorority sisters, and *definitely* way out of his league. "So do you guys go to University here?" John asked. *Whoa, good pick-up line, John*, his inner voice said.

"How'd ya guess? Yeah, we go to University of Colorado. We're both in second year of Management. The party life is just awesome at UC!" the redhead, Brittany, said.

"What's the University life like these days? Gotta say it's been awhile...." John stopped himself from both aging and embarrassing himself with his *I remember back in my university days* speech.

"Awesome, totally awesome. The atmosphere is fantastic. We love everything about life right now. We work hard, study hard all week, then party twice as hard on the weekend. What can be better?" Sherry—the brunette—shouted, as the music seemed to be getting louder.

The night progressed with Steve, Dale, Sherry and Brittany drinking pretty heavily. John kept ordering diet Cokes at the bar, but lied and told everyone there was Rye in the Cokes. John wasn't unaware of the numbers game here: three guys and two girls. John tried to keep an intellectual conversation going with Sherry, who seemed to share his passion for foreign films. Steve and Dale were apparently both vying for the attention of Brittany. This suited John just fine.

Two a.m. came pretty quick, and the bouncers were quick to force everyone out.

Sherry had stopped drinking by one a.m., but Brittany kept going. John and Sherry were the only ones slightly sober. "You guys are like total party poopers," Brittany shouted. "I'mma gon' join these guys in their hotel room for some drinkin' games!"

Sherry called Brittany over and the two of them huddled together for five minutes, seemingly working out their plans for the rest of the night. The three guys waited patiently, like dogs waiting for a treat from their owners. Sherry re-joined John and asked him if he wanted to still hang out. "No shit," John thought to himself, and quickly agreed. Brittany caught up with Dale and Steve, as the five of them walked back to the nearby hotel.

✳   ✳   ✳   ✳

John was on the tenth floor, Steve and Dale on the fifteenth. When the elevator opened up on John's floor, the door opened and Sherry and Brittany shared a look. The boys looked at each other in eager anticipation of what was to come. John was pretty happy he had the numbers game in his favor. He had no desire to be a part of a threesome, especially one that was male-dominated. *Yuck*, he shuddered at the thought. *Have fun, boys*, he thought to himself, if in fact that was the way things were going to go for them.

Sure enough, as John exited the elevator Sherry was the only one who followed. The elevator closed, leaving John and Sherry all alone in the hallway. John walked silently towards his room in the well-lit hallway and noticed Sherry right beside him. He fumbled for the key and opened the door.

"So what do you wanna do?" John asked stupidly as they entered his room.

"Uhh, gee, I don't know. What do you think, handsome?" Sherry asked, seductively moving her face within two inches of his. At six foot one, thin, with short, dark hair that was always kept very well groomed, John knew he was a decent looking guy. His recent dry spell with women, however, was taking its toll on his ego.

Sherry put her arms around his neck and started kissing him. John was shocked, and somewhat taken aback, but his libido took over and he eagerly responded. Their lips parted and his tongue found hers, and the tongue dance continued for several minutes. The taste of alcohol was prominent in Sherry's mouth. Normally, this would bother John but he was so turned on that he let it pass. He realized that they had been standing by the door in their embrace for far too long. He grabbed her hand and led her to the bed. Sherry is so *young*, John thought. He couldn't believe his luck; here he was getting it on with a college chick! They fell on top of each other and continued kissing.

Kissing turned John on immensely. There was something so sensual about it—to him it almost beat the act of taking it all the way. They began letting their hands roam around each other's bodies. Clothes were still on but John was unsure how to proceed. His recent lack of sexual experience rendered him uncharacteristically apprehensive.

Just as he had maneuvered his right hand under her bra, there was a knock at the door. Fuck! John cursed to himself. He jumped up, adjusted himself, and answered the door. To his amazement, there stood Brittany. "What are you doing here? Are you okay, Brittany? How did you find my room?" he asked, very surprised to see her standing in his doorway.

"I knew you were on the tenth floor, so I've been knocking on doors. I've only had to wake three people—your door was the fourth one I tried. So, umm, can I come in or what?" Brittany asked, appearing flustered.

"Please do. So is everything okay?" John was concerned.

Brittany came in and sat on the bed beside Sherry. John joined them. Brittany explained that she joined Steve and Dale in their room and continued drinking, playing various drinking games. Things were going well until Dale decided to change the rules of the game so that sex became a prominent factor. Although clearly inebriated, Brittany argued that she really had no intention of anything happening sexually between the three of them.

Sherry stood up from the bed and fiddled with her bra strap. "What did you expect, Britt Britt?" Sherry asked incredulously. "They *so* looked like pervs to me … I think if I wasn't drinking as much as I had, I prolly wouldn't let you go with them. Sorry Britt."

"It's okay, Sher. Dale was just being really creepy. He was touching me all over and I just left before it got out of hand. I wasn't raped or anything, it wasn't like that, but I didn't want to stick around long enough to see what they had in mind!"

John felt tinges of both guilt and responsibility. "Yeah, Britt, I'm sorry too. I don't really know those guys well but I'm sorry it happened to you. No woman should be put in that awkward position." John meant it. He was speaking out of pure kindness; his libido was obviously taking a nap. He told them about how he met Steve and Dale and how he really wasn't quite sure about them either.

"You're so sweet!" both girls gushed in stereo. John's ego surely wasn't suffering tonight, boy.

Brittany turned towards John and kissed him on the cheek. John smiled at her. Brittany looked into his eyes and gave him this odd, doe-eyed, you're-my-hero kind of look. John just stared at her. Brittany kissed him on the lips. John was in so much shock—the fact that Sherry was right beside them just didn't register. He instinctively reacted to Brittany's kiss and they began kissing passionately.

"Hey, no fair," Sherry grunted, "He was mine first. You interrupted *us*!"

Sherry grabbed John towards her, but John's limbs were currently entwined with Brittany, thus creating the result of John ending up on top of them both. He couldn't help but feeling like Leonardo DiCaprio in Woody Allen's film *Celebrity*, in which Leo enters into a threesome with two young starlets.

The three of them continued kissing and touching for what seemed like forever. John had never felt so *alive*.

Sherry interrupted the proceedings. "So, okay guys, are we going to get this going or what? We're all here, we're all adults, we've come this far, let's get down to business!" Sherry removed her top and bra with such abandon it almost made John's head spin.

For reasons absolutely unknown to him at the time, and forever more, John stopped Brittany from taking Sherry's cue and following suit.

"Guys, seriously, I don't think we should do this. You've both been drinking and as much as I love this, and as turned on as I am," he jutted out his pelvis for effect, "I don't think this is right."

"Are you fucking kidding us, John? The fuck is wrong with you, *boy*?" Brittany exclaimed, still spread out in a provocative position on his bed.

"No, I'm not kidding. You guys have been drinking and your judgments are probably somewhat impaired. I hate to sound like such an asshole, or square, but I always hoped my first threesome would be with all parties being *sober*."

Sherry came to John's rescue. "Britt, Britt, Britt ... I didn't even drink as much as you did and even *I* still feel a buzz. Maybe John's right. I totally would have gone along, but think about it—how would we feel about it tomorrow? I dunno. I actually think this guy is a gem. How many dudes our age would step up like that? Fuckin' no one. Something to be said for older men."

"Okay, okay," Britt acquiesced, "I guess you're like, kinda right. I'm just horny as all hell right now."

"You can always just masturbate each other and I could watch," John joked to lighten the mood, and it was clear he was joking when he said it.

"Ha fucking ha," Sherry replied.

The three of them laughed together. They hugged. They exchanged email addresses and said goodnight.

As soon as they left, John went over everything that happened this glorious night. John wasn't sure whether he should have stopped it or not. He clearly blew what probably amounted to his one and only chance at a threesome in this lifetime. Still, he felt that it was the right thing to do. Plus, how many guys got to kiss two college girls at the same time in their hotel bed? For some reason, he felt more on top of the world. Sleep came eventually, but took its time, as he was way too excited. He was *da man*, no doubt about it.

CHAPTER 6

▼

John returned from Denver with his head filled with much more than he bargained for. He didn't expect to learn so much about intrusion detection, and certainly didn't expect to have an almost-threesome. He was smiling from ear to ear
as he entered the security area. He went right to Dan's cubicle and dropped all
the learning materials on his desk. There was a huge thud that resonated throughout the whole IT area, turning several heads.

"What the hell did you learn there, cowboy?" Dan asked, eyes popping out of
his head looking at all the books.

"Too much for any one individual to handle in six days, I tell ya!" John
responded. *You don't know the half of it,* he thought to himself.

"We should go for coffee and you can tell me all about it," Dan suggested.

"Sure, sounds like a plan, Dan the Man."

They took their normal walk down Tahquitz. They often argued about the
pronunciation of the street name. Dan insisted that the real pronunciation is
Tah-Kwish and John would counter, pointing out that while that pronunciation
is correct, everyone just calls it *Tah-Kwitz*, both locals and tourists alike. John
told Dan everything he learned at the course. He left out all the
still-fresh-in-his-mind fascinating details about Sherry and Brittany. He wasn't
sure if he should share that experience with his boss, even though he truly considered Dan more like a friend as time went on. They planned on putting in a better
intrusion detection system as soon as possible, and decided that the more immediate need was for an email and web monitoring solution.

*   *   *   *

John spent the next few months working on implementing the new projects he had been planning with Dan. Patrick Bowman, IT's big cheese, was uncharacteristically optimistic of these new implementations and provided his seal of approval for a practically carte-blanche budget. John felt incredibly free to work however he pleased, and did not face the typical obstacles that many IT workers faced when researching and implementing new projects. Thankfully, Dan was fully supportive of John's efforts and pretty much allowed him the time and freedom to ensure things were researched properly.

John worked closely with Lee on the intrusion detection project. Despite having an infinite amount more knowledge of network packets after taking the course in Denver, John still lacked the overall genius embodied by Lee's techie brain. At least now he was able to speak to Lee more like a peer instead of just a wannabe. Between the two of them they were able to quickly put in place a low cost solution that worked rather well. In time they would be able to trash their current commercial software implementation and save the company thousands per month.

The project was a full three weeks ahead of schedule. This impressed John tremendously. He would now have more time to devote to the web and email-monitoring component of the project. To celebrate, he thought he would devote some time to catch up with Tara. Their weekly lunches hadn't maintained their regularity due to the both of them being really busy with work.

From: Davis, John
To: Williams, Tara
Subject: Hey you

Tara! Whatup chickiepoo? When was the last time we talked? Been far too long. Seriously. So are things any better with the bf? Still thinking of kicking him to the curb (God I hate that expression—please forgive me). Are you sick of all these questions? So anyway, I was shopping last night at the Palm Desert mall and on my way back home I stopped by the Blockbuster across there and rented a movie called The Devil's Backbone. It's a Spanish horror flick ... awesome stuff man. You gotsta see it, if you haven't already. Let me know if you have. So what do you think of going for a walk tonight? Let me know!

Write back—SOON!

Johnny D.

Tara was quick to reply:

From: Williams, Tara
To: Davis, John
Subject: re: Hey you

John!

Man—it's totally been too long. I think we're due for a walk, and soon, but I'm afraid the bf and I have scheduled some time to talk. As I write that I realize how odd that sounds. Scheduling time to talk. But he's like that. He's just such a GUY. It's really like I gotta schedule talk time. Should be fun ... hahaha. I'm convinced that I'm going to get it out of him tonight, if there's anything to get him to admit to. I just wish he'd admit it already. It's like our relationship can't go any further until we get this out. Before you're quick to reply and ask me why I'm even in it when I know damn well that it's not a great relationship ... I'll save you the trouble. I can't explain it, OK? Oh yeah, Devil's Backbone. Oooooh Santi's gonna get you! Good flick eh? Course I saw it! K dude I gotta get back to work. Lunch next week for sure!

L8r,

Tarawara

Dammit. John was really pissed off that Tara couldn't find a way to get out of her relationship. Regardless of how much of an ego boost the Denver trip was, he still couldn't shake the blow to his ego from Tara's unwillingness to progress with their friendship. It's not like he was asking for a full-out relationship with her, he just wanted to see her more. He'd have to think about it some more and figure out a way to get through to her.

✳   ✳   ✳   ✳

October and November was spent heads down researching the web and email monitoring solution. John became wrapped up in this project more than any other project he had ever been involved in throughout his career, because he recognized that this was the first time he felt fully in control of every aspect of the project. Everything was up to him. As long as he was able to properly communicate his findings and recommendations, Dan, Patrick and the rest of the company would pretty much go along.

Once he had things narrowed down to two vendors, he brought Lee in to help him with his testing. They spent a week testing out the various antivirus, antispam, content filtering, monitoring and reporting features of the programs. Both solutions were very solid and choosing between the two was difficult. Because he had developed a great relationship with the sales and support staff from one of the vendors, that vendor was chosen and now all John had to do was write a report on how his conclusions were based.

John wrote the report and Dan signed off on it. All that was left is for Patrick to bring it up at the Board of Directors meeting and get the VP of Finance to approve it for this year's budget. He knew that this process, while simple in theory, could take weeks, even longer. Waiting was difficult: this was John's baby.

Patrick came by the security area for a rare visit to tell John that it was *in the bag*. He expected Gary Jefkins, the VP of Finance, to approve the purchase of the software before the calendar year end, in order to fit the project into this year's budget. John was elated with this news. As hard as he tried to contain his excitement in front of his big boss, he just couldn't do it. Patrick picked up on this, and although he didn't let on, John couldn't help feeling that he saw John's excitement as weakness, and not worthy of leadership material. *Whatever*, John thought.

CHAPTER 7

▼

John woke up this day in mid-December with a feeling of elation. Today was the day that they would put their email monitoring system *live*. He couldn't wait to see what they would find. The system they had in place couldn't monitor internal email—that would be something that may come into place later in time, depending on how Human Resources feels about it. This system couldn't exactly *monitor* email, but anytime it came across an email that met certain criteria, such as having a virus, spam, confidential information, or inappropriate content, the system would flag it for review. This was going to be fascinating.

John joined Dan and Lee in the server room where the server with the software system resided. They plugged it in to the core switch and flipped on the power button.

"We're live, boys and girls!" Dan exclaimed cheerfully.

"Should be interesting—we tested the virus engine last week so I'm not really concerned about that," Lee said, hitting ctrl-alt-delete on the server so that he could put it in lock mode. "I just can't wait to see how it handles all the spam we're getting. John, you'll have to monitor it pretty closely over the next few hours to make sure it's working okay. This server is now our mail exchange, so all corporate email is hitting this box first. Since the server is running on Windows, I'm not as comfortable with it being our first line of defense in terms of our email. But we'll watch it and see how it goes," Lee clarified for them.

"No problem, I'll be monitoring it closely for the next few weeks. Yeah, I wish we would be able to have a system that ran on a Linux box too, Lee, but this one doesn't have that capability. Oh well. It did win out on our eval, so at least we have the best software solution, despite the OS platform," John said.

John created folders on the server for the various types of email that needed to be dealt with. Each folder would contain emails trapped by the system and would easily be able to be viewed by whoever had the password to the server, which at this time was, well, just him. He would have to create accounts for Dan and possibly Lee.

Within an hour, the virus and spam folders filled up pretty quick. The system was doing a great job in capturing spam; almost all the email that he checked was correctly flagged as spam by the system. The false positive rate was pretty good. Of about fifty emails that he checked, only one turned out to be a valid email that the system incorrectly labeled as spam. Not bad, hopefully this will be indicative of how the software works.

He opened the folder that he labeled as *Nasty*, which would hold all of the emails that contained inappropriate language. The software came with dictionaries that contained almost every dirty word and phrase he had ever heard, plus a few new ones. The half hour he spent on that dictionary alone was well worth the education. He saw a few phrases he had never heard of before, and chuckled to himself loudly after jumping on the Internet to look up what they meant. Who invented the term *dirty sanchez* anyway???

In the Nasty folder he saw an email with the subject *hey hot stuff*. He double clicked on it and the entire contents of the email was displayed on his screen:

Hey hot stuff,

I'm sitting here in this class that they make us employees in the finance department take. God it is so goddam boring. Why do we have to endure this shit? So anyway I'm sitting here in the back, my screen can't be seen by anyone and there's nobody sitting beside me. The guy teaching this class is such a blowhard, he keeps talking and talking and not getting anywhere. So I decided I'd email you to make this class a little more fun.

Guess what I'm doing right now? I'm moving my body slowly up and down the front of the classroom chair, and my pussy is rubbing against it. As I continue these wonderful movements, I'm getting wetter and wetter by the moment. Goddddd I am getting so wet and horny. Wanna put your tongue on me and taste my wetness? Yeah I know you do. Fuck, even writing this is getting me hot. What are you gonna do to me when I get home later? Grrrrrrind grrrind grind this is getting good. Can you believe nobody is noticing this? Ahhhhhhhh.... I'm gonna cum soon....

Write back ...

What the ...? John couldn't believe what he was reading. *Here we are, only one hour into going live with this system, and already we have this awesome email.* He read it again. The second time he laughed aloud. *This was too good.* He had to call Dan over.

"Uh, Dan ... you're really going to wanna come to my desk!" John called out.

"Something interesting to see?" Dan was clearly curious. John noted that whenever Dan raised his bushy eyebrows it was a clear sign that he was excited/curious/interested in something. He almost wished he were still playing poker so that he could invite Dan—that eyebrow raise was one of the most obvious tells he had ever come across.

"You might say that," John replied.

Dan joined John at his desk and they read the email together. Even after reading it for the third time John still got a kick out of it.

"Holy shit, who is this lady? I don't know her, do you, John? I don't think she comes from head office here. Maybe she's from a branch office. Look her up in the corporate directory," Dan suggested.

John looked her up. Yup, Glenda was a long-time employee from the Indio branch. *Oh boy, this was going to be good. He would have to compose a really good warning email to her.* "So I guess you want me to send her an email warning then? I know our corporate communiqué stated that they were going to get a two week grace period," John tried to clarify.

"Yep, she'll just end up with a warning. Just imagine the look on her face if there was no grace period and her manager called her in on that one. Oy!" Dan laughed his hearty laugh. "Put together an email for her and just send it to me to go over quickly before you send it. Wonder what her response will be?"

"Hehehehehe ... I don't know, but I'll be sure to let ya know!"

Before John did anything else, he called Jill over to his desk. He noticed her looking over while he and Dan were laughing and could easily deduce that she was wondering what all the fuss was about. He knew that Jill could be trusted to keep everything confidential. After all, she was in the security department. Jill knew a lot of people here, and there was a good chance she knew this woman. *Oh well, that's life.*

"Oh my goodness, oh my *goodness!*" Jill shrieked. "This is certainly not what I'd call proper email etiquette."

"Yeah, that's putting it mildly, Jill. Please tell me you don't know her!"

"Can't say I do. And thankfully so. I'm not judging, but c'mon ... this stuff is best meant for *personal* email! So what are you going to do about this?"

"Just send her a warning for now. That's all we can do until the two-week grace period is up. Then it's a copy of the email to their manager. Wouldn't that be a good one to have to explain, huh?" John said glibly.

John did his best to be as diplomatic as he could in writing his warning. He started, but out of the corner of his eye he noticed the Nasty folder was growing. *Man, what is with these people?* John thought. Can there be more of the same? His answer came as he clicked on the third email down the list, as the first two were clearly dirty jokes being sent from outside the company. He made a mental note to read them later on his break.

From: Thomas, Billie
To: Sanders, Greg
Subject: yesterday

Gregory o Gregory … where should I begin? I came home last night and hubby was all jealous and shit as usual. I told him I was out with Sara but he didn't believe me. Yeah, of course, he has every right to be jealous but this has been going on far before you Greg. I think I seriously may leave him this time. Sex sucks with him. He just fucking LAYS there. What a bore. If we were at least able to, ya know, COMMUNICATE, then maybe the sex thing would be something we could work on. But when both just aren't happening then I don't know what to do.

So last night just rocked my world … what did you like better? I loved it when you tickled my throat with your cock. Did you love it when I licked your balls? Mmmm that face you made when you were about to cum and I just grabbed you hard so you couldn't cum yet?

The email went on for several pages. John's eyes popped out of his head as if he were one of those cartoon characters—all that was missing was that canned 'boing' sound. This message reminded him of those so-obviously-fabricated *Penthouse Forum* letters that he used to read as a horny teenager. Why oh why were people using their business email to air out their sexual fantasies and lord knows what else? The system has only been in place for a few hours and look what we've got already. *This is going to be more than we bargained for,* he said to himself.

Now he would have two warning emails to write. He didn't want to call Dan over for this one yet; he really wanted to get the warnings done. After a few revisions he was able to come up with a good one:

Dear Glenda:

Today, the information security department put into place a system, which filters email, primarily for the purpose of fighting viruses and spam. This system also flags any emails that contain inappropriate language and confidential information.

At 10:12 a.m. this morning, the monitoring program captured an email sent by you as it contained language deemed inappropriate for business use of our corporate email system. A copy of the email in question is attached.

This email serves as a warning only, as DesertFinancial employees are given a two-week grace period while we get used to the new system. Should you continue to use your corporate email for that which violates policies found in our corporate directive IS322, your manager will be carbon copied on the warning and they will deal with you as directed by corporate policy.

I realize that the contents of this email are very personal in nature, so please be assured that your confidentiality is maintained by the security department. At this time, I am the only one who is able to monitor the emails and nobody else is aware of this.

If you have any questions, feel free to email me, or call at extension 512.

Sincerely,

Jonathan Davis, CISSP

Cool, that sounds about right. John felt slightly guilty for lying to her about being the only one to have seen the email, but he didn't want to embarrass this woman any more than she was sure to be. He sent it off to Dan and the email was quickly approved. He would send the two emails out later this afternoon, as he really didn't want these people to spend their whole workday freaking out. He actually felt almost sorry for them, despite knowing that they really should know better. Messages like these should really never make their way onto corporate email systems.

∗   ∗   ∗   ∗

"Ooooh, Travelchick is looking awful hot today. John, look, she's wearing your favorite top!" Aaron Gold pointed out. Aaron and John had been taking their morning coffee breaks together over the last few months. Aaron was a programmer who often had to consult John for security issues for some important upcoming software projects. Aaron was happily married, but the two had a mutual affection for the admiration of the stronger sex. They would walk across the street to the new mall that had opened there, sit at the Starbucks and discussions would begin with the quality of the *scenery* around them.

They made sure that they established a first-name-basis knowledge with the coffee house baristas. All the women that worked in the surrounding stores however were simply known by the store they worked in. The cutie at the travel agent was Travelchick; the cutie at the toy store was Toychick, etc. They had yet to come up with a naming scheme for all the beautiful female patrons that frequented the Starbucks however. Aaron vowed to change that.

"So how was the weekend, man? You know what? Sometimes I have to live vicariously through you. I would never trade my married life for the world, but it's great hearing the stories of life as a swinging bachelor like yourself," Aaron said, as his eyes glanced toward a beautiful woman who was ordering her daily caramel macchiato.

"Weekend was good. I saw Tara last night. She came over crying over having just broken up with her boyfriend. She came home from work early one day and actually caught him in bed with another woman. You've seen Tara, right? If *I* were that guy, there'd be no fuckin' way that I'd cheat on her," John declared.

"Show me the most beautiful woman in the world, and I'll show you a guy who's sick of fucking her. Most men just aren't faithful. They don't have it in them. As a guy that's been happily married for five years and always been faithful, I'm probably like a rarity. It really isn't worth it, man. A few minutes or hours of pleasure to fuck up a whole lifetime of happiness in a relationship? But then again I definitely suggest sewing your wild oats before getting married. I know I sure did. I think sometimes it's the guys that never really got their freak on enough, that end up in trouble," Aaron rationalized.

"Good point. I probably have had enough freak experiences. I think I'm ready to settle down. It's just gonna take the right chick," John said, before blowing hard into his straw to dislodge the large piece of ice that was blocking the flow of blended goodness. "Tara may or may not be the one, hard to say, though right now she's pretty vulnerable. I'm taking it super slow. We haven't even really done anything yet. We sat on the couch and watched *Blue*, one of the three Kieslowski *color* films. Great French movie, dude. Anyway, we're sitting on the couch and she's just cuddling beside me. I tried to lean in for a kiss and I just got a weird response. I didn't even follow through. I don't think she's ready. That's cool, the cuddling was nice. Made for a pretty damn cold shower when she left though. I tell ya, that chick is killing me."

"Just take it slow dude. It'll pay off for ya in the end," Aaron said optimistically.

"Fo rizzle, mah nizzle," John agreed. Aaron shared John's appreciation for African American pop culture. Even though they occasionally used Snoop-speak, they knew it was still something that white people should rarely, if ever, attempt.

"Bust anyone lately?" Aaron asked. John had told Aaron about having to send warning emails to a few employees. John valued his job, not to mention his fellow employees' confidentiality, so he kept all the details pretty much obscured from Aaron. He even felt awkward for saying anything at all, but he figured that he wasn't compromising anything by simply stating that warning emails were being sent out.

"Yeah, yesterday there was a guy who was obviously unhappy with his manager. He went on a swearing rampage in an email to his buddy. F'in this and f'in that … f'in everything all over the email. Pretty bad. Too bad for him that the grace period is over. That's all I can tell ya."

"Who was it? Ya can't tell me? C'mon John. Buddy. Ol' Pal," Aaron pleaded.

"Good luck, asshole. No way. I've probably already said too much. If I say anymore I'm gonna have to kill you." John always wanted to say that. Okay, he's said it way too often since starting at DesertFinancial. Dan used that one frequently, and John found he couldn't prevent himself from using it.

＊   ＊   ＊   ＊

John returned to his desk, and like a bad habit, went right to the Nasty folder on the email monitor software. Lots of dirty jokes floating around. Nothing to bust anyone for, not that he was on a fishing expedition or anything. It was late January, and for some reason business at work was abnormally slow for this time of year. When business was slow, the security department didn't find itself bogged down by the normal barrage of requests from various other departments. John felt it was time to set up a meeting with the VP of Human Resources, and go over some of the emails that they've captured, and ensure that the proper message was being communicated in their corporate policies.

He had created a *Saved* folder for the purpose of demonstrating to HR what was being captured, and what sort of emails were being sent out. He found the worst five offenders, opened the emails, and then cut-and-pasted the contents into a Word document. He replaced all of the names with a series of Xs, in order to protect the not-so-innocent. No need for the VP of HR to know who was guilty—yet. If the VP wanted to know, he could ask, and John would have no problem providing the info.

He printed out the document with the five offending emails, and although he had read them countless times, he was still pretty shocked. He was amazed that people would use their corporate email accounts for such nefarious purposes.

✳   ✳   ✳   ✳

Victor Nunez was the Vice President of Human Resources. He commanded respect from all around him. He was the classic example of a leader who was firm, yet fair. Rumors around the office had him being groomed for the position of CEO. John had yet to meet Victor, so he was rather anxious about this meeting. When the initial information security policies were created, John had not yet started; the policies were hammered out by both Victor and Patrick Bowman, IT's big cheese. Victor had emailed John personally to see if he would bring in some sample emails so Victor could see what they were dealing with.

John left his desk with abundant time to spare, and took the long way in walking to the Human Resources department. He wanted to be prompt, yet needed time to collect his thoughts and prepare himself for this important meeting. He arrived five minutes early and was ushered towards the boardroom by one of HR's administrative assistants.

"Sit down, John." Victor pointed to the comfy chair across the huge table found in the middle of the modern boardroom residing in the HR department. Before John sat, Victor extended his hand for John to shake. John recalled many lessons that advocated a small pump, with a firm grip. John shook Victor's hand and sat down. "Thanks for coming down to see me, John. I wanted to meet with you alone first to get a good perspective of what we're seeing in the monitoring software. From what I understand, you are the main point of contact for this project." Victor stopped talking, and although John wasn't asked any question specifically, he decided he should speak up.

"Yes, Mr. Nunez. I pretty much spearheaded the whole project from research to implementation. I honestly feel that we have the best that money can buy right now, and the support from the vendor is top notch," John explained, while trying to study Victor's face for any sign of validation.

"Victor. Call me Victor, John. Mr. Nunez just doesn't sound right to me. I used to be a teacher, way back, and I really haven't been called that since then. Anyway John, what do you have for me? According to Dan there have been some pretty racy emails being sent out from here. If that's the case, we're going to have to get more specific with our acceptable use policies. But, I'm getting ahead of myself here." He looked at the yellow folder John was clutching in his hands and nodded towards it.

"Well … err, Victor, here are five emails that I've printed out that contain some pretty questionable stuff. I've crossed out the names to protect the not-so-innocent." John flipped the folder across the large boardroom table.

Victor chuckled as he opened the folder and began looking over the emails.

John figured he should speak up. "I don't know what you were expecting, but I'm warning you in advance. I hope you aren't offended by anything there," John offered, as he really wasn't sure what Victor would consider offensive.

They sat in silence for several minutes while Victor looked over the emails. Victor broke the silence well before he finished looking over all the sheets.

"Well. John. I'd say we have a problem. This certainly is not good. What concerns me most is that these emails are getting out there with our company name all over them. Not only does our domain name appear after each person's email address, but they have their email signatures attached to the emails as well. Our company name cannot be associated with content like this. Can you imagine what would happen if this made the news? I can't have that, John. This is pretty bad. This one individual who uses the 'f' word about twenty times in his email, I'm assuming it's a he, has he been talked to?"

Gee, Victor sure uses my name a lot, John thought. "Oh yes, a first offence message was sent to both he and his manager. The manager may very well decide that his term will not be renewed here."

"Well, that's good … So what you've brought me here, five emails, is this a mere sampling of what has been caught or is this pretty much it?" Victor asked, almost rhetorically, as he more or less knew the answer.

"It's a sampling. There's more where these came from, but not only that, there's a lot of dirty jokes floating around. Not to mention the dirty pictures," John confirmed.

"Okay," Victor said, pausing for a moment while deep in thought. "I think next week I'll book a meeting in Outlook for myself, Dan, Patrick and yourself so that we can hammer out a new policy. We certainly can't have stuff like this go on any longer. Consequences will have to be laid out."

John stayed with Victor for ten more minutes discussing the situation. After leaving, John felt great. Here was Jonathan Davis, having a meeting with the man who would likely be leading the company soon, and they were getting along great. John was treated like a regular person, practically a contemporary. This was *so* different from some of the big brass of other companies he'd worked for in the past. Now he'd have to go and tell Dan how everything went.

CHAPTER 8

▼

Jennifer Billings had just logged off her MSN, but this time—much unlike most chats she usually participated in—she felt despondent. There were several girls in her class who took exception to the way she had been flirting with the guys at school. Two of them, Jessica and Brianna, started an MSN chat with her and started making some pretty serious accusations. Name-calling that started with "cocktease" had degenerated to terms like "dirty whore", "fucking slut", and "HIV-case-waiting-to-happen". These girls, who were once much more popular than Jennifer was, were just so obviously jealous of her, Jen hypothesized, that they had to resort to cyber bullying. Still, Jennifer was terribly distraught.

The girls had threatened to spread rumors all over the school about her sleeping with as many as ten guys since breaking up with Brad. This was just *so* untrue and unfair, since the truth was she hadn't slept with *anyone* since Brad. Even when it did happen with Brad, it was only twice. They broke up soon after. As had become habit recently, Jen rushed to Mom's medicine cabinet and downed two Prozac. It had been five weeks since Jen first started experimenting with Prozac. Initially she would only try a few per week, but over the last week she had moved up to at least one per day. Prozac was most certainly making her calmer, and helping her sleep better. Thankfully no side effects. Soon though, her mom would find out. Jen couldn't have that—her mom would literally shit herself.

Jen called her friend Cassie to tell her what had just happened with the girls at school. "Like I'm totally serious, Cass, that's what they were calling me. They said they were telling people that I've been slutting around the school. Brianna said it was only going to get worse. That fucking beyotch. I swear I just wanna *kill* her … Can I kill her, Cass?" Jen asked, returning to her room from a trip to the fridge for a Diet Mountain Dew.

"Oh my god, J, that's so fucked up. I can't believe those bitches. What can we do to get back at them? Should we just give them a dose of their own medicine? What do you say? Tomorrow when we have Spanish class I think I'm going to do something. Those white trash little skanks!" Cassie shouted angrily into the phone.

"No, no. I don't want to stoop to their level. They're not worth my time … I don't wanna talk 'bout it anymore, k? So who's on TRL today?" Jen changed the subject. Her and Cassie loved watching Total Request Live on MTV whenever they could, and often either stayed on the phone or on MSN while watching so they could give the props or disses whenever required.

"I think Usher is on. Now *that* will keep your mind off those bitches. Mmmm he's got such a bod, girlfriend. I could lick his abs all night," Cassie drooled.

Despite the supposed caffeine burst from the Mountain Dew, Jen was drowsy. "Yeah, that could take my mind off things for a bit. I'mma flip it on, but I'm not really in the mood for talking right now so I'm gonna let you go, k? I'll see you online later." Jen had no intention of putting MTV on. Even with Usher. She just felt like positioning herself—fetal-like—and crying.

Within minutes of lying down, she drifted off to sleep. Soon after drifting off, she was woken up by her mom.

"Jennifer, wake up. You're always sleeping when you get home. Is everything okay at school? You seem to be pretty withdrawn lately." Her mom was clearly worried.

"Okay, yeah, I'm just always tired," Jen tried to explain.

"Jennifer. What's wrong with you? I know there's more to it than being tired. I *am* your mother, you know. Please … tell me what's eating you," Mom pleaded. She sat down on the bed next to Jen and softly placed her hand across her daughter's forehead.

Jen responded favorably to her mom's soft touch. "If I told you, do you promise you won't say much about it, and just *listen*? Honestly. If you'll listen to me and try not to judge, or give any maternal advice, then I'll tell you," Jen asked, wiping her eyes and preparing herself for a long talk.

"Of course! I just want to know what it is, okay?"

Jen sat up, and told her about what was happening at school with all the jealous girls. She had no plans to tell her everything, but once she started she couldn't stop herself. Jen hadn't revealed so much personal stuff to her mom, in, well, maybe ever. Her mom just listened intently, and when Jennifer was finished, all her mom did was give her a huge hug and didn't say a word. "I'm so sorry. Is there anything I can do for you?" was all her mom said, after one of the warmest hugs she had ever had with her daughter.

CHAPTER 9

▼

John went home after his successful meeting with Victor feeling pretty damn good about himself. He figured that this was probably the high point in his career—he could *feel* it—something was changing for him and it was all for the good. The future's so bright …

John's new salary was surely sufficient to go out and get a nicer town home or something, but he couldn't bring himself to leave the area. Plus, he would have to resort to a high-risk lender for a mortgage with the bad credit he had accumulated from those damn gambling debts.

When his grandparents both passed away a few years ago, they left their condo to John's mother. His mother already had a home of her own in Rancho Mirage, and didn't want to leave. Since John was the only child, his mother had no problem bequeathing the condo to him. Having been clean from gambling of any sort for almost two years, he literally shivered as he remembered that night being down twenty large at Morongo—he actually considered selling the condo just to make up the losses. *Who was that John guy I used to be? Gambling is not all that different from alcoholism. The similarities are numerous.*

He had been visiting Seven Lakes ever since his grandparents moved there. He was very close to them and to this day missed them dearly. Some part of him felt that leaving the condo would be tarnishing their memory somehow.

He loved living in the Seven Lakes community, which was just off Gene Autry, East of Highway 111. It was an area of very nice town homes that surrounded a lush, beautiful, beginner-level golf course. The majority of residents were seniors, which did not at all bother John since he had been visiting there for years. They all knew him and he enjoyed chatting with them whenever he would run into them on his daily walk, or when he would take a swim in one of the many public swim areas that were scattered throughout the community.

What was now *his* place was still very much like how his grandparents left it for him. He made some well-needed decorating changes, but the overall feel—or energy of the place—still resembled the warm dwelling he remembered visiting. It was undoubtedly way too much space for one person, but that didn't bother him at all. Plus, he loved being a part of a gated community, where there was a security guard posted at the gates twenty-four/seven.

John had two computers, one laptop and one PC. He used the laptop whenever he wanted to roam around the place wirelessly but most of his computing was done on the Dell computer that he kept in the den, complete with a 21" LCD screen. Go big or go home, he always thought. He fired up the PC and logged on to MSN to check if anyone was on. He really didn't use MSN, or any other chat program for that matter, very much. He grew out of that in the 90's after spending many hours on bulletin board chatting systems that were prominent in the pre-internet boom days.

John didn't consider himself at all a desperate guy, but when it came to his love life he was feeling rather unsettled about it. Things with Tara were at a standstill with no real possibility of things progressing past the friendly cuddling. As much as he loved it, he wished they could take it a lot further. He found that he was either taking too many cold showers or masturbating too much, even for his liking.

He decided that he would give the Internet chat rooms a try. *Being single is tough*, he said to himself. *Maybe I'll see what's out there.* There was a local area chat room for Palm Springs singles that he had overheard a few hotties talking about at Starbucks earlier. He found the **PSi<3u** room and looked through the participant list. Several of the female chatters had webcams enabled, so he figured that he'd have much better luck actually being able to *see* who he was chatting with. He had yet to purchase a webcam, but thought of getting one sooner than later.

John picked one at random. The name *jennaybobennay* just jumped out at him, even if she didn't have her camera on. *What a cute name*, he thought. Let's see what she's all about …

johnnyD:	*hey u*
jennaybobennay:	*hey*
johnnyD:	*how's things 2nite?*
jennaybobennay:	*not bad I guess*

johnnyD:	*why just guess?*
jennaybobennay:	*don't ask. How r u?*
johnnyD:	*good! chillin', thrillin', killin', ya know, scary movie 3*
jennaybobennay:	*yah, good flick yo*
johnnyD:	*name/age/sex?*
Jennaybobennay:	*wouldn't u like 2 know*
johnnyD:	*as a matter of fact …*
jennaybobennay:	*guess*
johnnyD:	*ok, well, im pretty confident in the name and sex—jenny and female*
jennaybobennay:	*oooh he's good, but not quite. just jen*
johnnyD:	*ok, jen. I'm john. duh. male of course*
jennaybobennay:	*umm how old r u?*
johnnyD:	*30, u?*
jennaybobennay:	*guess*
johnnyD:	*y?*
jennaybobennay:	*r u gonna b difficult or wut?*
johnnyD:	*oooo testy chick*
jennaybobennay:	*yeah wuts it 2 ya?*
johnnyD:	*ok ok I'll play*
jennaybobennay:	*now we're talkin*
johnnyD:	*I say 20*
jennaybobennay:	*omg omg r u like psykik or something*
johnnyD:	*am I right?*
jennaybobennay:	*shyah dude!*
johnnyD:	*sweeeet*
jennaybobennay:	*does it bother u that im like 10 yrs younger than u?*

johnnyD:	*no*
jennaybobennay:	*perv*
johnnyD:	*no way*
jennaybobennay:	*way*
johnnyD:	*come here often?*
jennaybobennay:	*tell me u didn't just say that*
johnnyD:	*ok I didn't just say that*
jennaybobennay:	*shut UP!*
johnnyD:	*hahahahahaha*
jennaybobennay:	*so what do u do?*
johnnyD:	*I work at a financial services company in the IT dept*
jennaybobennay:	*keewl*
johnnyD:	*what about u*
jennaybobennay:	*I work as a waitress at the OG ... luv the breadstix there*
johnnyD:	*hey ru gon turn on ur cam or wut?*
jennaybobennay:	*no. if u had one then id turn mine on but until then ferget it*

John and Jen continued their chat for about forty minutes. John asked twice more if she would turn on her webcam to no avail. Despite both having lied several times, both about their age, and Jen about where she works, the conversation flowed pretty well. They talked about work, movies, and the current state of rap music. John figured that knowing as much as he does about rap made him seem younger. They ended their chat by promising to both log on soon.

*   *   *   *

"Shit, do you think Travelchick's shirt could be any more revealing today? If she continues this we're just going to have to go and book a trip or something," Aaron said, smiling from ear to ear as his eyes were practically Velcroed to Travelchick's lacey bra that was showing through her low-cut top.

"Dude, I say next time we go over there and just start talking to her. You start the talking, then you can introduce me. Maybe my luck with women will start to change. Things with Tara are stalling big time," John added, frowning for effect.

"Bust anyone lately?" Aaron asked, as was always the case on each and every coffee break.

"Nothing good, nothing good. I'm kinda shocked to see a bit of a lull in that department. Maybe people are wising up," John replied.

"Could be. Hopefully. You would think they would know better, especially with the new policies you guys set up last week."

"So Aaron, I gotta ask ya. What do you think of me trying to meet someone online?" John moved his stool several inches closer to the table to demonstrate his interest in Aaron's answer.

Aaron did the same. "Depends … I actually met my wife through an old school bulletin board. We were set up by a mutual friend. But I don't really know if that counts. Our relationship didn't really start by chatting online. Why do you ask? Did you finally check out the PS I luv U room?" Aaron asked.

"Yeah, I did. Ended up chatting for forty-five minutes with some girl supposedly named Jen. Said she was twenty but who knows. What do you think the percentages are of people who actually tell the truth about their name, age and sex?" John asked curiously.

"Probably 50%. Crapshoot, really. You know how often guys will pass themselves off as chicks just to goof on people. Plus you've seen those *Dateline NBC* shows where they catch the online predators, those pedophiles who are trolling for young stuff. Gotta love that Chris Hansen guy. He's money … Anyway, it's really hard to say. Never know what you're gonna get, Forrest," Aaron said with a grin.

"Yeah, but those pedos are pretty much being set up with girls or guys that say they're like twelve or thirteen. This girl said she was twenty. My gut says she's for real, though I'm not sure about her age."

"Just chat with her again. Find her online and try to get more out of her. What if she was under twenty? Would you go for it?"

"I doubt it, even at eighteen, that's a stretch. I'd really like someone more my age, but, if this chick is twenty like she says then maybe, we'll see, guess it depends how hot she is."

"Have you got a webcam yet?"

"No. But I think I may go buy one tonight," John said.

"Good idea, dude. Does she have one?"

"Yep. That's why I'm going to get one. We can *see* each other then."

"Can't wait to hear how it turns out!"

"I'm sure you do. You still love living vicariously through me, don't you Aaron, Mr. Married Man?"

"Yeah, like I said, wouldn't trade ya. Just don't stop telling me all your stories!"

*   *   *   *

It was a rare rainy day in Palm Springs. John hated the rain. The fact that the desert area of California got very little rain was one of the main reasons John loved living there. But on those few occasions when the rain came down, he found himself in some sort of mini depression that didn't quite last a whole day, but long enough to bother him. He heard of a psychological disorder called Seasonal Affectation Disorder, or SAD, which affected many who lived in climates where sunshine was far from abundant. He likened his symptoms to this disorder, but was thankful that his suffering seldom lasted more than several hours.

Before heading to work, he stopped to get a Venti Caramel Frappucino just to brighten his spirits. Mmmm, that would help his mood. Arriving at his desk, Dan caught him before he turned on his PC.

"Johnny boy, I need to talk to you. Looks like we're going to have some changes here in the security department," Dan said, with an aberrantly serious look on his face.

John swallowed hard and took a deep breath. *Was there something wrong? Had his performance not being up to par?* John was pretty sure his status with Dan was practically unshakable, but perhaps he was wrong.

"What's up Dan? Have you finally realized I'm a no-good criminal that's here only to steal industry secrets?" John joked, in an attempt to lighten the mood, in the event that the mood did in fact require lightening.

Dan grabbed a chair and wheeled it towards John's desk. "Har har, cowboy. I could fire you for even *saying* that, but we know you're joking," Dan said with a warm smile. "Anyhoo, the deal is, Marilyn is retiring next month and we're going to need to replace her. The skill set isn't terribly technical, but there's quite enough that she's been responsible for to keep the replacement busy. What's going to happen is: we're going to get a guy named Ray from the Indio location. He's been their unofficial IT guy there and he's more than qualified. He's going to start later this week, and guess who is going to be training him?"

John laughed. "I'm guessing that person isn't you. Passing the buck to me, huh?" John asked, shaking his head in mock-disgust.

"Yep. You guessed it Johnny. I'm too tied up in meetings all the time, so it'll have to be you. Ray's a great guy—I think you'll like him. He's about forty-five and has quite the sense of humor. I'd say you should probably let him sit with you for the first few days, then you can get him up to date on our processes and procedures here. Things will work out well I think."

"Awesome, no problemo, Dan. Done deal." John turned away from Dan for a moment to turn his PC on.

"Great. Jill will help you after the first few days and get him up to snuff on some of Marilyn's other duties. She and Ray go way back, as they started out here around the same time."

"Cool. Looking forward to meeting him!"

John and Dan continued talking for a good forty minutes, just catching up on some work stuff, but generally just shooting the shit. John was really happy with how he and Dan got along and were able to talk freely and easily. Although Dan was not his official 'boss' (Patrick was), he considered Dan to be the best supervisor he has ever worked with. His overall easygoing-ness along with his attempted hard-ass approach to serious matters made him a most interesting supervisor. John didn't want to do anything to ruin their working relationship.

When John finally reached his desk and opened the Nasty folder on the monitoring system, once again he found an email that was way in violation of corporate policies. This email was different than the others in that it was almost five pages long. The first few pages were an obvious rehash of the author and recipients' previous evening's sexual escapades. The next three were an extremely detailed description of the author's wishes for the festivities that were about to take place that evening.

Emails that came into the system were analyzed for their content and all of the words contained within the message were given a score. Certain words or phrases were attributed different scores than others. The way John had it configured, one or two instances of the word 'fuck' would not set the monitor off, just by themselves. An email would need to have a score greater than one hundred to flag the email as inappropriate and send the message to the Nasty folder. Outside of the email that showed up earlier on that was primarily comprised of f-bombs, the previous 'high score' for an email was 550. This five-page classic that appeared on his screen was scored at 1150. Almost every dirty word he could think of was here.

Even more troubling than the language was the overall tone of the email. There was a running theme of bondage that wasn't in the least bit subtle. This woman was a great believer in pushing the proverbial sexual envelope. John wondered what the folks in HR would say if they knew what was lurking deep in the minds of their employees. If that were in fact the case, nobody would ever be hired!

After reading it three times over just to make sure he got the true gist of this message, he tried to decide how he was going to handle this. Despite knowing damn well that employees should know better, and that when it comes to usage of corporate assets there is no expectation of privacy, John couldn't bring himself to act according to procedure on this one. What would this lady do if she were called into her manager's office, faced with the realities of what she wrote being dangled in front of her face in plain view for she and her manager to discuss? And to make matters worse, or simply more uncomfortable, this prolific author of porn was herself a supervisor. *What the hell was she thinking?* John wondered over and over.

He looked back and across to ensure Dan, Marilyn or Jill hadn't somehow seen what was up on his screen. He figured he would wait until lunch time—when hopefully the three of them would be out of the area—to call this lady and try to give her a diplomatic heads up on corporate policy. He would see what she says and take it from there. He knew this should be dealt with punitively but couldn't bring himself to embarrass someone to that degree.

It was just past noon and John was alone in the security area. He dialed her extension at the Palm Desert branch and hoped she would answer. Some voyeuristic part of him couldn't wait to talk to the person responsible for such erotic prose. This was sure to be the highlight of his week.

She answered on the second ring.

"Is this Victoria?" John asked.

"Speaking. How can I help you?"

"Hi Victoria. This is Jonathan Davis from the information security department at head office on Tahquitz—"

"I know who you are," Victoria interrupted. "You're the one who sends out all the virus warning and other security information emails!"

"In the flesh, or, umm, maybe not. In the voice I guess. I'll cut right to the chase, Victoria." John cleared his throat and prepared himself for what was sure to be the most embarrassing moment of this person's life. "Yesterday afternoon you sent out an email that set off our email filter. The content was pretty, er, questionable for corporate email." John felt uncomfortable already. How humiliating for this person!

"Please, oh please, *please* tell me you didn't read that email."

"I'm afraid I did. Whenever an email hits our system that contains quite a bit of questionable language, the system flags it and it is our responsibility to occasionally look into the contents. In many cases we don't bother, but yours was, well, let's just say … unique," John said, congratulating himself for his choice of the word 'unique' as the most a propos for this conversation.

"Shit. Shit! Sorry for the language John, but right now I think I can honestly say that I am experiencing the most shame I have ever felt … Umm … Oh boy … okay, I have one question for you, John: The body of the message really didn't have anything in it, but I put the message in a Word document. How come it still set the damn thing off?"

"The system is pretty sophisticated. It doesn't matter if the content is in a Word doc, an Excel doc, or even a PDF. Nice try attempting to get around the system though," John quipped, trying to lighten the mood a bit and alleviate her embarrassment.

"Sorry. If I knew it was going to be seen by more than the intended set of eyes, there is no way in hell I would have sent it. Oh my God, John, I just remembered what your policy is for violations like this. Are you going to send a copy to my manager? Do I have to *beg* you not to?"

"Begging will get you nowhere," John teased while chuckling. He was getting a cheap thrill out of this conversation, which troubled and excited him in equal measures.

"Flattery?" Vicky countered.

"Probably further than begging. But still, I gotta tell ya, Victoria, this stuff was pretty intense. Do I have to say that you should know better?"

"No. Totally guilty, embarrassed, and scared. I don't know what to say. I still can't believe you read that. Not that it's any of your business, but since you pretty much know way too much about me already, the guy is someone who lives out of town who I rarely see. When we see each other we try to make the most of it," Victoria explained.

"I don't really need to know all this. I just have to decide what to do about it." John was feeling more and more Godlike as the stimulating dialogue progressed.

"Please tell me that you're the only one who knows about this. If you're not, then just shoot me now and put me out of my misery, okay?"

"Just me, Victoria. I can't promise that it'll stay that way though." John had to lie. He couldn't have her knowing that her private life was being exposed to more than just him.

"Oh God please John please please please. Can't you just let me off with a warning, officer John? I don't know what I would do if my manager found out.

She's kind of a prude, and wouldn't understand. She's the branch manager here and I don't know if I would even have a job anymore."

John had to think quickly. "That's not true. I don't think she could fire you for this alone, though I guess if she's a prude then things between you would never be the same. If your work is good otherwise I don't think HR would allow the disciplinary action to be that severe."

"Still. What do I have to do to convince you *not* to take this further?" Victoria asked, in a rather sexy voice, John thought. Was she actually trying to come on to him? *Nah, no way*, John figured.

"Nothing. I think your embarrassment is likely punishment enough," John said, at this moment making the executive decision that she was going to get away with a warning. "But Victoria, please, don't *ever* do this again. If I find another email from you like that I will have to act according to our procedures." John stood up and looked over his cubicle wall to ensure nobody was lurking nearby to eavesdrop.

"Thank you thank you thank you. I can't thank you enough. John, you have been a pleasure to deal with. You have handled this matter professionally and diplomatically. You are a good person."

John blushed, and sat back down. "Thanks Victoria. I'm sorry that you're embarrassed, but I promise you, this time it's between you and me. Nobody else knows. Take care Victoria, and please watch your emails from now on."

"I will. Bye, John."

"Byeeee Victoria." John stretched out his *bye*, perhaps in an attempt to flirt back. He had no idea why he ended the call on that note.

It was almost one o'clock and John was starving. Aaron had already taken lunch and Tara took hers at eleven thirty, so John was going solo today. He ran out of the office, jumped in his MDX and drove down the Highway, and although it was still raining, he found that even the weather could not bring him out of the great mood he was now in. He knew he was just doing his job in dealing with Victoria, but he still wondered whether she was coming on to him. He had no clue what she looked like, but she *sounded* hot and sure as hell wrote emails that were titillating to say the least.

John stopped at El Pollo Loco to get his chicken fix. Each time he ate there, he couldn't help wondering what it would have been like to be a fly on the wall at the marketing meeting that eventually decided to name a chain of restaurants *The Crazy Chicken*. He snatched his bag of food from the drive-thru, parked in the nearby Target parking lot, stayed in his car and ate his meal. He enjoyed watching all the people with grimaced faces running frantically into Target to escape the rain. *Hello? It does rain here, people!*

He cursed the rain a few hundred times and drove back to work.

Just before he was about to leave for the day, he got an email from Victoria:

From: Wallace, Victoria
To: Davis, John
Subject: Jokes?

Hey John … I'm still trying to get over my embarrassment earlier. I think my face is still red. REALLY red.

The reason I'm writing you this email is because, well, I get a lot of dirty joke emails. I wanted to know if I'm going to get in any more trouble for having dirty jokes in my Inbox. I want to be a good girl, ok? Help me out here.

Let me know how.

Vicky

Vicky. Hmm, John thought, *now it's Vicky.* More informal now. Okay. No problem. He decided he'd reply before leaving:

From: Davis, John
To: Wallace, Victoria
Subject: re: Jokes?

Vicky,

Thanks for wanting to be a good girl. Very commendable of you!

As for the dirty jokes, I'm surprised any are getting through to you. Our email filter should be blocking them, but maybe you're referring to the pre-filter days. Either way, I don't think it's a good idea to keep too many dirty jokes in your inbox. Remember, they're stored on our email server in YOUR name. If you get them—I'd say, read them, laugh (or not laugh) then delete them.

That's my best advice. Other than that, I hope you really can be a 'good girl' from now on. I'd really hate to have to see you more embarrassed than you already are.

Take care,

John

There. Not too formal, yet informal enough to sound friendly. He went home smiling a permanent smile like *The Joker* from *Batman*.

*   *   *   *

The next morning, John came in to work, kicking himself for not looking Vicky up in the corporate directory yesterday to see what she looked like. He tried to picture her in his mind last night; was she as hot as the stuff she wrote? He wasn't getting his hopes up, as the last few female naughty email offenders were rather unattractive.

He fired up the corporate directory on the company intranet and typed in her name. Her picture popped up on his screen. John figured she was in her late thirties (the pictures were taken for the online directory last year). Victoria had dirty blonde hair, soft features, piercing light blue eyes and had a nice smile. *Definitely MILF material*, John thought. *Nice.*

Not a mere ten minutes had passed by before his phone rang. He looked on the internal call display before picking up: It was her!

"Knock, Knock," Vicky started the conversation.

"Okay, I'll play," John went along. "Who's there?"

"The Interrupting Cow."

"The Interrup—"

"MOO!!!" Vicky shouted.

John thought for a second, then laughed out loud. "Good one! I like it. Almost revives the whole knock knock genre!"

"Yeah, I thought you'd appreciate a *clean* joke to start the day," Vicky said.

"Awesome. What can I do for you that I haven't done already?" *What a loaded question*, John thought to himself as soon as he said it.

"Never mind. I just wanted to thank you for yesterday. You have no idea how grateful I am that you handled it the way you did. So, thanks again, John."

"Like I said, no problem. Just be a good girl, ok?"

"Will do."

"Have a good day, Vicky."

"You too, John."

CHAPTER 10

▼

Jennifer Billings was sitting in the principal's office for the first time since starting Cathedral City High four years ago. Jen had always been a good student, even in her wild years, and never had reason to visit this dreaded location of the school. But here she was. Not that her purpose for being here was disciplinary in nature—no, not at all. She was here to do something about those vile bitches that were trying to spread awful rumors about her.

"Jennifer Billings?" the secretary called her name. Jen was shown to Principal Garcia's office. She had met principal Garcia on several occasions but didn't really *know* her that well. Jen was somewhat anxious.

"Jennifer. Nice to meet you. How can I help you today?" Principal Garcia asked, with a friendly smile.

Jen took a look around the office and couldn't believe how outdated it looked. *Ohmygod, this office is so 70's,* she thought. "Well, umm, well, there's these girls in my class who are spreading rumors about me. They're making life here at school pretty difficult to deal with. I'm here to see if there's anything you can do. You're my last resort. I *really* didn't want to come here, but I don't know what else to do," Jen said.

"Why don't you tell me as much as you can, and we'll see if there's anything that we can do for you here. Okay, Jennifer?"

Jen told her as much as she could, explaining all the names that she was being called, and pointed out that the bullying didn't stop at school either—this was happening online as well.

"I'm sorry, Jennifer. That's a horrible thing to go through. Is there anything specific you would like me to do with these girls?"

"I don't know. You tell me. You're the Principal!" Jen barked, almost sarcastically. She couldn't help it. She felt like this conversation was going nowhere fast.

"No, no, you're right. I will certainly talk to all the girls involved. I will try to do everything I can to ensure this stops. As soon as possible," the principal said.

"Thanks, Principal Garcia. Whatever you can do."

*   *   *   *

A week passed and most of the bullying at school stopped. This was great, Jen thought, but things online just got worse. Every time she would ban a Hotmail ID from being able to chat with her, the girls would just create a new Hotmail address, add her, and start the bullying again. Jen was becoming more and more distraught and equally reliant on mom's Prozac. She decided to visit the principal again.

"But can't you do *anything* else, Principal Garcia?" Jen asked, pleading, trying desperately to hold back the tears.

"I'm afraid when it comes to cyber bullying, which is basically what's happening to you, Jennifer, my hands are tied. What can I do?" Principal Garcia leaned in towards Jen and looked at her with kind eyes.

"I don't know, but there's gotta be something. And you can't tell me that I'm the only one that this kind of thing is happening to."

"I'm not at liberty to say, Jennifer. Your own specific situation is all I can freely discuss with you. And I'm so sorry, really, I truly am, but all I can do is try my best to make sure your experience at CCH is as enjoyable and trouble-free as possible. I can't act as the cybercop as well."

Principal Garcia really did feel terrible. Jen's situation was certainly not that uncommon; there have been other cases of cyber bullying that have come up. She knew that this was a growing concern for schools across the country, and it was going to be a big topic that would be covered in the upcoming educational convention she was to attend. Still, she feared that the problem would never go away and could truly never by solved by the schools. This was an issue that schools didn't have the resources to handle.

*   *   *   *

It had been two days since he last heard from Vicky. He'd been thinking about her a lot lately, but was trying not to over think things. Sure, he thought she was attractive, and he enjoyed their banter, but it wasn't as if there was anything to really get himself excited over. Plus, the whole bondage thing in that email still bothered him. His heart skipped a beat though when the phone rang and the call display showed her name.

"Knock knock … just kidding. How are you, John?"

"I'm well, *Victoria*. To what do I owe the pleasure of this call?"

"I was wondering … this is going to sound really forward of me, but I was, er, wondering, what you were doing after work today? Care to join me for a drink-iepoo at the Cheesecake Factory?"

"Well, well … I don't know … I'm not sure what it would do for my reputation if I were to be seen in public with corporate troublemakers like yourself," John replied. His heart was suddenly beating faster than an acid techno song.

"Oh come on now, you know I'm a rehabilitated good girl now. I think I deserve a drink. Hey you already know way too much about *me*. I think the least you can do is tell me a bit about *yourself*."

John thought about it for a moment, and perhaps against his professional judgment, decided to go for it. "Okay, you got me there. It's a deal. What time?"

"Is there a way you can sneak out by four? I think we'll need to get there well before five. Traffic to Rancho Mirage shouldn't be too bad if you leave at four. It's not far for me, so if you're late that's okay. I'll be at a table in the lounge at four thirty."

"Good deal, Vicky. See ya there!"

John was elated. He was not used to being the hunted. He was usually the one doing the chasing. *This could be different. Is she anything like what she wrote in that five-page masterpiece?*

He called Aaron and told him the news. Aaron was happy for him and told him to be a good boy.

John couldn't promise anything.

$$* \qquad * \qquad * \qquad *$$

John and Vicky had a wonderful time together. Before their meals arrived, John had two chocolate martinis and Vicky had three. The conversation flowed freely and openly. Arriving early at the restaurant provided them the luxury or securing a comfortable corner booth. By the time they were downing their second drinks the place was jam-packed as usual, the huge lobby swarming with beautiful people.

Vicky described to John about the pain of her divorce, the difficulties in being a single mom, and provided further details behind the now famous email. Her *boyfriend* from the email was nothing more than casual. The mere mention of the word divorce transported John's mind to a time when he was fifteen.

*   *   *   *

Sitting in his room listening to music on his ultra thin Bang&Olufsen headphones, John couldn't help overhearing his parents arguing in the room across the hall from his. This was bound to be a doozy—Prince was blaring at full blast in his eardrums, and both bedroom doors were closed.

John was sick of the arguing. He didn't mind his parents having disagreements, but the constant shouting was getting to him. Why couldn't his parents be like most of his friends' parents? They seemed to always get along so well, and were so touchy and lovey with each other. He tried to drown them out by jacking up the volume even louder, but there was no point. He may as well eavesdrop and see what the point of contention was this time.

"I won't stand for this anymore," he could hear his mom say. "Come on, she's barely twenty years old. It's disgusting to me. You're becoming disgusting to me!" she yelled.

His dad had a way of not quite raising his voice, but in that odd, calm, demeanor, was able to convey a certain tone that pissed people off even more than as if he was screaming at the top of his lungs. The tone was in full force tonight.

"Look dear, listen to me, all we did was go for coffee. She was having trouble with one of the supervisors at the office and needed someone to speak with about it. Contrary to your beliefs and insinuations, I am not having an affair with her. I'm not that kind of man, you know," his dad said, his tone present in each and every syllable.

John had heard enough. He didn't have any proof, but his gut told him that his dad had cheated before, and was likely doing it again. At fifteen, John could easily understand kids his age cheating on their boyfriends/girlfriends, cause what is cheating when you're fifteen and in the early years of high school? He was definitely not innocent, especially after that night with Kim in the bushes last summer when he was supposed to be with his girlfriend Debby. But isn't the point of marriage to stay faithful and monogamous? He worried that when it was time to grow up and find the one, he may not be able to keep that promise to be faithful. Regardless, he vowed to never be like his dad.

"Fuck, you are just so arrogant," mom said. "To hell with you and your righteous indignation. I want you out of here tonight, and don't come back until you can be a man and own up to your indiscretions!" Mom actually sounded like she meant it this time.

There was no reply from his dad. Just a few moments of silence, followed by the violent slamming of the back door. Whoa. Is dad really leaving?
This was the beginning of the end of the relationship for John's parents.

✳   ✳   ✳   ✳

John fought back the tear that was fighting to make its way out of his right eye, and told Vicky as much as he could about his past, without revealing *too* much of himself in the process. He would suppress his experiences as a poker addict for another time; that was too much to get into for an informal setting such as this. To even the score on the sexual revelation department, John described in painstaking detail the whole Denver experience. He even exaggerated somewhat just to make the conversation more interesting and stimulating. John found that his exaggerations seemed to work wonders on Vicky. As the evening progressed, she became more and more *touchy.* No complaints there.

Having finished their dinners, they decided to share a caramel cheesecake. Two bites in, John decided to bring up the *bondage thing.* "Vicky, I gotta ask, what's up with the S&M?"

"Pardon me?"

Awkward moment alert. John knew that Vicky heard him, and was obviously put off by the question. Against his better judgment, John didn't give up. "That part of the email you wrote ... are you into that stuff? If you don't want to answer, you don't have to, I just, umm, thought I would ask." John spotted a beautiful waitress walk by, and did his best not to watch her from behind.

Vicky smiled. "Let's just save that for another time, okay?"

"Deal," John said, relieved that his question hadn't pissed her off, even though he didn't exactly get an answer to his question.

As the seven o' clock hour approached, Vicky looked at her watch and frowned.

"Looks like I have to go. Gotta pick my daughter up from her basketball game."

"Yeah, no problem, totally understand. Let's blow this popsicle stand. Hehehe, don't you just love that expression?" John asked.

"Yeah, but not as much as I like blowing popsicles!" Vicky exclaimed, with a naughty twinkle in her eye.

"Ooooh baby—I thought you said you were going to be a good girl from now on. Now you realize you have me in a quandary here. I don't know whether I want the good Vicky or the bad Vicky. How 'bout you try to maintain your newfound status of good girl at the office, but you're free to be as nasty as you wanna be in your free time?"

"Wouldn't you just like that, Jonathan Davis? We'll have to see about that."

They each paid their share of the check (Vicky insisted on going Dutch) and they walked slowly around the shops of the River—which just happened to be centered around a river—before making way toward their cars. The River was a relatively new addition to the Palm Springs dining and shopping scene, and although it had the same faux qualities as the new hotels in Vegas, John viewed it as a welcome addition to the local nightlife.

As fate would have it, they were both parked very close to each other in The River parking lot. As they approached Vicky's car, she grabbed John's hand.

"Thank you for spending time with me this evening. You are a true gentleman, and I enjoy your company. I'd like to get to know you even better, John. No, not *that* way. Well … maybe *eventually*. But you get the picture. I just think you're a kind soul."

"Awww, you're sweet. Thanks, Vicky. I had a really nice time. You're a good person too, ya know," John responded, smiling a friendly smile.

"Well, ain't we just full of admiration for each other tonight. Now shut your trap and kiss me goodnight, darlin'!" Vicky said in a mock southern accent, which actually came out sounding pretty damn authentic.

John didn't waste a beat. He turned towards her, looked her right in her light blue eyes and kissed her gently on the lips. Vicky kissed him back, but with a ferocity that John had rarely experienced. He wasn't exactly one for public displays of affection, but here they were in the middle of a fairly busy parking lot going at it. This had got to be one of the hottest kisses ever. After two minutes of heavily making out, John pulled back. He felt like he was in eighth grade again.

"We should really stop this before we get outta hand for everyone to see. We'll chat tomorrow, okay?"

"Okie dokie," Vicky said as she wiped her lips with her left hand. "Talk to ya tomorrow. I'll email ya!"

They both got in their cars and drove off. Instead of going home, John kept driving the other way down Highway 111 past Palm Desert and almost as far as Indio before turning back west to head home. He couldn't stop thinking about that kiss. Man, he wondered, maybe there's something to be said for older women. Vicky was thirty-nine, five years older than he. He was spending all this time trying to hook up with younger chicks, when all the while perhaps what he really should have been looking for was someone older. He hoped in this case, with Vicky, maybe experience would breed talent. In bed, he added, just like that old joke of adding *in bed* to each fortune found in a fortune cookie.

∗　　　∗　　　∗　　　∗

John returned home just before eight and turned on the PC. He couldn't wait to tell someone about this. He hoped that Aaron was on MSN. He and Aaron hadn't got to the point in their friendship where they talked on the phone yet. He didn't even know Aaron's phone number.

Unfortunately, Aaron wasn't on. Jen was though, and he hadn't seen her on lately. *I'm feeling like quite the stud today,* John said to himself. Why not a little more harmless flirting to round out the night? What's the harm in that?

johnnyD:	*hey u, havent seen ya on here 4 awhile*
jennaybobennay:	*I know ive kinda been avoiding the msn l8ly*
johnnyD:	*y?*
jennaybobennay:	*cuz*
johnnyD:	*good answer, what r we, like 6?*
jennaybobennay:	*hahah very funny asshole*
johnnyD:	*what? no jk, or smiley? were u serious?*
Jennaybobennay:	*kinda*
johnnyD:	*ooops*
jennaybobennay:	*sry, I'm just kinda bitchy these days*
johnnyD:	*anything u need 2 talk about?*
jennaybobennay:	*y?*
johnnyD:	*I asked u*
jennaybobennay:	*just these cunts that r trying to ruin my rep … had 2 go to the principal and get her 2 try 2 stop them*
johnnyD:	*principal????*
jennaybobennay:	*shiittttt*
johnnyD:	*like how old r u jenny?*

jennaybobennay:	*17, soon 2 b 18, seriously I'm in my senior year*
johnnyD:	*fuk*
jennaybobennay:	*whaddyamean?*
johnnyD:	*doesn't it bug u that im 30?*
jennaybobennay:	*no, we're just chattin*
johnnyD:	*tru dat*
jennaybobennay:	*yep*
johnnyD:	*omg ur 17*
jennaybobennay:	*almost 18*
johnnyD:	*but shit now i feel like a perv*
jennaybobennay:	*like i said were just chattin*
johnnyD:	*yeah. do u still feel like talking about it?*
jennaybobennay:	*what?*
johnnyD:	*ur problem—with your 'friends' at skool*
jennaybobennay:	*yeah, i don't know what to do. if they don't' bully me at skool they do it online. i'm not even lookin forward to prom or anything*
johnnyD:	*oh that's said. what senior doesn't look forward 2 prom?*
jennaybobennay:	*this one*
johnnyD:	*sad. tell me more. what can good ol Johnny D help u with?*
jennaybobennay:	*Idunno. maybe I should start with when me and my bf broke up*
johnnyD:	*ok, sure I'm all ears, or shall I say eyes*
jennaybobennay:	*hahaahaha … ok … here we go….*

Jen spent the next hour telling John all about her problems. John listened, or more appropriately, read, what she had to say and provided commentary and/or advice when requested. He could tell that she really needed a male opinion. Even though he thought of offering to call her to make it easier to get things off her chest as opposed to just having to type everything, he decided it probably wasn't a good idea.

One, he figured that most young people these days for some reason preferred MSN to actually talking; and two, he realized that he was twice her age and didn't feel quite comfortable making chit chat on the phone with someone that young. Even if all he was doing was essentially being a friend to this girl. All of a sudden the thought of starting something with her, particularly after the events that had transpired earlier tonight, seemed like a not-so-great idea.

When she was done she thanked John for listening to her and for his advice. She asked if he didn't mind talking to her online when they were both on, given that he was so much older. He wasn't sure how to answer but just replied with a "yeah, for sure". He felt guilty that she didn't know that he in fact had *also* lied about his age. Not that there's any difference between thirty and thirty four, when Jen was only seventeen.

✳   ✳   ✳   ✳

"Whoa whoa whoa, fuck dawg, you are the D-O-double-G! What a night for Johnny. Good going, my friend." Aaron was clearly excited for John. He hadn't even touched his frappucino since John began his recap of last night's date.

"And I haven't even told you about what happened online when I got home," John said, clearly bragging now. His eyes followed a beautiful woman he had never seen before as she strolled by their usual table at Starbucks. He was going to kick Aaron under the table to subtly inform him of the hottie walking by, but decided against it.

"Holy shit. What now? Is there more? Did you guys have like some good cybersex online after? Just to finish up where you left off in the parking lot?" Aaron was becoming a *tad* too excited now.

"No no no no no, nothing like that. Wasn't even Vicky. Remember that girl Jen who hasn't been online the last few days? Well, she was on last night. Get this though—she's only seventeen!"

"No fucking way! Are you kidding me? Please tell me you guys didn't try to hook up or anything."

"Hell no, dude. Johnny don't play dat game. Johnny's a good boy. I just kinda listened to her while she told me all about her problems at school," John clarified.

"Can you hear yourself, dude? You just said *problems at school*. John, the girl is seventeen. You're thirty-four. Do the math. Even if you *were* just chatting online, don't you think you are setting yourself up for some trouble?" Aaron asked, finally noticing the woman that John was staring at earlier.

"No. I don't. Aaron. Don't worry. I was just trying to help her out. I was feeling, ya know, in a giving mood after all the fun with Vicky."

"Ohh kayyeee, if you say so. I'm just trying to look out for you, brother. I say things look really promising with Vicky. I wouldn't even go there, at all, with Jen. Try to brush her off or something. Did you happen to turn your cams on?" Even though Aaron was advising his friend to stay away from her, he still was curious to know what she looked like.

"No, I forgot to ask in fact. We just chatted."

"Think she's hot?"

"What the fuck is with you, Mr. Married Man? Who just told me to stay away from her? Are you like going schizo on me?" John asked, half seriously.

"I'm just screwin' with you. Honestly, John. I'm excited for you that things are off to such a great start with Vicky."

"Good … me too. Hey, look who's at the counter in a short skirt. Insurance agent chick!"

"Nice."

After having the nice coffee chat with Aaron, John returned to his desk to check the work tickets that had been piling up over the last few days. The company has been on somewhat of a hiring frenzy lately, and with the new employees come new requests for access to network resources. These requests were always quite time-consuming, and John wasn't too fond of having the security department do the work. Dan and Jill shared his sentiments. Thankfully, this Ray guy would be starting on Friday so that will be a big help.

His phone rang, which brought him out of the daze he seemed to be in as he was looking over all the work that he needed to do today.

"Hey Stud!" It was Vicky.

"Hey Good Girl Gone Bad."

"Whatcha doin this afternoon?"

"Work. And lots of it."

"Can it wait?"

"Why?"

"I called in sick today … why don't you come over?"

"Are you serious? Really? What am I going to say to get myself out of here?" John's heart began doing the 100-yard dash.

"I don't know, you're a smart guy, you'll figure something out," Vicky replied.

"Shit, you make it *really* hard for a guy to say no. I can always come back after and work late I guess." John's mind was quickly made up. "So where do you live?"

She told him her address and said to come by after lunch. John realized he was pitchin' quite the pants tent, so he quickly thought of Snufalupugus and it went down right away. Someone had once told him that if he ever wanted to diffuse a boner, thinking of that strange creature from Sesame Street would do the trick. It almost never failed him.

John hated lying to Dan, but somehow the ends would definitely justify the means, so it was easier than he thought. Last minute cancellation at the dentist: always seemed to work.

✳   ✳   ✳   ✳

He arrived at Vicky's place and took a deep breath. *What am I getting myself into here?* John wondered. Do I really know this woman? She *seems* really genuine and stable, but what if she's a psycho? He couldn't get that email out of his head. Just knowing what she was doing with some other guy not too long ago drove John a little bit bonkers. *What have I got to lose?* Nothing ventured, nothing gained.

Vicky answered the door in a pair of really short, red, silky workout shorts and a grey t-shirt that was so short that the slightest bending of her body would be certain to reveal flesh or undergarment. He quickly realized there were no undergarments to speak of there. He also didn't fail to notice her pierced bellybutton, which to him was the icing on the visual cake. As she motioned for him to sit down on the couch, he got a great look at her perky breasts. Okay, they weren't Gwen Stefani small, but they were almost perfect. *Shit*, his pants tent was back, and this one was not going away even with the help of Snufalupugus.

They talked for twenty minutes, or it could have been a half hour or more; John wasn't really paying attention to the clock on the wall. He felt very comfortable sitting here with her, talking away, much like he felt last night. He started thinking about work and lying to Dan, but those thoughts quickly faded away, never to appear in his mind again.

She grabbed him by the hand, draped her leg over his and brought her other arm around his waist and held him against her. He pulled in even closer. They began kissing, continuing where they left off last night in the parking lot. He knew at this very moment that he had never, ever, been so turned on in his life.

She bit his ear rather lightly, then used her tongue to effortlessly lick around it. He was breathing heavily now. He almost felt like he was ready to pop.

"You're totally driving me crazy, Vicky."

"That's the plan. Now why don't we move to my bedroom?"

She led him to her modern, minimally decorated bedroom. They practically swung themselves on to the bed and he got on top of her.

"Are you going to take off your clothes or what, big fella?" She asked, nodding towards his groin.

John ripped off his clothes. He took the initiative and slowly moved Vicky's shorts down her legs—revealing a pair of soft, cotton, pink panties with hearts on them. John rubbed himself across her panties. He eventually ended up *there*, and thrust himself towards her.

Vicky removed her shirt. With the exception of her panties, they were now both completely naked. It was apparent that they both wanted to get right to the main attraction, but an unspoken understanding emerged between them that they were going to take this slow. *Lots of foreplay.* No problem, John decided.

John took the initiative and began nibbling at the dangling piece of jewelry from her navel. Vicky moaned in pleasure, signaling to him to keep doing what he was doing.

After twenty minutes of intense foreplay, the likes of which John had never experienced, he decided it was time to close the deal. He slid her panties to the side to give himself room.

"Stop. John, stop," Vicky pleaded, visibly upset for some reason, almost in tears.

"What? You don't want to? Are you okay?" John was now concerned. Hard, and horny as hell, but still concerned.

"I don't know, John. I like you. I really really do. A *lot*. I just don't want to ruin this. I've been divorced for a while now, and since then I've pretty much kept things casual with men I'm dating. I'm not a slut, John. I hope you know that. But I've always just had this, well, *wall*, that I keep up and haven't let anyone in for a really long time. I know this sounds totally cliché and everything, but it's true. There's no other way for me to say it." Vicky paused to catch her breath. John carefully slid himself off of her and lay at her side.

Vicky continued: "The thing is John, like I said before, I really like you. And I don't want to ruin what we've started. I know we're just starting this, umm, relationship, but I feel you may just be the person to turn things around for me. Maybe we should wait just a bit before we have sex … make love … fuck. Is this okay with you? Do I make any sense whatsoever? Or am I just rambling?"

John adjusted himself and slipped on his underwear. "No, you make perfect sense. I don't want to push you into doing anything you're not ready to commit to. Even if I'm as turned on as I am. I like you too, Vicky, and I don't know you enough to really make any predictions as to our future, but I see great potential. I do." John was only partially speaking the truth. Although he understood her, a very small part of him was concerned that maybe he was dealing with someone who wasn't quite 100% stable. Nevertheless, he wasn't ready to give up on this budding relationship.

"Thank you for understanding. I'm not as much of an emotional wreck as you think. Really I'm not. I can't have you think that I'm some whacked-out freak of a woman, that's always going to be this unpredictable. Spontaneous, yes, but I'm not a psycho or anything. So we're cool?"

"As a cucumber. Now what do we do?" John asked.

"Well, first I'm going to finish you off. We can't leave you *hanging* like that. Then let's just stay in bed and cuddle for a bit, k? Then Mr. Big Diplomatic Security Officer can return to work and not get into too much trouble. How's that?"

"Perfection."

✳   ✳   ✳   ✳

John came into work early the next morning, having been unable to sustain any semblance of restful sleep. Thoughts kept swirling through his head about the future of his relationship with Vicky. He really wanted to get laid yesterday. He almost *needed* it. He understood that she was vulnerable, and really had no choice but to understand. He did understand. He just hoped that everything she said about not being psycho was true. Hopefully things would settle down and their relationship would flourish with the passage of time.

There was an empty work area behind him that had always been used to store departmental procedures and documentation. Overnight it had obviously been cleared up and re-done to make room for Ray, who was starting today. As John sat down at his desk, he noticed Dan talking to a guy who was likely Ray. Dan walked over with him and made introductions.

"John, this is Raymond Douglas. He'll be working with us for at least the next six months. Don't let his wicked sense of humor put you off. He's a good guy. I think you guys will get along," Dan said.

"Nice to meet you! Are you ready to get lost in the highly secretive, super-wonderful world of information security?" John asked, extending his hand.

"Yeah, I am. I'm actually just here so I can wreak havoc with all the systems we have. I hear you guys have the most access than anyone in the whole company. I want that prestige that comes along with being in your department," Ray said.

"You came to the right place. We're the place to be. Did Dan give you the long-winded confidentiality speech?" John asked.

"Of course. Ray knows that everything he sees in here, stays here. We're just like Vegas here in security," Dan said.

"No slot machines, no neon lights, no smoking, no overpriced designer restaurants, no hookers … yeah, sure Dan, completely like Vegas," Ray said sarcastically.

"Hmmm, everything I like about Vegas," Dan replied. "Anyhoo, John, I guess you'll spend the morning letting Ray sit in with you and showing him the proverbial ropes."

"Yep, definitely. Ray, have a seat and I'll take you through our most frequently used apps and stuff," John said, sitting down and motioning for Ray to join him.

John spent the morning with Ray, allowing him to watch as he went through his day-to-day tasks. There was an email from Vicky, but since Ray was able to see everything John did on his screen, he had to read it briefly and compose a quick reply. He invited Ray to join him for a walk at coffee. They walked down Tahquitz and enjoyed the sun. Ray looked completely at home with his very loud Hawaiian shirt. John admired Ray's chutzpah in showing up for the first day of work at head office in a bright red Hawaiian shirt.

They talked mostly about work. John was surprised to find out that Ray had actually worked in IT for several years quite a while back before being promoted to a better-salaried position at a branch office. This was great news; Ray actually knew a lot of the people at DesertFinancial, and would probably be a good resource for personnel stuff.

As they were heading back towards the office, Ray asked what he had obviously been meaning to ask for some time: "So, I gotta ask, I couldn't help noticing the email from Vicky Wallace. I take it you guys are some kind of *item*?"

"You could say that. It's an interesting story."

"Oooh this should be good. That is if you're willing to tell me."

Yeah, sure, John thought. John began telling Ray all about the email monitoring system (he hadn't shown him yet) and how we found an email sent by Vicky. He left out the details, and thankfully had earlier destroyed the evidence. He realized they were now about to enter the building, so he suggested they continue their walk for a few more minutes. They continued their walk on the immaculate grounds of the Wyndham Hotel, which was situated close by on Tahquitz.

"Are we allowed long coffee breaks?" Ray asked.

"One of the unofficial perks of being in IT."

They walked around the perimeter of the Wyndham, John explaining the whole Vicky story, sans the gory details. Ray seemed happy to be getting the low-down. John liked Ray, but didn't want to divulge too much just yet. Plus, they needed to head back to work.

In the afternoon, John demonstrated the ins and outs of the email monitoring system to Ray. He could tell that Ray loved this thing. They spent some time going over some of the dirty jokes that were trapped in the Nasty folder, and had a great time laughing.

"Okay, Ray, now that you've seen this stuff you gotta realize it's extremely confidential stuff. You're going to see things you didn't want to see from people you may know. I'm sure I don't have to tell you this, but I thought I'd mention it anyway," John said, with the company line firmly in tow.

"I know. My lips are sealed. Until I find someone to spill this shit to. Ha ha ha. No, I know what I signed up for. I don't even have to see any of this, actually. Right now I don't have any access to anything anyway."

"You didn't get the security clearance on your userid yet? I'll make sure Dan takes care of it," John said.

"Don't worry, it's only my first day. Just as long as I can sit with you and train a bit more, I'm happy. Next week I'll want to practice on doing some stuff on my own, if that's okay with you."

"Of course, next week we'll put you to work," John said, looking at his watch and noticing it was coming up on four thirty. He began closing the programs on his workstation. "Pretty much weekend time. We'll see ya Monday. Have a great weekend, Ray!"

"You too. Thanks for showing me the ropes today," Ray replied.

They left together and chatted about various topics as they approached the parking lot. They were both looking forward to continuing the training on Monday.

*   *   *   *

"Whoa … my … John your place is absolutely lovely. How can you *afford* this? Forgive me for asking that, but wow, this place is fantastic," Vicky said, as John walked her through the foyer into the living room.

"It was my grandparents' place. They left it to my mom and she said I should have it. Kinda lucky, huh? I just can't see a reason to ever leave here," John replied.

"That's pretty frickin' obvious. Still, Designer Vicky says the place could probably use some modernizing. It still kind of has a late 80's/early 90's motif. Ever think of doing some re-decorating?" Vicky asked, clearly wishing she could put all that time watching TLC and HGTV to good use.

"Yeah, yeah, I know you're hooked on *Trading Spaces* and all those design shows. I think you told me five times the other night. Maybe, just maybe, one day, I can get you to help me redecorate."

As they walked through the rest of his home, Vicky was amazed how large this place was for just one person. "How big is this place, two thousand square feet? Holy shit, it's large."

"More like 1,600. It looks a lot bigger than it really is. The open layout is deceiving. I love it though. I have so many good memories here. Come outside on the patio. We can sit outside on the loungers and watch the golfers struggle to sink their ball on the seventh hole."

"You *are* on the golf course. You are living large, King John!" Vicky said.

They sat together outside, each on a comfortable lounger, each wearing shorts and a t-shirt. The sun was beating down on them, and within five minutes, they were already starting to get warm. John pointed up to the orange tree that hung just above their heads to the right. He asked her to pick a few for fresh orange juice. John went inside for a moment, and returned promptly with a juicer. They sat together, drinking orange juice, enjoying each other's company, and admiring the fantastic view. Vicky hadn't seen so much green before. Between the greens of the golf course and the many surrounding trees and plants, *green* was certainly the prominent word that came to mind as one took in the visuals.

Conversation was flowing just as easily as it was at the Cheesecake Factory— even without the benefits of alcohol. John's cell phone rang, putting an abrupt end to their smoothly flowing dialogue.

"Johnny D in the place to be."

"John? How's it goin'? It's Tara."

"Tarawara! Whatup, girlie?" John was happy to hear from her.

"Not much. What are you doing today? It's gorgeous out. Perfect weather before it starts getting well into the 90s. Wanna go for a hike?"

"Ahhh, no can do Tara. I'm kinda preoccupied."

"Preoccupied huh? That sounds like polite-speak for *I'm about to get my freak on.* Is there something you haven't told me, John?"

"Perhaps, but we'll talk later, k? Gotta go. I'll call ya later this evening if you're gonna be around."

"Awwrite. Later dude."

John flipped his cell closed. He looked at Vicky apprehensively, unsure of how she was going to react given the excitement in his voice when mentioning Tara's name. John apologized for taking the call. Vicky remained silent. They resumed their conversation as if the phone hadn't even rung.

It was about fifteen minutes later that Vicky brought it up.

"So who's Tara? Not that it's any of my biz."

"She's a friend from work. And yeah, it's *kinda* your business. We do seem to have something going together, you and I. And if it were me, I'd wanna know too. So. That's about it. We've been hanging out almost since I started at DF."

"Cool. Did you sleep with her?"

"Wow. No beating around the bush for the Vickster. Not that *that information* is any of your business, ha ha, just kidding. Really. But no, we haven't even done anything sexual," John said, digging his heels into the concrete and pushing his lounger back so his was in line with Vicky's.

"You say that with a hint of disappointment in your voice, John. You like her, don't you?" Vicky asked, unable to mask the mild anger in her voice.

"Liked. Past tense. I'm telling you the truth. Her and I will be friends, but that's it. Right now I couldn't be happier with the way things are going with you. That's the truth," he said, looking her right in the eye to somehow enforce what he was saying. "Do you believe me? I can't be any more serious." John spoke with absolute conviction, although deep down, there was a small part of him that still wanted Tara. He wouldn't compromise his relationship with Vicky for it, but it scared him somewhat to admit to himself that there was something unfinished about his relationship with Tara. He put those thoughts away and prayed to the God of Deep Seated Unresolved Feelings to abolish those feelings forever more.

"I do believe you. That's what I find so attractive about you. Your convictions, your honesty, and your overall kindness. Oh yeah, and you're kinda hot too."

"Kinda?"

"Okay. Hot with a capital H. There, satisfied?"

"I *guess* so. You can show me later," John said, grinning ear to ear. He usually believed in himself as a good looking guy, but always thought that he was a bit too skinny. He worried that women didn't find his body *masculine* enough. Oh well, regardless, it seemed like his stuff was working well with Vicky.

They spent the afternoon together sunning, talking and fooling around. All in all, a perfect Saturday. This was going to have to be it for the two of them for the weekend, as Vicky wanted to spend the rest of the time with her daughter. John understood; right now he wasn't in the right frame of mind to completely commit all of his time to someone anyway. Things were going really well, and the apprehension John had felt earlier about Vicky was fleeting with each hour spent together. Life was good.

CHAPTER 11

▼

Training with Ray was going incredibly well. After three days, Ray had picked up on more information and procedures than John had ever expected. The two of them were getting along like they'd been friends for a long time.

John brought Ray along to coffee break with Aaron. After a few days of coffee breaks together, Ray was fitting in wonderfully. The three of them were already like the Three Amigos, thoroughly enjoying the male bonding experience. Ray most certainly shared their admiration for all the various *chicks* that they pointed out along the way.

Aaron and Ray loved getting all the details surrounding John's love life. Ray joined Aaron in his enjoyment of living vicariously through John's adventures.

*   *   *   *

Wednesday afternoon, John opened the Nasty folder and found what was probably the best email ever so far. He couldn't believe his eyes. This one beat Vicky's by a mile. He called Ray over to take a look. "Yo Ray, peep diss ovah here. This one'll blow you away."

"John. Look at your skin. Is it black? No? Really? Well, why do you talk like you're black? You're so sad," Ray said, somewhat jokingly, but with Ray it was always hard to tell.

"I swear I have black blood in me somewhere. Anyways, get over here and look at this!"

"Okay, but please, promise me, no more of that rapspeak," Ray begged.

The email came from a rising Hollywood star, Pope Harris. Ever since getting his breakout role in last year's blockbuster, *Sexy Ugly*, Pope was quickly becoming one of Hollywood's "it" boys. He had only been in one big film, and already the gossip mags were already pegging his salary for his next film at ten million.

"What the fuck kind of name is Pope anyway?" Ray asked.

"Don't ask me. I'm sure his parents didn't name him that way. Read this though," John said, as he double-clicked on the message, opening it up in a new window.

The email was sent to an employee in the Long Beach branch, a new branch that had just opened recently as the company expanded further north. It was their furthermost northern branch in California, twenty-five miles south of Los Angeles.

It wasn't the sexual content of the email that raised their eyebrows. Well, not really. Threesomes *were* mentioned. What really got their attention: the cocaine use, the fact that the third person in their *ménage* was a male, and the illegal procurement of weapons. This one had certain legal implications. John looked back and noticed that Jill was busy working and Dan must still be in one of those IT supervisor meetings. He turned to Ray.

Ray spoke first: "I don't know about you, but I have no frickin' clue about what to do. I've gone over the IT Security policies over and over, and there's really nothing that quite covers something like this. This Pope guy is one sick fuck, though."

"Yeah, that's for sure. I don't know what to do. Who's the chick he's emailing? Let's look her up," John said.

They looked her up. Heather Sweeney. No picture. Which means she hadn't been an employee long enough for a picture to appear in the online directory.

"Damn. Well that wouldn't really help anyway. I guess our curiosity just wants to know what this chick looks like. What do we do? I have no idea, Ray. Perhaps we should bring it to the Legal department."

"You're the boss, man. I'll do what you wanna do."

"My initial gut reaction is to leave it for now … We'll release it from the Nasty folder jail, so that she gets the email. She'll reply and then we can start a whole separate folder just for this. This is too good to nip in the bud and have it end before it gets better," John said, having already made up his mind.

"Are you sure? Shouldn't we tell anyone?"

"Yeah, we'll tell Dan later on when nobody's around. *Everyone* knows Pope … the less people that know about this the better."

John took the next step and called Lee. "Lee, I'm going to need to change the admin password on the email monitor box. I know we just changed it last week, and it's not due for a password change for another three weeks, but something came up and it needs to be changed." John didn't want to take any chances with someone hacking into that system. "Is there anything you need access to it for? If so, let me know, if not, I'm going to change the password now. I thought I should let you know. Ray knows as well, but I don't want to set off any alarms if you start wondering why I put through a password change."

"I don't need it. That's your baby. The less I know about that stuff the better. I hear you've had some interesting stuff come up in there. No, I don't wanna know. Nothing would surprise me, anyway. Okay, change the password; go ahead," Lee said.

John highlighted the email from Pope Harris and clicked on the green light button on the tool bar to release the email. "Now, let's see how far this email conversation is going to go," John told Ray.

*   *   *   *

Jennifer Billings was walking home from school, and finally feeling more like her normal self over the last few days. She decided to take a shortcut and walk across the sand swept and tumbleweed-infested land situated behind her neighborhood. Memories of wild, out-of-control partying with all the cool kids flooded her mind as a strand of tumbleweed grazed her left leg with a harsh sting.

The abuse she had been taking from those bitchy girls had almost *stopped*, both in school and online. Could I finally get back to my *life* now? She wondered. Those thoughts were quickly halted; as she noticed Britney, and another girl she didn't really know, approach her. She swore out loud, noting that she was only a few more minutes away from the comforts of home.

"The fuck do you want with me, bitch?" Jen asked, more angry than scared.

"Slutwhore," the other girl said.

"Stay out of it, you fat beyotch!" Jen ordered, not understanding who this girl was and why she was with Britney.

"Yeah? What you gon' do about it?" Britney said, speaking for the first time.

From out of the blue, the other girl took a sucker punch at Jen. The girl's index finger connected with Jen's nose. Unfortunately for Jen, the girl was wearing a thick ring on that finger, thus sharpening the impact.

Before Jen could say anything, or even think of retaliating, the girls ran away.

"Yeah, run, you fucking slobs!" Jen yelled after them.

Jen noticed she was bleeding from the nose and searched her handbag for a Kleenex. She applied the Kleenex to her nose and held it there for several minutes, looking up at the beautiful mountains to the north. If this place weren't so damn gorgeous, she'd love to beg her mom to move. *If I can just get through the next few months, I can graduate and then go to UCLA or something,* Jen thought.

She got home and cleaned her wound. It still hurt a bit, but not too bad. She'd live. Looking in the mirror however, she noticed that she didn't look all that great. This was going to leave a mark, and going to school tomorrow was going to suck. She wasn't sure what to do about that girl that punched her. She was obviously from another school or something. What could she do to get back at her? She'd have to think about it.

Right now all she wanted to do was nap. She fell asleep for about an hour, woke up and turned on the computer. Firing up MSN, she hoped Cassie was on so she could tell her about what happened. Maybe Cassie's brother Assface could help her out and find that girl. He knew a lot of people in Palm Springs—maybe he would be able to track her down.

Cassie was on, but her status was set to *Away.* She tried to message her, but Cassie wasn't replying. Several chat windows opened up from other friends, but she wasn't in the mood for chatting with them so she set her status to *Busy.* A small window on the bottom of her computer screen popped up saying John had just logged in; maybe he would be good to talk to.

She double clicked on him and a new chat window opened.

Jennaybobennay:	*hey U*
JohnnyD:	*heya*
Jennaybobennay:	*wutup*
JohnnyD:	*just got home from werk, otherwise not 2 mucking fuch*
Jennaybobennay:	*heheheheeh good one I like that*
JohnnyD:	*kewt eh?*
Jennaybobennay:	*yep. hey can u turn ur cam on?*
JohnnyD:	*y?*
Jennaybobennay:	*cuz I wanna show u something*
JohnnyD:	*whoa. should I ask?*

Jennaybobennay:	*nothing like that asshole. turn urs on and I'll turn mine on.*
JohnnyD:	*ok, why not.*

John started his webcam and Jen followed. Now their live *feeds* appeared beside each of their names on the right hand side of the window.

Jennaybobennay:	*nice to put a face to the screen name*
JohnnyD:	*yeah fer sher*
Jennaybobennay:	*ya know ur kinda kewt actually for an old guy*
JohnnyD:	*hahahaha … ur kewt 2 fer someone who's still way 2 young*
Jennaybobennay:	*hey I'm gon b 18 soon*
JohnnyD:	*kool. hey what happened 2 ur nose?*
Jennaybobennay:	*that's what I wanted to talk 2 u about. i needed 2 tell someone*
JohnnyD:	*ouch. ru ok?*
Jennaybobennay:	*yeah, but it hurtz. i swear i think i wanna kill someone tho. i'm just so fucking angry.*
JohnnyD:	*tell me what happened.*

Jen told John the story. John advised that the best thing would be to just try and avoid the bitchy girls at school, and for the next while not to walk home alone. If the girls ever showed up again, at least she would have someone to back her up.

Jen could tell from John's facial expressions that he really cared. She found herself strangely attracted to him; perhaps it was his caring nature and sense of humor. Plus, he was a pretty decent looking guy. It wasn't like older guys weren't attractive to her either. When she was with her ex Brad, everyone compared them to Brad Pitt and Jennifer Aniston, Hollywood's Super Couple. She thought Brad Pitt was super hot, and wasn't he like forty?

Jen tried to flirt a bit with him to see how he would react. He seemed visibly uncomfortable with it, but still flirted back in a reserved kind of way. She didn't really want to push it too much because right now she really was just enjoying having an adult male to share her feelings with.

Her mom arrived home, and Jen knew she would have to explain her new look. She ended her chat with John, turned off the computer and went downstairs to deal with mom. Hopefully she wouldn't freak out too much.

*   *   *   *

"Mmmm, Travelchick, will you marry me?" Ray joked with John and Aaron as they collectively stared with appreciaton at the girl who worked at the travel agency. It was becoming customary to begin their morning coffee break with a brief analysis of the travel agent's wardrobe, hairstyle, and perceived mood. Eventually they hoped to walk across and introduce themselves, as it was painfully obvious to her that she was the subject of their conversations.

"Yeah, she's got it goin' on today I tell ya. Very nice. Hey do you guys ever watch that *Ali G Show* on HBO? The guy who does it has this character named Borat. It's hilarious, ya gotta check it out," Aaron said.

"Holy shit, that guy is so funny," John agreed. "I've seen it a few times and it's so hilarious. I wonder if it will take off, though. The guy is money!"

"Never seen it. We don't get HBO, so I'm kinda screwed. Oh well," Ray said.

"So anyway boys, yesterday I go online and that young chick Jen is on and she asks me to put on my cam. I wondered why, then she put hers on and revealed this really awful bruise on her nose. Seems she was jumped by some psycho bitch."

"Now that you've seen her, is she hot?" Aaron asked, somewhat tauntingly.

"Fuck, enough with that. Don't you even care about her well being?" John asked.

"Do you?" Aaron quipped right back. "I mean, sorry, I know you *must* care about her in some way, and I actually think it's kinda sweet what you seem to represent for her, but seriously … just answer me … is she hot or what?"

"Okay! Yes, she is kinda hot. But she's not even eighteen yet. And even if she were like nineteen or something, I'm too paranoid to do anything that would fuck up what I have going so far with Vicky. Nuh uh. I mean, I'll chat with Jen once in a while, flirt a bit even, but nothing more," John declared, in a slightly defensive tone.

"My two pesos? I say if she starts coming on to you, you're going to be all wound up and you won't know what to do. Advice: just keep it really platonic. You don't want to end up in a situation that you really shouldn't be in. Even if she were eighteen, or even twenty-one. Not worth it. Vicky's a hottie, John. Keep things on the up and up," Ray advised.

"I agree with Ray. Be careful with this one, my gut says you're almost asking for trouble, even chatting with her. Especially with the cams on," Aaron said.

"Okay, okay, I get the picture. Shit. Anyway … what else?" John said, changing the subject.

"Bust anyone lately?" Aaron asked.

"Not really. Nothing good," John said, looking at Ray with a subtle grin.

"You guys suck. C'mon guys, gimme some good stories. I love hearing stories of our employees gone wild!" Aaron exclaimed.

*   *   *   *

Later that morning, John's eyes almost popped out of their sockets when he checked the Nasty folder just before lunch. Yet another email exchange between Heather Sweeney and Pope Harris:

From: Sweeney, Heather
To: thepopester@gmail.com
Subject: re: last night

K, so I think I may be able to meet u again tonight. I enjoyed the other night too. Do you really think you're ready to commit to me already? I know we've only been out a few times, and I'm flattered, but you're just so always in the spotlight. Do you really think your fans will accept you with a girl like me?

I know I can do it for you, you made that pretty obvious. But isn't it pretty easy to hold a guy's attention by blowing him like crazy? You love the deep throat though, don't you. Can I admit something to you? I've never done cocaine before. It was such a rush. That combined with having two guys fill each hole was one of the greatest pleasures I have ever known.

I'm a little concerned about you carrying a loaded weapon with you all the time. Isn't having a bodyguard enough protection? Sure the paparazzi can be pretty low, but I don't think it will ever escalate to you requiring the use of a piece. Whatever I guess. I can't wait to see you again later. Let me know when — and we'll meet at your crib. Are you bringing Tyler along again? Even if you don't, I'm ok with it. I'm sure we'll be good to go either way.

Let me know what's up … write back soon!

Heather

Wow. This was awesome! John read on, though Pope's reply was rather anti-climactic:

From: popester@gmail.com
To: Sweeney, Heather
Subject: re: last night

Heath,

Yes you do it for me and no it's not just the deep throat. Meet me at 9, we'll hook up. Tyler can't come, so it's just you and me and the blow and the blow hahaha. Don't say anything about the piece to anyone, remember it's not registered. Cya l8r.

"What do we do?" Ray asked.

"I don't know. I say we just let this continue. Dan is pretty cool with it. When we talked about it yesterday we agreed that this was pretty sensitive stuff, and once it gets really crazy we'll have to turn it over to Victor Nunez in HR. Perhaps even the legal department. We should probably take it to Patrick as well; he always likes to be kept up on these situations. He'll probably get a kick out of it. But man, how stupid can someone be to mention an unregistered firearm in an email?"

"Damn, I should just ring my friend Joey Styles at *Tattle Inc.* magazine and hand this to him. He'd shit himself!" Ray exclaimed.

"You know someone who works for that rag? That mag is pretty nasty. Don't they get sued by the celebs all the time?"

"Sure, but they make so much fucking money it doesn't matter to them. People love getting their gossip fix, man. It'll never go out of style," Ray said.

✻   ✻   ✻   ✻

John decided that the end of the day was the best time to present the information on the Pope emails to Patrick Bowman. At four thirty each afternoon, the IT area pretty much cleared out. John wandered through the sea of empty cubicles and arrived at Patrick's door. Patrick looked busy as always, his desk buried in paper. John knocked on the door.

"Come in!" Patrick yelled. John opened the door and sat down in a chair on the other side of Patrick's monstrous desk. The concept of having chairs that sat much lower than that of the big boss was not lost on John. He knew it was a managerial power play that made subordinates feel lower than their boss.

Patrick began the conversation. "So what can I do for you, John? I'm just trying to finish up some paperwork here, but if you have something important to discuss, I'm all ears," he said.

"Umm, it seems like we have another email incident that should be brought to your attention," John said. He tried to sit up as straight as possible to be at eye level with his boss. Even though John was probably a good five inches taller than Patrick, the difference in chair heights was still favoring the manager.

"Another incident. Wow, as one who really enjoys the study of human behavior I must say I'm not surprised. People will never learn, will they?" Patrick asked, not expecting an answer. "So what's the deal on this one?"

"This one's kind of juicy," John began. For the first time since meeting Patrick, he felt that he was being treated as an almost-equal by the big, bad IT Director. "Seems like that new Hollywood star, Pope Harris, is involved in various acts of sex, drugs and weapons, and has no problem revealing his lifestyle in email messages. He's got a thing going with one of the employees here, her name is Heather Sweeney, but she's not at this branch. Not sure how to proceed. I wanted to let you know though."

"I've heard of the guy, but I try not to follow all of the Hollywood gossip. So have you done anything with the emails?" Patrick asked, shuffling a stack of papers into a file folder on his desk.

"No, not yet," John replied. He wasn't quite sure whether he should admit to having let the emails go through instead of having them blocked as per their policy. Might as well be honest though. "But I'm allowing the emails to flow through, not keeping them held in our email jail, just so we can see what they're up to. I hope that's ok."

"Of course, I would do the same myself. I would just keep monitoring it—we can't really do anything much about what Pope says or does, but eventually we may need to bring Legal in. Not sure. Please keep me up to date on this, though."

"Will do," John said with a smile. Patrick's body language indicated that the meeting was likely over, and any attempts at making small talk would be futile. He stood up and kept the smile on his face. "Have a good evening," John said as he made his way out of Patrick's office.

"You too," Patrick replied, already moving on to more paperwork.

*   *   *   *

Patrick Bowman shut the door about a minute after John left and picked up the phone.

"Seems like your boy Pope is more of an idiot than I thought," he said to his friend on the other end of the line.

"Don't even tell me about it, I don't want to know," his friend replied.

"The guy is lower than scum, and each time I hear his name it just pisses me off more. I wish he would just go away. What he did that night was unforgivable," Patrick growled.

"He's money though, Patty. Pure gold. I wish it had never happened to her, but what can I do?" His friend said, with as much of a consoling tone as he could muster.

"Bastard," Patrick said, hanging up the phone.

Patrick knew many of his minions didn't like him, but he didn't believe that they actually *hated* him. Hate is such a strong word. He hated Pope though, and that was a certainty.

*   *   *   *

John and Vicky were supposed to get together that evening but she called him at the end of the day to tell him that she wasn't feeling that great, and she'd make it up to him tomorrow.

I could handle that, John thought.

As John's thoughts wandered, he couldn't help but thinking of another thing he and Vicky had talked about earlier. She mentioned to him that her once casual boyfriend, he of the infamous email, wasn't happy with her calling off their relationship. He wanted to keep seeing her and couldn't understand how she can just end things so abruptly, especially for a guy she had only gone out with on a few dates.

Was this the reason for her canceling their plans tonight? Was she seeing him tonight? Even if it were to break it off in person? For whatever reason, John couldn't help himself from having it consume his evening.

What he did next surprised him, even as he was doing it. He promised himself he would never do it, regardless of how curious he ever got. But here he was, using the Terminal Services program on his PC to log on to the corporate email server. He went right to Vicky's email box, and checked to see if there was any incriminating evidence about her activities this evening. To his relief, there was nothing suspicious whatsoever.

Still, it was certainly possible that she erased any personal email at the end of the day, as many employees often did. His mind wouldn't be put to rest. Maybe he should call her just to see how she's doing. If she's not home, then bingo—she's caught.

He called her and she answered. She told him she was doing okay, still had quite the headache, but was happy that he called. They talked for about ten minutes; John was pretty sure that *he* was not there, and his suspicions were put to rest. *Whew.*

Who else's email could he check? He swore to himself that this was going to be the last time he would ever do this. For the next two hours, John picked people he knew at random and inspected the contents of their mailbox. He found evidence of several office affairs, which was probably the most salacious of evidence. Otherwise, nothing that serious. The voyeuristic thrill he received while doing this was overwhelming. Nevertheless, he swore again that this was going to be an isolated incident. Never again.

✳   ✳   ✳   ✳

By Friday, John was feeling pretty much back to normal. Things over the last few days with Vicky were pretty blissful, in fact. They went out for lunch once and shared a wonderful evening together. They were planning to spend the weekend together—Vicky was going to loosen up the apron strings a bit and allow her daughter to spend the weekend alone in the house.

"So what are we going to do this weekend? What do you have planned for me, Johnny?" Vicky asked, calling John before the end of the day to see what he had in mind for them.

"I have a few great things planned. I know you like hiking, so we're going to spend the morning tomorrow at Indian Canyon trails. Then we're going to head north to LA to get a taste of the Hollywood experience. I recall you having not really experienced Hollywood, even though you've only been a few hours away for most of your life."

"I know, isn't it sad? Man, that sounds pretty awesome. Where are we going to stay in Hollywood? What are we going to do there?"

"Just leave it up to me. It's gonna rock! I promise," he said, unable to conceal his excitement.

✳   ✳   ✳   ✳

They woke up early on Saturday, and not surprisingly, the weather cooper-ated. It was already seventy-six degrees by eight o'clock. By noon it would proba-bly be too hot for hiking. John hopped in his Acura MDX and swung by Vicky's place to get her. She jumped in the car and within the first minute it was obvious the two were eager to have their first weekend together.

Hiking at Indian Canyon trails was a wonderful experience. Vicky had never been there before, and John was more than happy to share this beautiful place with her. He often hiked there whenever he felt he needed to think and didn't feel like driving, he would come here. The trails were not terribly difficult, even for the amateur hiker. The views of the mountains and the valley below, the gor-geous canyons, lush foliage and various creepy crawlies made for an unforgettable experience for Vicky.

"I can't believe I've lived here all this time and never done this. This was incredible, John. I would have never thought to do something like this," she said, kicking off a chunk of gravel that accumulated on top of her shoe. "I'm not even that *tired*. If this is how the weekend is starting, I can't wait to see how it goes from here. Where have you been all my life, hun?"

John grabbed her hand and lifted her up from one of the steeper hills on the climb. "Don't know, but maybe this is fate. Maybe this is how it's supposed to be, and we were meant to meet when we did. But what do I know. I do know I'm really enjoying. Now lets go climb down and hike back, then we can get lunch on the way out and head to LA."

"Lead the way. I'm just your loyal follower this weekend," Vicky joked, pok-ing John in the ribs and then grabbing him towards her for a passionate kiss.

As they approached the 101 before turning onto Santa Monica Blvd., John finally gave in as to where they were staying. Vicky had been trying to get it out of him ever since they left Palm Springs.

"We're staying at the Montrose. It's a relatively small, boutique-like hotel right in the middle of Hollywood. It's super close to Sunset Boulevard. You can, like, walk there in about two minutes. The suite-like rooms have a kitchen, a bal-cony, and a raised bedroom. You gotta see it. Plus, the best part … the view from the hot tub and pool is to *dah-eee faw*," John said, finishing in his best *Linda Richman* impression. "You can almost see all of LA. You will freak, Vicky."

"Wow, I can't wait. Sounds awesome. This is almost too good to be true … Hey wait a second, how do you know so much about this hotel? Did you bring another girl there?" Vicky asked, as her face went from glorious smile to despondent frown in an instant.

"Vicky. Look at me," he tried to look deep in her eyes while trying his best to concentrate on the road to make sure he didn't miss his turn. "I have never been here with a girl. I came once with a few guys when we came to party. I loved it and said to myself that I would bring someone special here. That would be where you come in."

"Really? You mean it???"

"Yes, I do. I'm not lying, and yes, you're special. Now sit back, relax, and enjoy our in-car entertainment." He flipped the radio to Power 106, wondering to himself why he hadn't thought of that earlier. He knew Vicky didn't really like rap, but she told him she would keep an open mind and try to appreciate it.

Vicky was really freaked out during the initial part of their drive down the famous Sunset strip. She couldn't believe how many homeless people were scattered all over the street. She had always seen them on the news, but it was different being there to observe it for herself. She felt helpless that not much could be done to help these people who lived their lives on the street. Her heart went out to these men and women who were likely living normal lives at one time or another.

Once they parked the car and checked in to the hotel, they took a stroll down Sunset. She loved seeing all the sights, the people, and the bright lights. The whole experience. They found a great Thai place on Sunset, and instead of eating at the restaurant—which didn't really look too shit hot anyway—they decided they'd take out and eat at the hotel. She remarked how Sunset Boulevard was something everyone should experience at one point in their lifetime.

After savoring every bite of their wonderful meal, they sat on the balcony and chatted for a while. Vicky wished the view from the balcony were better, but she knew she shouldn't complain. They held hands and enjoyed the light breeze that was giving a nice chill to the air that they hadn't experienced in Palm Springs for a while now. When Vicky got a bit too cold, she grabbed John by the arm and led him to the bedroom.

Not a word was said. They made love for the first time. It was a fantastic experience for both of them. It was two hours of unbridled passion that had been held back for far too long. To John, it was the best mix of making love and fucking that he could imagine. It was one part gentle, one part kinky. Bondage didn't even enter into the equation. He was spent. Vicky was energized.

"I think I'm falling in love with you," Vicky gushed.

"I think I am too—falling for you, that is. Can we love each other at this point in our relationship?" John wondered aloud.

"Why not? What is love anyway? Whatever it is, I think I'm feeling it."

"I am too. Mmmm Vicky, that was fucking awesome, pardon my French."

"Oui oui!!! I agree!" Vicky said.

*   *   *   *

They had planned to hit a club on Sunset to get a true Hollywood vibe going, but they were enjoying just laying together. They decided they would lie in bed for a while, and if they changed their mind, they could always still head out. It was only eleven o'clock.

At 11:15, John's cell phone rang.

"This is John."

"Still want to meet?" The caller on the other line said.

"Yeah give me about twenty minutes," John said quietly, not wanting Vicky to hear.

"Okay, I'll be on the corner of Sunset and Larrabee, right across from the Viper Room. Did you bring it?"

"Yep. See ya."

John hung up. He lied and told Vicky it was his buddy Aaron, who wanted to get together and forgot that they were going out of town. He told Vicky he was starving after their marathon session, and was going to head down to Sunset to grab a chicken sub at Subway. Vicky was okay with it, and just asked that he bring her one too, and not to be too long. She was hoping for an encore.

"If the food re-energizes me, we're good to go for one more round!" John exclaimed.

*   *   *   *

John waited for Joey Styles from *Tattle Inc.* magazine where they had planned to meet when John called him last night. John was a few minutes early, despite having to pull the papers out of his suitcase without arising any suspicion from Vicky.

"You John?" Joey asked.

"That's me. So how much is this worth to you?"

"Like I said, if this shit's real, it's worth seven large for you. If those emails continue, you and I can be really good friends. You're going to be making more money from me than you ever will with that geek job of yours. Let me see the printouts."

John handed him the emails he had printed out from home last night. Joey read them over and his grin got bigger and bigger with every turn of the page. *Could this finally be the solution to my financial problems?*

Joey handed John an envelope with his remuneration. *Yup.*

"Fuckin A man—you are the king, Sir John. This is going to look so fucking good on the front page of the mag next week. Sheee-it. I think I'm gonna gizz my pants, dude," Joey said, clearly excited with John's *contribution.*

"You aren't going to print the actual emails, and you won't reveal your source, right Joey?" John asked, wanting to ensure his ass was covered. Both of their heads turned to examine the two scantily clad headbanger chicks about to enter the Viper Room.

"Nice stuff, hey John? Wow." Joey's eyes were still glued to the girls' chests. "Anyway, why would I ruin this cash cow that you represent to the magazine? Hell no. All we say is that this shit is coming for a very reliable source. So reliable, that we have proof. Pope is such a fucking idiot that he won't know that his email has been compromised. He'll just keep doing it. We can get new shit on him every week, as long as he keeps bangin' your employee there. I gotta run, Sir John. We'll chat next week."

With that, Joey was gone.

John ran to Subway, ordered two oven roasted chicken subs, and returned to the hotel. Before heading up to the room, he took the elevator to the small parking garage and hid the envelope full of cash in the trunk of the MDX. This would go a long way into paying back the huge line of credit he had with the bank. Plus, if things kept up the way they were going with these emails, he may even make enough to pay his mother back. He hated owing money, especially to family.

This is more of a thrill than gambling, anyway, he thought.

CHAPTER 12

▼

The first month of John and Vicky's relationship continued on the same path as it began. John's initial distrust of Vicky's former casual fling had dissipated quickly. The weekend they had spent consummating the relationship, so to speak, pretty much cemented what had now become a very solid ground for the connection that they shared.

John had met Joey Styles twice more since their initial meeting on Sunset. In less than a month, John had already made enough money from the incriminating emails to repay his mom and part of the line of credit from the bank. The frequency of electronic correspondence between Pope and Heather had slowed somewhat, but they still emailed at least twice per week, with varying levels of guilt-ridden content.

It was an intensely hot day in April, one of those days where the desert area is blanketed with heat seen only in the middle of summer. What made it difficult to deal with for residents of the Coachella valley was the moderate humidity that accompanied the high temperatures. Definitely not Florida-like humidity, but because it was so rare for the area, you'd be hard pressed to find any of the locals mutter the overused "but it's a *dry* heat" expression. DesertFinancial had a business casual dress code, so jeans and shorts were not appropriate. The air conditioning was especially strong in the IT area, so IT staff just always felt cold. Not today. No level of artificial cooling was going to relieve the Cinnabon-like stickiness experienced from spending even a few moments outside.

After the morning coffee with the three musketeers, John and Ray broke away from Aaron. Ray suggested that they needed to talk.

"Yeah sure, what's up man? Did ya catch anything really good?" John asked. Two weeks ago Ray had been given the proper security clearance required to access the monitoring server and software.

"Not really, but this shit is pretty confidential. I don't think we should talk here. I hate to suggest it today of all days, but let's take a walk at lunch," Ray suggested.

"Yeah, sure, if you think that's best, but man is it ever hot today. I hate this humidity. I went for a walk early this morning and even at six thirty I couldn't stand it. Let's walk downtown where there's more shade on the one side of the street."

"Right on."

They made small talk for the first part of their walk. Once they found the comforts of the shade, Ray spoke up.

"Dude, I gotta tell ya something. I heard from my buddy Joey Styles last night. He said you guys have been, er, collaborating on a project."

"Oh shit. Umm, yeah, I guess we are …"

"Fuck, John, I told you about that in confidence. I'm actually not mad at you personally. You haven't really done anything to me. Don't worry about that. I'm just worried about how it may look professionally if anyone found out."

"What are you saying???" John asked, worried now.

"Not what you're thinking. I would never say anything. I think you're a great guy, man. You've made me feel really welcome here, and I enjoy hanging with you. What I'm worried about—is Joey. I think you're playing with fire here. He's not exactly a reputably moralistic individual. Look what he does for a living," Ray said.

"I see what you're saying. I don't know what I was thinking. I guess I got caught up in the whole Hollywood thing, feeling in some way like I'm doing my part in shaping the Hollywood celebrity landscape, ya know?" John said, as they were passing the Palm Springs Follies theatre. He had never seen the show, and always wondered what it would be like, even if it seemed to draw crowds of only those aged sixty and over. The Follies just didn't seem to belong anymore to the *new* Palm Springs, his vision of Palm Springs.

"I do. I know what you're saying. I've been an extra in a lot of movies. I'm sure I've told you that before. I'd love to make it as an actor, but hey. Whatever. I see where you're coming from. But what if Joey ever decides that he's going to reveal his source. He's got the emails. He's the kind of guy that will do whatever it takes to serve his own purpose, regardless of the effect it has on others. I just don't want you to get in any trouble at work."

Even walking in the shade, it was too hot. They ducked into the lobby of the Hyatt Regency on Palm Canyon to resume their discussion in comfort.

"Right. I'm kinda pissed that the guy told you anything at all. He promised my confidentiality," John said.

"John! Look at what he represents. Do you think the word confidentiality is even in this guy's fucking vocabulary???"

"I guess. So what are you doing being friends with him?"

"I just know him from another friend. We've seen each other at parties and stuff. I wouldn't put him on my list for people to hang out with, that's for sure. You however, are. I'm just looking out for you. I've got your back, man," Ray confirmed.

"Thanks. So what should I do? Cut Joey off? No more fodder for him?"

"That's a start."

Ray had convinced John to cut all ties with Joey and stop selling the emails. John felt terrible; this was something he questioned himself on every day. Despite needing the money, he always considered himself an otherwise ethical guy.

John still kept this information from Vicky; he surely didn't want her to know that he would be so foolish in compromising his future with DesertFinancial. This was really the only thing that he kept from her though. Outside of this one issue, his life was pretty much an open book to her. He finally felt that he was in a relationship that wasn't just 50/50, or 80/20. It was as close to Dr. Phil's recommended 100/100 as he thought possible. They were equal in their contributions to their relationship.

When John came home after that rough day at work, paranoia still poisoning his thoughts, he just wanted to sleep. Despite the heat, he came home, threw his clothes on the floor, grabbed his bathing suit and ran out the door to the hot tub. He needed to melt his tense muscles. He sat there for twenty minutes, allowing the jets to alternate between his shoulder blades and lower back, where the tension was most intense. The heat of the late day sun shining on his body combined with the heat of the hot tub seemed to do the trick in dissolving his anxieties.

He took a walk around the pathways that weaved in and out of the large townhomes that made up the isolated community he was so comfortable with. He cleared his head enough and came to a feeling of relaxation that had eluded him all day since having the chat with Ray.

John made himself dinner and ate while surfing the Internet. Jen MSN'd him and asked him to chat. John wondered what she wanted—their online relationship had declined to a chat once per week, just to catch up. Her problems with the girls at school had seemed to go away, thanks in part to her friend Cassie's brother. Jen couldn't say for sure, but she was fairly confident that *Assface* had something to do with it.

Jen said there was a new problem in her life, and she wasn't comfortable discussing it online. Jen begged to see John in person. She promised that everything was on the up and up. She really needed to talk to someone. In person. And John was her last resort, she said. Against every shred of his common sense, John reluctantly agreed to pick her up at the Taco Bell on Highway 111.

✳   ✳   ✳   ✳

Jen saw John's MDX and approached the car.

"You're John, right?"

"That's me. Jen, hi. Nice to meet you. Hop in if you like."

Jen jumped in. "Let's just drive for a bit. I won't take much of your time. I really appreciate this. I really do. Totally," Jen said.

They made small talk for the first five minutes or so. John was really uncomfortable being in this situation. His heart was pounding so loud that his ears were pulsating. He told himself that he was just doing a good thing for someone in need. Every minute or so, he caught himself looking to his right and noticing how naturally pretty this girl was. *Stop it, John. You're in a really good relationship. Don't even think these thoughts. Stop!*

Jen told him that her friend Shawn, from math class, a guy she had been friends with for a long time, had finally confessed his love for her. She admitted to having feelings for him as well. The problem was, he couldn't get over the rumors about her. No matter how often she would explain that they were not at all true, he couldn't seem to let them go, at least in his mind.

John couldn't help making a comparison to his own feelings about Vicky and that email, especially the part about the bondage. He wanted to tell himself it was in the past, but a part of him was unable to get over it.

"*Chasing Amy*," was all John said.

"What????" Jen asked, obviously confused.

"The Kevin Smith movie. Rent it tonight. Similar plot. Boyfriend can't get over the rumors about his chick. You haven't seen it?"

"No. I saw *Clerks* though. That rocked," Jen said.

"Well, *Chasing Amy* may just be his masterpiece. Rent it. But instead of just telling you to get your advice from a movie, I guess you want something more," John said, as they continued driving down Highway 111. His eyes remained focused on the road. "There's really not much more I can tell you, Jen. He's really gotta realize that you aren't defined by what is said about you. A mature guy would realize this, and see you for who you are, and those things … worries and feelings, would just go away. Ya know? Time will tell, Jen. You either give him time, or you don't. You deserve to have a guy who isn't going to question your past. Especially if the present is really good." As the words left his mouth, he realized that he should practice what he was preaching to Jen. Vicky deserves that consideration. "You guys have a good time together when all that shit isn't hanging over your heads?" John finally asked, taking a deep breath.

"Yeah, we do. That's what drives me so fuckin' crazy. I think I love him, I know him so well, but … deep down I know he thinks I'm this slut that I'm totally not. It really sucks. I see what you're tellin' me though. That makes sense. You kinda rock, you know. Your girlfriend is totally lucky to have you, man," Jen said, with a hint of flirtation in her voice that was not at all lost on John.

"I'm flattered, Jen. I think this Shawn guy is very lucky to have you, too. He just has to realize it."

"Awww … too bad you're not like more my age. Why do guys seem to get better as they get older? It's not at all fair," Jen said, punching John in the shoulder as she said it. "And, you're *so* the tall, dark, and handsome type. Good dresser as well. Nothing like the guys at school. Oh well," her voice trailed off.

John remained silent. He suppressed the desire to just grab her and kiss her. He felt like he was in high school again, driving with his girlfriend, thinking of a place they could go and make out. He felt so *young. Stop it, John!*

John made a U-Turn at Frank Sinatra Drive and drove back towards the Taco Bell where he picked her up.

"Did you want me to drop you at home?"

"No, I'm meeting Shawn at the McDonalds next door anytime now. So you can just drop me back there. I appreciate our talk. You're a great guy." She punched him in the shoulder again.

Was she flirting with me? John wondered. *Is she teasing me? Either way, I ain't buyin. I'm just here to help her. That's it.*

✳   ✳   ✳   ✳

"So where do you guys want to go?" Travelchick asked, as John, Ray and Aaron stood across from her desk.

"I don't know, really. We were hoping you were going to suggest something. If we want to get away for a bit before summer, what have you got for us?" Aaron asked her, taking the lead for the three of them, who were all standing around rather sheepishly.

"Are you all going like, *together* together?" she asked with a wink.

"First of all, I'm Aaron, this here's my buddy Ray, and this is John. It's very nice to meet you—" Aaron paused, waiting for her to fill in the blank.

"Samantha. I see you guys all the time across at Starbucks. Nice to meet you all," she told them.

"We're really not creepy or anything, really we're not. We're just two married guys and one getting-in-a-serious-relationship guy, who, well, you can just say we can look at the menu but just won't order. That's us. We're really good guys!" Ray piped up.

"I see-eee," Samantha the travel chick said, drawing out the word *see*. "From where I'm sitting, you guys must be really, really hungry cause you're doin' a lot of menu lookin'. If you aren't orderin' anything, I hope y'all get to eat at home. Umm, please pardon that pun. Forget I just said that, okay? So are y'all really looking to go away together or are you just here to introduce yourselves?"

"A little of both, to be honest. I think at various points in the next six months all of us may require your services. *Travel* services, Samantha, don't get any ideas. Ha ha. Let us take some of your brochures and we'll be on our way. See? Aren't we just fine, upstanding young gentlemen?" John finally spoke.

"Two out of three ain't bad," Samantha joked.

"Which two?" Ray asked.

"I'll give you upstanding, and you'll just have to guess the other one. Have a good day, boys," Samantha said.

The guys walked across to Starbucks and lucked out on getting their favorite table.

"So yoyoyoyo check it out, I gotta tell you guys somethin'," John said, unable to conceal his enthusiasm for what he was about to reveal.

"John. You are *not* Randy Jackson, and you're not a dawg. Awww-ITE? You crack me up," Ray quipped in his sarcastic tone.

"Ray, you're just pissed because you have no insight into the hip hop culture. You feel left out. That's okay. We understand. But hey, we can always *school* you for free," Aaron said somewhat sarcastically, coming to John's defense.

"What fucking *ever*. Enough of the rap shit. John, we're waiting. Your life is just one wicked event after another. You're giving new meaning to the term vicarious. Aaron, what would we do without this guy, hey?" Ray said.

"My life is pretty frickin' cool, isn't it? Okay, *get* this, guys. Yesterday I had a pretty bad day at work. Ray, you can attest to that I'm sure."

"Yeah, you were severely busy. Security isn't always fun and games, Aaron. Not always glitz and glamour," Ray interrupted, assisting John in their attempts to ensure Aaron doesn't find out about John's recent missteps with corporate confidentiality.

"Okay, okay, will you guys let me tell this? So I get home, take a hot tub and chill. Then Jen comes on MSN and tells me she really needs to talk, needs a male opinion …"

"I'm really scared about where this story is going. Ray, you feelin' me on this one?" Aaron said.

"Yep. But dammit, we want to hear it anyway, don't we Aaron?"

"Sure as fuck do. John, continue."

"*Anyway,* I pick her up and we just drive around and chat. She supposedly has a new dude, a guy she's been friends with for quite some time and now wants to make it more of a real thing, but he can't get past all the nasty rumors that are floating around about her," John said.

"Okay, now I *really* feel like we're in high school," Ray quipped.

"We will always be in high school. Adult life is just high school for grown-ups. Once we realize this fact we'll all be better off," Aaron pointed out.

"Would you guys just quit interrupting my story? Holy shit you guys can be irritating sometimes. So we drive around and I give her my advice. I don't act like a pervert at all—I'm just there for her. She's a sweet person. I kind of feel for her. Being a high school student is not the same as it was for us. Think of all the extra shit they need to deal with every day … Anyway, before you say anything, no, nothing happened. At all. She punched me in the shoulder a few times, nothing at all sexual, but the way she looked at me, it was kind of, like, I don't know, almost like she's testing me or something. Or teasing."

"Okay. Understood. So what's your problem? Are you asking for advice on anything?" Aaron asked.

"I don't know," John said. "Do you think she's trying to test me to see if I'm going to make a move on her? I was a total gentleman. If I had my way I'd just try to stay out of her life."

"Why do you say that? Do you not trust yourself around her? That's what it sounds like to me," Ray said, in the sarcastic tone that only Ray could get away with.

"Do you want us to forbid you from seeing her? We're not mommy and daddy, *little Johnny*. Here's the big question, yet again: Is she hot?" Aaron asked.

"Okay. Yes … Yes she is. But guys, do I need to remind you that a) she's seventeen and b) I'm happier now with Vicky than any relationship that I've ever been in?" John was actually growing frustrated with the grilling his coffee buddies were giving him.

"No need for reminders buddy. I just think that there's something about this girl that you're drawn to and it seems like you can't shake it. Look, girls these days look a lot older than they did when we went to school. Remember that *Seinfeld* when Jerry and George are at the network exec's place, and they catch a look at his fifteen year old daughter? *There was cleavage!*" Ray and John nodded in agreement and all three laughed. Aaron continued. "Remember what we said to Samantha today, we can look but can't touch? If you want to stay monogamous and happy, we gotta live by that. Are you having an almost-mid-life crisis, John?"

John didn't admit to having a mid-life crisis at all, but did admit that there was a strange attraction he felt for Jen. He promised that he wouldn't act upon his base male desires, and try to keep contact with her to a minimum. He wondered whether Ray and Aaron ever faced situations like this, and if so how they handled it. It really seemed like they were two guys who were really happily married, and have been able to keep their relationships healthy and lively. Was there something wrong with him? Was he addicted to drama? With every fiber of his being, John wanted things with Vicky to be as perfect as could possibly be. His trust in Vicky was growing with the passage of time; he probably trusted Vicky more than anyone else in his life right now. If only he could trust himself as much, his life could be so easy. *But would it be exciting?* John would need to dig deep and answer that question for himself.

The three of them returned to work and John continued working on his daily tasks. He couldn't seem to get Aaron's comment about a mid-life crisis out of his mind. Maybe the Nasty folder would have some interesting stuff to keep his mind occupied.

John had developed an uncanny ability to keep at least six program windows open and active on his desktop. He would switch between them with such ease it was something he became very proud of: this was multitasking at its best. John could maintain his focus on each task without losing his train of thought as he switched between them, even if it had been half hour since working on the previous task.

Nothing in the Nasty folder except for some really good dirty jokes that made him laugh out loud. He noticed the message light on his phone was lit up, dialed his voicemail password and listened to a message from Vicky inviting him over for dinner tonight to meet her daughter. John was to show up at six thirty, and if there was a problem he should call her back to reschedule. No need to call her back.

Cool, John thought. Finally get a chance to meet Vicky's daughter. He really didn't know too much about her. This was the only thing that John found odd about Vicky; for some reason she didn't talk too much about her daughter. It was obvious she was proud of her, but it was unusual that her daughter wasn't brought up often. John chalked this up to the nasty divorce. Maybe Vicky was just being very protective. Come to think of it, he really didn't even recall her daughter's name. He remembered Vicky mentioning it briefly when they had their first *date* at the Cheesecake Factory, but that's about it.

I guess I'd better be on my best behavior tonight, John told himself. Definitely want to make a good impression. After all, if everything goes well, he and Vicky could live a great existence together and he would end up playing an important role in her daughter's life.

In her message Vicky told him to just dress casual, as this wasn't some formal dinner or anything. After taking a swim and a nice long shower, he threw on a pair of Diesel jeans and a nice Zegna button-up shirt he had got on eBay for thirty bucks (one of his better eBay acquisitions) and headed out.

✳   ✳   ✳   ✳

He approached Vicky's place, found a parking spot and parked the MDX. For some reason, his heart was pounding. He wanted so badly to make a good first impression for Vicky's daughter. The way he figured it, if he could score some brownie points with her daughter it would go a long way in keeping his relationship with Vicky in great standing. It certainly didn't hurt that he was having some pretty good luck lately relating to the younger generation.

As soon as John approached the door to ring the doorbell, Vicky opened the door and appeared before him. She was obviously waiting at the door for his arrival. "Hey handsome, don't you look awesome," she said as she gave him a really nice kiss. "Come on in, I have most of the dinner almost ready but I sort of forgot the bread … I'm such an idiot sometimes. I'll call Jen down and we can chat for a bit, then I'm going to need to run to Vons for a minute," Vicky explained while leading John into her home.

"Sounds good. But really Vicky, I don't think you have to make a special trip just for bread. We don't have to have bread. I'm sure the rest of the dinner won't mind if the bread won't be around to join it."

"Yeah, probably not, but *I* will," Vicky asserted.

John looked around and gave the house his once-over. *Not bad for Cat City.* Contrary to popular belief, even amongst locals, there are a lot of nice-looking homes in Cathedral City. Vicky's home was built in the seventies, but somehow Vicky managed to take a modern approach to decorate the interior to seamlessly resemble current chic. Vicky sure sparkled as a would-be interior decorator. *What a contrast from the home's exterior,* John thought.

Vicky called upstairs for her daughter to come down and meet John. "John is here! Come on down. We can chat for a bit then I'll run and get the bread!"

As soon as he saw her, John's heart sank right into his stomach. A huge surge of fear came over him unlike anything he had encountered before as Jennifer Billings came down the stairs.

"John, this is my daughter Jennifer. Jennifer, this is John, the man that I've been seeing. He's a sweetie, isn't he, Jen?"

Jen was obviously speechless as well. She and John shared a look of utter confusion and uncertainty. "Yeah, he definitely *looks* like a good guy. Nice to meet you, John," Jen said, while contorting her face at John to reveal her discomfort. John looked over at Vicky to make sure she didn't catch it.

The three of them sat down on the couch and made small talk for about fifteen minutes. John tried his best to calm his nerves and maintain as much normalcy as he could. Jen did the same.

John hated himself for thinking it, but he couldn't wait for Vicky to go and get the bread so he could try to work this out with Jen. This was going to be really messy, and he didn't know what to do. He knew that he hadn't done anything wrong in the least; in fact he had been nothing but a friend to Jen. But his instincts told him that Vicky would not understand.

Vicky stood up and announced she was going to get the bread and shouldn't be any longer than twenty minutes. "See ya guys shortly, just tawk amungst yawselves, and enjoy," Vicky said, in a surprisingly good *Linda Richman* impression.

"Okay, Vicky, see ya soon," John said, trying his best to conceal the panic.

"Bye, mom," Jen said.

Vicky went out the door and left them to sort out this new crisis that had presented itself.

"So … you're Jennifer Billings. Mom's name is Wallace. I take it your dad was Billings, and you took your dad's last name," John said, starting it off with the obvious.

"Yep. You got it. So you're thirty, eh? Way to go, asshole!" Jen said, half joking.

"Sorry, Jen. I guess I wanted to appear younger. Forgive me?"

"I have no choice, do I? So what in the world we gonna do here? Are we going to tell her?" Jen asked.

"I don't know. Holy shit, this has got to be the most awkward predicament ever. I'll do what you think we should do. She's your mother, so you know her best. I really love her, Jen. I don't want to fuck anything up."

"Ohmygod—why do these weird things always happen to me? I just can't seem to catch a break or anything," Jen said, knocking her head against the brown leather sofa for effect. "I'm not sure what to do about my mom. I think it's best we like don't tell her anything. As time goes on, I'll just tell her that I added you online and that you give me advice on shit once in a while," Jen suggested.

"That actually sounds like a really good idea. Let's go with that. Man, you *are* wise beyond your years, Jennifer."

"Thanks. So anyway. Man, this is awkward. Can I confess something?"

"I'm afraid to hear it, but go ahead. How much weirder can this get?" John asked, subtly moving a few inches away from her.

"If you don't want it to get weirder, then maybe I should just shut up."

"No, no, go ahead. Speak your mind."

"The other night? When we were out driving? I would have kissed you. I was almost insulted that you didn't make a move on me. Tell me it was because of your love of my mom. Any other reason just won't cut it," Jen said, squinting her eyes.

"Wow. Jen. Yeah, now things got weirder. Thanks. Yes, it was *exactly* that reason. Plus, you're not even eighteen. That's a biggie too. I really love your mom, you have to know that. It's only been just over a month, but I want a life with her," John said, hoping the explanation was sufficient.

"Okay, I understand completely. When you dropped me off I thought there was something wrong with me. Do you know how many guys would have totally made a move? Men your age are such *pervs*. I'm not saying you're one of them, but you wouldn't believe the shit I see in my MSN chats. There's something wrong with these guys. Do they not realize that we're in fucking *high school*? My friend's sister is thirteen, and guys that are older than you hit on her all the time. *He-llo!* Goddam pervs. It's disgusting," Jen said, unmistakably infuriated.

"I know. I can't speak for them though. Can't tell ya what's going through their mind. I guess most figure that they can get away with it, sitting at a keyboard hiding behind an online identity. It's the guys who try to take it a step further that you should worry about. Please tell me you've never met with an older guy you've chatted with."

"What? Other than yourself? Jealous much? Ha ha, I'm just kidding, yo. No, but I have had some interesting chats. It's just fun teasing them."

"Just watch it, okay? I don't want to see you get in trouble. Seriously."

"Okay, mister. So ... we're cool with stuff with my mom, right?"

"For sure—I think I hear the door. We'll just say we've been getting acquainted and it'll be our little white lie. You're a cool person, Jen," John told her, just as they heard the sound of the front door opening.

Vicky came in and dinner went off without a hitch. Vicky was elated that her new boyfriend and daughter seemed to be getting along fabulously. She had a smile on her face that just wouldn't go away. After they finished dessert, Jen asked to be excused so she could go finish her homework and go online.

John and Vicky moved to the couch and watched TV while they let their dinner digest.

"So what do you think of Jennifer?" Vicky asked.

"She's really sweet. You have a really nice daughter. I can see that the apple doesn't fall far—"

"Awww, that's so sweet," Vicky interrupted. "She is very much like me, and I try to be the best mother I can. Being a single mom is harder than it looks. Ha ha. Everyone says that, but it's so true. Especially with a teenager in grade twelve. I'm so glad you guys got along. I'm so *happy*, John."

"Me too. I had a really nice time. Great dinner, too." John pointed to her, as he looked her up and down. "All these looks, plus she can cook. I hit the jackpot!" John kissed her. Vicky kissed back, but opened her mouth and licked John's lips all the way around. John became instantly aroused.

"Whoa, I think we should stop. We shouldn't get too intense with this, what if Jen walks in on us?" John asked, slightly worried.

"Once she's up on the computer, she's good to go. I likely won't see her down here for the rest of the night. We can fool around a *little* bit. Vicky ran her hand up John's leg.

"Okay, but I don't want to make too bad of an impression on her. I have to be a positive role model for her!" John said. He left out the part about still feeling incredibly awkward about the whole situation. This was going to take awhile to get comfortable with. Getting busy with Vicky at this point just didn't feel right at all. He would have to do his best to fend her off a bit tonight.

CHAPTER 13

▼

Coffee time the next day. Same time, same place, same table. Never before had the guys been this lively however.

"You have got to be absolutely fucking kidding me. This is the best thing I have ever heard in my life. Dude, your status has just increased to *Godlike.* You da king!" Aaron was excited, and enjoying the life that John was living vicariously for him. "Ray, let's bow down to him," he joked.

"How does this happen to you? I couldn't even dream of having this shit happen to me. Can you tell us the story again, huh, can you, daddy? Please. I won't even ask for my milk and cookies," Ray joked, using a high-pitched voice of a six-year-old.

"It's true, boys. I can't make this shit up," John confirmed.

He continued to tell the guys the story. He tried to include as many details as possible to make sure the boys got as much as they could from the situation, given that he did have a vicarious life to live up to. Ray and Aaron didn't really have any actual advice for him, but they agreed it was probably best that he and Jen pretend that they just met that night.

No point in rocking the boat, especially since Vicky appeared to be so damn happy. It was probably Vicky's heightened sense of happiness that allowed John to get *some* sleep last night. Regardless, he still felt uncomfortable about everything.

The next week went by without a hitch for everyone. John visited Vicky's home again, spent some time with her and Jennifer, and things appeared to settle into a comfortable place again. Happy times were back.

*   *   *   *

John was sitting at his desk, training Ray on a new procedure that was unloaded upon the security department from mainframe guys. Often there would be jobs that were handled by other IT departments that became somewhat of a security risk. If Patrick Bowman decided that these tasks were best handed over to the security department to handle, it was usually a quick turnaround for the transition to occur. That department would train the proper individual in security and the task would now become under the responsibility of the security department.

This was happening far too frequently, John thought. *Oh well, at least now I have Ray to help me out.* As he was showing Ray the proper Unix commands to execute for the initial query, his cell phone rang.

"Hey, Sir John, where the hell ya been, mah man?" Joey Styles asked.

"Joey, Joey … dude … I don't quite know how to say this. So I'll just come out and say it." John was nervous but he wasn't about to let it show in his voice. "I can't compromise myself any longer like that. One shot deal. You got what you needed, and that's where our, uh, business relationship has to end. Sorry, Joey," John said, walking outside of the IT area into an empty hallway with nobody within earshot. He had made more than his fair share of money selling the emails. He had reached that point where it was no longer worth the risk.

"John, are you like naïve, or what? That's not the way I work. I can't have one of the best fuckin' sources I have ever had jump ship on me like that. Those stories we ran on Pope, they went over so totally well. Readers ate that shit up. The thirst for all the best *goss* is unquenchable, and I'm getting pretty fucking parched over here. Capiche? Pope is about to wrap his latest project, and the studio is going to start ramping up the publicity machine. Nothing would make me wet my pants more than getting some more of your goods, just before the movie opens."

"Wouldn't that kill the guy's career? How do you sleep at night?"

"Au contraire, my naïve deep-throat dude. At first, that was my intention. I've met the fucker and his arrogance is even worse in person. This guy brings ego to a whole new level. He gets more ass than a toilet seat, too. If I only got ten percent of his pussy, I'd be a happy man. But anyway, when we published the first few stories it was my way of sticking it to him. It felt great. But now I have another motive. The studio loved all the press the guy was getting over those emails. Because I held my end of the bargain and didn't actually print them or reveal my sources, they considered it to be merely hearsay. Pope freaked, threatened me and shit. But too fuckin' bad. So anyway, the studio wants more shit. And I can't make it up, or else I would get sued for sure."

"Hold on a second, the *studio* wants more dirt on him? Aren't they the ones signing his paycheck? This makes no sense." John knew he was out of his league here, and was quickly coming to the realization that he was in too deep.

"Of course it makes sense. Everything you've given me so far was nothing too terrible. It actually bumps up his street cred. Think of it that way. Look at all those gangsta rappers: more street cred, more sales. Same shit here. Simple stuff."

John knew Joey was right. Gangsta rappers always sold more than their clean-cut counterparts. He really loved the irony of Ice Cube as an actor in family friendly films, though. He missed the old NWA days. "What does Pope think about that? He can't be thrilled. I can't see anyone actually wanting their dirty laundry aired out like that," John said.

"He doesn't know that the studio is driving this. He would shit a bowlful. What he doesn't know can't hurt him. And I know *you* won't tell him. I just know that there's a lot riding on you right now, John. You opened up a huge can of worms that can't be closed. The can must stay open. Get me more stuff. I'm in a pretty giving mood too. Dollar values are tripled. Just call me Richard fucking Dawson."

"I can't promise anything, Joey," John said, a tad frightened now. What has he gotten himself into? As healthy as he was, his heart may not be able to handle all this *drama* lately.

"I know you'll help me out. Have something for me by next Monday. I have a golf game at Indian Wells that day. I'll even come and meet *you* this time. No excuses. Marriott Desert Springs, in the lobby, eight p.m. I'll see you then."

Before John had a chance to reply, Joey hung up. John didn't know what to do. Maybe Ray would be able to help.

He went back to his desk and grabbed Ray. They went to the lunchroom, which was currently unoccupied. They'd be able to chat in secrecy there.

He told Ray everything Joey laid out for him. Ray maintained his stance that John should stick to his guns and not risk his job. John agreed, but was worried whether that would carry any *penalties* from the likes of Joey. Ray didn't know Joey all that well, but didn't think he was capable of carrying out any harmful threats. Although this was meant to comfort John, it didn't help. John felt pretty powerless.

*   *   *   *

By the time Monday rolled around, John had decided not to give Joey any-thing. He realized he was essentially calling Joey's bluff, and he would end up having to see what Joey's next move was going to be. He figured not showing up would be the ultimate piss-off, so he decided to head down to the Marriott and talk to him in person.

*   *   *   *

The Marriott Desert Springs always held great memories for John. *Was there any other hotel that had real boats that ran through the lobby?* The hotel was sur-rounded by water, and the lake actually flowed *inside* the lobby of the hotel. John and his buddies would often hang out here for drinks, and would sometimes *get their groove on* at the nightclub downstairs. Somehow he knew that meeting Joey here was a perfect opportunity to tarnish those memories forever.

Joey was standing right in the front of the lobby waiting. He approached John right away. "I don't see an envelope on you, John. And you're not wearing any-thing that could conceal it. So I take it we have a problem," Joey said, looking rather angry.

"You're right. I don't. I can't do this, Joey. I've worked too hard to get where I am right now in my career and it's not worth it. I've established a really high level of trust with the exec at DesertFinancial and I've already compromised it. If I push it any further, my career as an information security professional is over. I've breached the code of ethics big time, and it doesn't feel good. So, sorry Joey."

Joey didn't understand. He told John that he was making a big mistake, but eventually he'd come around. John asked if that was a masked threat and Joey said nothing. This wasn't going well. Joey still looked angry, but he just kept say-ing that John would come around.

"I won't come around, Joey. What's going to change my mind?"

"You just will. Trust me. I'm sorry you don't have anything for me this time, but I'm pretty sure next time will go much better. Have a good evening, John."

Joey walked away. John sat there, stunned. He went to the bar and ordered a drink. He was fucked and he knew it. He called Vicky and asked if she would see him. He was going to have to tell her what was going on. He hadn't told her about any of this before, but he needed her opinion. Hopefully she'd understand.

The drive to Vicky's seemed to take forever; in reality it only took twelve minutes but John's head was spinning so much that time was nothing but a foreign concept. It was as if he was in the middle of a nightmare that wouldn't end. He prayed to the God of Understanding Girlfriends and hoped that Vicky would bring him out of this unease that was taking over his psyche.

✳   ✳   ✳   ✳

John had just come off a huge weekend at Morongo. If he could just take some of those winnings and multiply them, one more lucky night, he could pay off most his debt. It was a dull Wednesday at work and he had long finished that coding project. He decided he'd take off early; he'd bring his buddy Howard along and show him what a high roller he was.

"Seriously, Howie. We'll leave now, get to Morongo, have some beverages, I'll make some serious dough and we'll go party some more," John said.

"What the hell. Let's do it," Howard said.

They took off for Morongo. As soon as they entered, Bill, the pit boss, approached and welcomed John. "You're back already, John? Good to see you though. What can we get you and your friend to drink?" Bill said.

"Just a simple rum and Coke for me, and whatever my man Howie wants," John said, enjoying being able to show off for his bud.

"Dirty martini, three olives for me," Howie ordered.

Howie followed John to the Blackjack table. John had always been a poker guy, but his recent luck at hitting twenty-ones led him right to the Blackjack area. Within two minutes, a beautiful waitress came by with their drinks.

"See? Life is good, ain't it dude?"

They finished their drinks as John started in slowly, only playing two hands of two hundred dollars per hand. As soon as their drinks were finished, the same waitress was right there with refills.

"Holy shit, John, you are quite the king here. I'm going to go gamble on the smaller tables for a bit, and we'll see you soon. We'll go for dinner at seven thirty, right?"

"You got it."

The next ninety minutes were hell for John. The two hundred dollar table was incredibly quiet, so he had the whole table to himself. Fourteen hundred sweep per hand. John was down ten thousand by seven fifteen. He only had two thousand left on his Visa. He would need to get a cash advance.

Howie came to get him for dinner. John was in no mood for dinner. He abruptly took a fifty dollar chip and flipped it at Howie's chest. "Go play for a bit and come get me in an hour," John said without looking up.

By the next day, John was down twenty grand. He would give it one more sweep of seven hands. He lost six of them.

"Fuck, what is wrong with you?" John swore at the dealer.

"John, it's not my fault. I'm sorry you're losing, but you're going to need to calm down."

John threw his chips against the table, making them scatter all over. "I don't need you to tell me to calm down!"

The dealer called the daytime pit boss for assistance. "John, you're a great customer, but I don't want to have to ask you to leave," the pit boss said.

"Motherfucker! I can't stand this anymore!" John was freaking out.

"Security. Can I get security to 2H," the pit boss said into his walkie-talkie.

"Look, I don't need to be escorted out. Please. Just let me be for a second," John said, mustering up all he could to calm down.

Howie approached and grabbed John. "Dude, let's go. Today just isn't your day, okay?"

It took ten minutes for John to snap out of his mini-tantrum. "Let's go, Howie."

The first fifteen minutes of the car ride back to Palm Springs was uncomfortably quiet. Howie broke the silence. "Bet ya a hun that you'll be back within a week."

"Ha. Very funny, asshole."

Howie was wrong. This would be John's last journey to Morongo.

✳   ✳   ✳   ✳

Vicky was happy to see him. She noticed right away that he didn't look quite right. She worried that he looked really pale, and offered to make him some hot tea. John would pretty much drink anything. Can you spike tea with anything? John wondered. She handed him a large cup of herbal tea and promised it would calm him.

John started from the beginning. He told her everything, without excluding a single detail. Vicky listened intently, eyes focused on John's complexion and wild eyes. As he came to the end of the story, concluding with the events that just transpired at the Marriott, he let out a loud sigh and slumped his body against hers. At first she kept quiet and just hugged him.

"Well, your fit has hit the proverbial shan. What are you going to do? Wow."

"What are you saying? I thought I was the one who's supposed to be talking like gibberish."

"Fit hits the shan. Like, it's just a polite way of saying *shit hits the fan*. I can't believe you've never heard that one before. Kinda like *not mucking fuch*. Not fucking much. Get it?"

"I'm glad you're able to lighten things up, when here I am in the deepest of shit. Honestly, I mean that. I'm not being sarcastic. I need your sense of humor". John was beginning to feel better now. He reached out and softly touched Vicky's face. Vicky gave him a loving look and began stroking his hand, building up to a soothing hand massage.

"Thanks … but I just don't know what to say. Maybe this Joey guy is just blowing smoke out his ass. He hasn't actually threatened you or anything has he?" Vicky asked.

"No, but you should have seen his face. That facial expression said more than any threat he could have made. It was like this satanic grin. It really freaked me out!"

"At least you're not alone. I'm with ya, Mr. Security Guy. So you've never really told me how much debt you were in from your days as the *old John*."

"I'm close to getting out of it. I'm still incredibly ashamed of the John I used to be," he said. He decided to recount the events of his last adventure at Morongo.

"That's quite the tale. I just can't see you throwing a tantrum like that. Not at all," Vicky said.

"It really wasn't me. It was almost as if I jumped out of my skin and looked down at myself and saw what an absolute *ass* I had become. I vowed I would never get to that point again, and the only way that could be achieved is by giving up on any type of gambling altogether. So far so good, right?"

"Hey, what's done is done, you stopped it and now you're just trying to do the right thing. Both with the addiction, *and* with Joey. I can't hold that against you. So here I am, offering my support. I don't know if I can help much, but I'm here for you, John." She gave him that same loving look yet again.

"Thanks, Vick. That's awesome to have you by my side. I know I haven't said it yet, but I think I love you," John declared, with more emotion than he had planned.

"I love you too, John. Don't worry, this will go away and you can get your life back to normal," Vicky replied, with equal emotion.

As Vicky went to the kitchen to refill John's cup of tea, Jen ran down the stairs and sat beside John on the couch.

"Are you going to be online later tonight?" She asked him.

"Probably, why?"

"You'll see. Go online. We'll chat."

"Wha?"

"Shut up, mom's coming. We'll talk online."

The three of them sat there for a few minutes making small talk. Jen returned upstairs leaving John and Vicky to resume their post-confessions-of-love cuddles.

*   *   *   *

John felt much better, but as he was driving home the feelings of hopelessness were revisited in his mind. It was ten thirty, much earlier than his normal bedtime of twelve thirty, but all he could think about was how he wanted to just head to bed.

He checked his email before going to bed, and just as he was deleting the tenth email message advertising Viagra that day, an MSN chat window opened from Jen.

Jennaybobennay:	*hey future stepdad*
JohnnyD:	*haha … what is it? jen ib really tired, was ready to go2bed*
Jennaybobennay:	*i won't take much time*
JohnnyD:	*ok wutup?*
Jennaybobennay:	*i couldn't help but overhearing part of ur convo with mom*
JohnnyD:	*ruserious? what did u hear?*
Jennaybobennay:	*about that fucko from tattle inc. and I thought it was a good mag*
JohnnyD:	*oh shit wtf … u werent supposed 2 hear that*
Jennaybobennay:	*2 bad, I did. i wanna help*
JohnnyD:	*how*
Jennaybobennay:	*2moro nite it's friday and lotta timez I sleep at my friend cassies*
JohnnyD:	*so?*

Jennaybobennay:	*ur gonna pick me up somewhere and we're gon get u outta trouble*
JohnnyD:	*the hell are u talking bout?*
Jennaybobennay:	*trust me.*
JohnnyD:	*ur putting me in an awkward position*
Jennaybobennay:	*funny … seems like ur already in a pretty awkward position*
JohnnyD:	*smartass*
Jennaybobennay:	*show up online 2moro at dinner and I'll tell u more*
JohnnyD:	*i don't get it*
Jennaybobennay:	*u will, itll make sense when I explain*
JohnnyD:	*whatevs—gotta run and sleep—l8r jen*

What the hell is she up to? How could she have heard? John was sure that his voice was pretty quiet when he explained everything to Vicky. Whatever, he was too tired to think about it. Within two minutes, he was asleep.

✳   ✳   ✳   ✳

Surprisingly, John slept for nine hours straight for the first time in a long while. Perhaps it was the relief that he felt having shared everything with Vicky. Regardless, he felt great. Never underestimate the power of a good nights sleep.

His workday was more or less uneventful. He wrestled with the idea of telling Ray about the latest Joey developments, but thought better of it. Maybe one day, especially if Joey decides to put any action behind his satanic grin. There was so much going on in his mind, even the latest scandal to pop up in the Nasty file failed to bring the regular rush of voyeuristic thrills. Ray was jumping all over it but John had to feign interest. He decided he would look after it Monday.

The day dragged on   for John, evening could not come fast enough. He was curious to see what Jen was up to. She sounded so sure of herself that she was going to help him out of his predicament. When he found her online she was still secretive, but again she promised that she would be able to help. Just pick me up at the Taco Bell again, at seven thirty, she said.

Vicky was to be taking her second class this evening in her accounting program she was starting. DesertFinancial was pretty high on education, and in order to move up in the company it was pretty much a given that you would need some sort of degree or diploma. Vicky decided that if she were to climb the corporate ladder, she would need to finish the accounting diploma she had started several years ago. She had asked John if he would join her for a drink after class, but he lied and told her he would likely be hitting the sack early again tonight.

He hated lying to her. If she knew that he was actually meeting her daughter she would have his head—and not the good one. Even if his meeting with Jen was purely platonic, and for the overall greater good of all involved. *No matter,* he thought, this was a one-time thing. He would hear Jen out and see what she had planned, then no more meeting without telling Vicky.

*   *   *   *

He drove into the Taco Bell parking lot and found Jen standing there. She jumped in and gave him a big smile.

"To the offices of *Tattle Inc.*, please. Driver Sir," Jen chuckled.

"What in the world are you talking about???" John asked, very confused.

"Oh, don't be so coy, John. We're going to break into Joey's office and fight fire with fire. Find some evidence on him and blackmail his ass."

"Are you feeling okay, Jen? How the hell do you figure we're gonna do this? And in case you didn't know, *Tattle Inc.*'s office is in LA somewhere." John turned the ignition off and pulled the keys out. This wasn't what he had in mind.

"C'mon. Don't pretend we're not going anywhere. Put the keys back. And duh, of course I know their office is there. Do you have anything better to do tonight? It'll be fun. It's only a two hour drive, and we shouldn't have to fight traffic."

"Yeah, I could be sleeping, or enjoying time with your mother."

"She's in class, and one night without her is not going to kill you guys. I know you guys are happy together, and I'm all for it. I think you're the first guy—since Dad left us—to come along that she really likes. Me too. You're a great guy. I knew the first time we chatted. But you're in a whole shitload of trouble, and I'm about to get you out of it."

"How are we going to break in? I know nothing about B&Es. But something tells me you do. I don't wanna know, Jen." John really *did* want to know, he just didn't want to admit it to himself.

"Leave it to me. When I was twelve," she said, pausing as she could *feel* his eyes glare at her. "Yes, *twelve*—I kind of fell in with a bad crowd. They taught me a lot. Let's leave it at that. Plus, have you like looked around on the Internet lately? You can find out how to do *anything*. Make a bomb, pick a lock, you name it. And … when I get us into his office, you have all da mad skillz to hack into his computer and find shit. Am I right?"

"Yeah, but this is really pushing it. Do you know how much trouble we can get in if we were to get caught? I don't know if I want to risk it for either of us. And I'm essentially responsible for you." John began driving towards Vicky's house to drop Jen off at home. He couldn't partake in this. "I'm taking you home, Jen. I appreciate your offer, but we can't do this. It's not right."

Jen looked at him with such a serious expression on her face, it literally made John fall back in his seat. "You're in shit already. We're just going to get you out of it. And don't worry, I *promise,* we won't get caught. Just drive and shut up about it already," Jen said with an equally serious tone in her voice.

John pulled the car over to the shoulder of the highway and thought about it. There was something about Jennifer that made him believe in her. Plus, she was Vicky's daughter, so how far could the apple fall from the tree? He knew it was a gamble, but this risk was one he was going to have to take. As scary as the notion was, Jen was his best hope right now.

*   *   *   *

John and Jennifer drove towards Los Angeles. John could not believe he was agreeing to this. His life had turned into some clichéd movie and he couldn't yell *cut.*

They talked mostly of Jen's relationship with Shawn. Jen told him about how they were getting along better, but there was still something holding Shawn back. The rumors at school had stopped, but somewhere in Shawn's mind they were being kept alive. It drove Jen crazy, but she could see something special about him and was willing to put up with it for a while. She figured he would eventually come around when he realized that she wasn't anything like what the rumors said.

After turning off onto Santa Monica from the 405, they pulled into the 7-11 parking lot and checked the phone book. *Tattle Inc.*'s offices were on West Olympic. They were only several minutes away. At least they wouldn't be driving aimlessly trying to find the place.

The time was ten after ten. Century City was pretty quiet: lots of office buildings, and hardly anyone working late on a Friday night. They approached the building where *Tattle Inc.*'s office was. The phone directory said the office number was 320, likely on the third floor. John was still wondering how the hell they were going to pull this off.

He parked the car and Jen opened her purse to reveal what appeared to be a rather complex lock-picking set. Before Jen could say a word, John piped up: "I don't even want to know. Just don't tell me. If it works, great. I still think we should turn around and go back home. I can drop you off at Cassie's and nobody would have to know anything."

"Would you just re-*lax*? I told you I was going to get you out of this and that's what we're here for. Now be quiet and let's go inside."

They walked toward the seven-story building. John had assumed that the offices of *Tattle Inc.* would be slightly more glamorous than the building that stood just feet away from them. This was more modest than he expected. Oh well, maybe that would be a good thing. Better chance of getting by any physical security measures that they would face.

Approaching the entrance, Jen stopped John and laid out the initial plan.

"Okay, here's how it's gonna go down … dayum, that felt good to say. Anyway, your part is easy. I'm going to distract the security guard in there that thankfully hasn't seen us yet. When I bring him outside to chat and have a smoke—and by the way, don't worry, I don't smoke—you can sneak in and take the stairs to the third floor. As long as you don't see cameras, just hang out in the hallway and wait for me. I'll take care of the rest. If there's a restroom on that floor, just hang out in there and when I'm up I'll knock on it and we'll break in," Jen said, somehow sounding like the consummate pro.

"Again, I don't want to know. Does your mom know about this side of you?"

"Are you kidding? Hell, no. And she *never will.* Right? Right."

"You don't plan on hurting this guy I hope."

"No, I'm just going to test out my power of persuasion. And hopefully it won't come down to using my powers of *persuasion*. I don't want to go there. But I will if I have to. Don't worry, I have pepper spray in my purse if he tries anything. I can handle it. Just hang out at the side of the door."

John obeyed. What was he doing here? This has gotta be the most ridiculous thing he had ever done. With his girlfriend's daughter, yet. Aye Carumba!

He watched as Jennifer walked in and started chatting with the lone security guard. After about two minutes of conversation, the guy started following Jen towards the doors. Jen opened the door for the security guard who followed her to the opposite side of the door where John was waiting. As the door closed, Jen stuck her leg out to stop the door from closing, and gave it a feather-light push so it would open slightly. John took his cue and snuck in quickly. The security guard had his eyes glued to Jennifer's ass, obviously too consumed with lustful thoughts to pay attention to his job duties. For a brief moment, John wished he were a woman.

Once inside, he ran towards the staircase, all the while making sure there weren't any security cameras overhead. Before climbing the stairs, he quickly looked outside to check on Jennifer. They were out of sight. Probably on the side of the building having a smoke. He figured he should take a risk and deviate from the plan slightly. He walked back towards the security desk to do some initial reconnaissance of his own. John wanted to see how many security cameras were implemented at this office building. Lucky for them, most of the cameras were placed in the elevators and the attached parking garage. Several of the closed circuit sets had a label called *Top Floor Offices. Must be some sort of clandestine operation up there,* he thought. That was pretty much it for cameras. *Whew.*

John rushed up the stairs to the third floor. He walked down the hallway and quickly found the offices for *Tattle Inc.* Old fashioned deadbolt. Awesome. Hopefully Jen would be able to pick it. He was surprised that a swipe card reader wasn't used. Then he figured that there might in fact be swipe cards employed once inside the office. They'd have to cross that bridge when they came to it.

John found the restroom and walked in. He looked in the mirror and noticed that he was sweating profusely. He also realized that he appeared to be rather pale. "This can't be good for my heart," he muttered to himself, slightly aloud. He turned the blue lever to start the cold water running. He let it run until it turned ice-cold then splashed it on his face until his hair became wet. There, that would provide some temporary relief.

The knock on the door startled him and made him jump. Was that her already?

"Okay, let's get busy," Jen said. John grabbed a towel and dried his face, then joined Jen in the hallway. He led her towards *Tattle Inc.*'s office door, and stopped in front of it.

"This I *do* wanna know. Pardon my French, but how the fuck did you get up here and what did you say to that poor security guard?" John asked.

"We just had a smoke, and while we were chatting I convinced him that I was Joey's niece, and that it was his birthday coming up—a big and important one. I said I needed to get up there to get some pictures of him so we can blow them up for his big party. He was pretty apprehensive at first. So we continued talking and eventually I started complimenting him and asking if he wanted my number. I flirted it up pretty good. He totally bought that I was twenty and that I was a student at UCLA. I gave him a fake name, a fake number, and a fake Hotmail address. Here's the kicker: are you ready for this? He gave me the keys to the main office, and even Joey's private office! Can you believe our luck? You *so* owe me big time!"

"Wow. You are something else, Jennifer. If we get anything good in here, I will forever owe you one. Gimme five, girlfriend!"

They gave each other a really spirited high five.

"How long did you say you were going to be up here and how do we explain my presence with you all of a sudden?"

"I'll come down alone, we'll go for another quick smoke, and you'll run out to the car. I told him I may be awhile. Hopefully he won't come up to check. Just in case, I'll stand watch near the door while you do your stuff."

They entered the offices. *Not too shabby,* John thought. Not a huge office space, but very contemporary and well decorated, which you wouldn't expect given the façade of the office building that it was a part of. Jen said she would sit on the couch by reception while John went to work on Joey's computer.

John turned on the computer and hoped that there wouldn't be a BIOS password required to boot it. Thankfully the computer booted right to Windows. *No password needed to log on Windows either. Sweet!* John spent the next fifteen minutes sweeping through Joey's hard drive and couldn't find a thing. He really hoped to find something, anything, somewhere on this computer that he could use against Joey one day if it was ever required.

He hoped to have better luck with Joey's email. He looked out Joey's office window towards Jennifer who was relaxing on the couch reading the latest issue of *Tattle Inc.* She gave him an encouraging nod and he shrugged his shoulders to signal that so far he hadn't come up with anything.

He opened Outlook and fired up Joey's email. *Uh oh, Windows Networking window asking for a password.* In order to crack Joey's network password, John would need access to the Windows domain controller. He stood up, wiped his forehead dry and looked around the office space to see if he could spot where they may store the file servers. There were several locked closets that looked like good possibilities, but John wasn't sure he wanted to go that far. He had a better idea.

He walked back to Joey's office and tried to open the desk drawer. No luck. Once again he stepped out of Joey's office and called over to Jen who seemed to be very much involved in her reading.

"Hey Jen, how would you like to help me with some hacking here?"

"Hacking? I thought that was *your* specialty. I know my way around the computer pretty good, but all that security stuff that you know is well beyond my understanding. Sorry to disappoint you." She resumed her reading.

"Nonono. Not that kind of hacking. I'm actually going to need your lock-picking skills to break into Joey's desk. I need his network password and don't want to take the chance breaking into the server area to get it. I'm willing to bet he's got his password written down somewhere in his desk."

Jen threw the magazine down on the couch and joined him in Joey's office. One quick look at the lock on Joey's desk drawer and she produced an apparatus from her purse that resembled a surgical scalpel. "This should do the trick," she said. Within ten seconds the lock was open.

"Awesome! You are one talented chick, I tell ya. Now let's see if this guy is like so many silly people who store their passwords written down right by the computer, even if it's in a locked area. Did you know that the best hackers don't have to know much about computers or programming or anything like that? They have what we in the biz call social engineering skills. Which you happen to have in spades, by the way. Look at how you got us into the building. You're one dangerous individual." John opened Joey's desk drawer.

"Awww, that's so sweet of you to say. I think. I know I don't have to remind you that my mom will never, ever know about any of this," Jen said, in a manner whereby a response was unnecessary.

They shuffled through several pads of paper and notebooks. Two minutes later, John found several passwords written in small letters in the back of a black notebook. Bingo.

"Okay, Jen, I think I'm good to go. You can go finish reading—don't forget to tell me what they say about Pope in there!"

He re-fired up Outlook and typed in the password, and Joey's email folders appeared on the screen. John's excitement was quickly extinguished as he opened folder after folder within and under the Inbox to reveal nothing good. *Fuck,* he swore out loud. Obviously Joey did a good job of clearing out his email on a regular basis. No luck with the Deleted Items folder either. Ditto with the Sent Items folder.

John's last hope was the Personal Folders. When he clicked on the plus sign beside the Personal Folders to open them up he was presented with another password window. *Hmmm,* John thought, *maybe he's hiding something.* He removed a USB drive from his pocket that contained several hacker tool programs. He clicked on the newly created drive of the computer and double clicked on the executable for the *Personal Folders Password Recovery* program. Personal folder passwords are one of the easiest passwords to crack. The *hash* that Microsoft uses to store the password is pretty weak, and can be decrypted quickly.

John got the password from the program and used it to open Joey's personal folders. John discovered lots of questionable stuff there, but nothing good enough to hold over his head. Typical porn and dirty email exchanges. He'd need something more substantial than that.

Finally he stumbled upon a folder called CPSC. When he opened it he was able to piece together evidence of a phishing email scam. Phishing was the act of attempting to acquire personal information by means of a fake email. Victims would be fooled into sending their information—like credit card data—to the scam artist phishers.

Apparently Joey was involved in a scam where he (or an accomplice) would send emails to about ten thousand individuals who had purchased the latest fitness toy, the ABSolute Best Machine. The email would purport to be from the Consumer Protection Safety Commission, and tell them that there was a defect found with the device, and that a recall would be imminent. An offer for refund would be mentioned and it would simply ask the recipient to send their relevant info, including credit card number, for an immediate refund. Joey obviously obtained a customer list somehow. Either way, John had enough within this CPSC folder to fully implicate Joey.

John went to the Outlook preferences, and found the location where the personal folders file was located. He closed Outlook and opened a new window for the USB drive. He opened Windows Explorer and found the .pst file, and dragged it into the window for the USB drive. He pulled the small USB device out of the computer and put it back in his pocket, then closed all the windows on the computer. He turned the computer off and gave Jen the thumbs up. Jen came to lock up Joey's office, they both walked out of the main door, then Jen locked up and told him to just wait about five minutes then she'd meet him at the car.

John waited five minutes then headed out the main building. Sure enough, the security guard was not at his post. *Wow. This was too much fun.*

Jen jumped in the car several minutes later, John peeled out of the parking lot and they started the trek back toward the desert. As long as they didn't encounter any traffic snags, which was still possible despite being late evening, they should be back before one a.m. John's adrenaline was on overdrive though and he hoped that the trip back would be relaxing so he could calm down.

"I really gotta hand it to you, Jennifer, that was some show you put on back there. I think I'm actually speechless. That was so awesome! I know it was totally wrong, but this shit we got on Joey is going to keep him off my ass for sure. He really is quite the slimeball."

"What a creeper. He looks like a fuckwad too. I'm glad we got all that. I think you should report it to the authorities no matter what. He should be thrown in the slammer. Send him to the Q!"

"The Q?"

"San Quentin. John, get with the program, awwwite? Do I have to teach you *everything?*"

"Ha ha. Just because you're the queen of B&E doesn't mean you know it all. But anyway, we gotta promise each other that this never gets to your mom," John said, realizing it really didn't need to be mentioned.

"You don't have to tell me. I mean, if she ever found out I'd be so dead. Then again so would you. So yeah, don't worry 'bout it."

For the next while, they both embraced the silence and enjoyed all the passing lights that never seemed to end. John thought about how you can drive all over southern California, for hours on end, and never come up on an unoccupied patch of land. This part of the country was so *populated.* It seemed to him that the whole area between San Diego and Los Angeles had become one huge megalopolis.

Jen broke the silence. She wanted to talk to him about her relationship with Shawn. She delved deeper into the story and pretty much told him everything. He was shocked, and for some reason relieved, to find out that they had yet to sleep together.

"Don't get me wrong, I'm not a prude or anything, but we're both just not ready. I want this time to be special. And before you ask, yes, I've done it already. With Brad. But I'm no slut. I hate how those rumors are still running around Shawn's head. Which really pisses me off, because even those girls don't say anything to me now."

"Did you ever find out what happened to shut those girls up? Or are you going to tell me that you had something to do with it, and that you have *connections?* Okay, if that's true just don't say anything." John was feeling much more relaxed now, almost as if he had just devoured a few Valium. Helping Jen out with her high school problems calmed him.

"What do you take me for? I know I may seem to you not quite as innocent as I did before, but I'm not *that* bad, okay? I think Cassie's brother did something, but to this day I have no idea. Doesn't matter. All that matters is what Shawn thinks, and I hope he gets over it."

They continued to chat about her and Shawn, with John providing as much advice as he could. John was relieved that she showed no signs whatsoever of flirtatious behavior. It scared him to think that if he were single and if Vicky were not in the picture, his intentions may be significantly different. The line between seventeen-and-nine-months and eighteen was pretty thin.

When they arrived in Palm Springs they were both exhausted. John couldn't wait to crawl into his bed and sleep until noon. He dropped Jen off at her friend's house and they said goodbye.

"Remember. Our secret forever," Jen reminded him as she was getting out of the car.

"For sure, Jen. Thanks for everything, you have a great rest of the weekend!"

John went home and didn't even turn any lights on when he got in the door. He easily found his way to the bedroom, threw off his clothes and was asleep within minutes.

CHAPTER 14

▼

Aaron and Ray were sitting at the regular table having their coffee on Monday morning, this time without John, who had called in sick.

"I don't think he's sick. I'm pretty sure he just needs a mental health day," Aaron suggested.

"Yeah, very likely. His life is pretty wild. Can you believe that guy? Mother and daughter? That's my fuckin' dream. Lucky asshole. Can you imagine being young again, knowing all that we do now? Sheeeit," Ray said.

"Oh man, no shit dude. We'd be lethal. Still wouldn't trade my life for his right now. All that drama is probably getting to him. I used to be addicted to drama in my life, and sure it's fun for a while, but in the end it's just too much. I'm actually worried about him. Slightly. You work with him, Ray, what do you think?" Aaron asked.

"I agree. He's not quite himself at work lately. It's almost as if he's on autopilot. Which is okay for him cause he sure knows a whole lotta stuff about everything that needs to be done for our department. But he could be so much more productive if he didn't have all this drama going on in his life," Ray said.

"Uh huh. You got it. It's almost as if he's living two lives. Like he's torn between the angel on his left shoulder and the devil on his right. Maybe I'm making it seem really black and white, but who knows? I hope he just settles down with Vicky. She seems pretty awesome. You know her, right Ray? How much do you know about her?" Aaron asked.

"Well, I don't know her too well personally, but I think she's definitely good for John. She's a hottie, too. MILF to the maximum. One thing I know is that she had a really nasty divorce. I mean really bad. I think she needed to take some time off work for it. Some gossip at work says she's still rather fucked up over it and hasn't quite recovered. But gossip is gossip, right? How much of it is ever true?"

"Maybe none of it. I just hope John's back tomorrow and is in a more relaxed mental state. Should be interesting to hear his weekend stories," Aaron said, taking his last sip of coffee while staring across into the travel office. "Now finish up your coffee so we can walk over and you can book your trip with Samantha. Or should we wait until tomorrow when she's having a better hair day? I hate when she puts it up like that, don't you? Plus that color she's wearing is just not her."

"What the hell is wrong with you and John? Sometimes I don't know how I got mixed up with you two homo, I mean, metro, sexuals," Ray said with a giant smirk.

✳   ✳   ✳   ✳

John woke up Tuesday feeling much better. He had really needed the weekend to chill and do next to nothing. Vicky had come over Saturday night and they shared a nice quiet evening together having dinner and watching a movie.

When he sat down to his desk he was inundated with emails. *You miss one day and look what happens.* He hated how the world was so reliant on email as *the* form of communication. What would we ever do without it? Heaven forbid that people would have to resort to actually *talking* to each other.

John went through all his email, which took about half an hour. Most of it was just updates on ongoing projects in IT, most of which he was cc'd on. He spent the next hour catching up with Ray, Dan and Jill. He loved the camaraderie that had developed between the four of them in the security department. They really did resemble one happy family, which was such a rarity among any department, let alone any other company out there.

Ray and John were about to head off to grab Aaron for coffee when John's cell phone rang. *Great,* John muttered to himself when he looked at the call display, *it's Joey.*

"Sir John. I hope you've had time to reconsider and that you have something for me. I need something by tomorrow. It's terribly important we meet tomorrow. I'll even come out there and meet wherever you want. As long as you have the goods, we're best pals," Joey said.

Little do you know who has the upper hand now, John thought.

"Hello to you too," John said. "Look, I don't know what part of *no more* you don't understand, but like I said last time we chatted—no more. Sorry, man.

Find your information from someone else." John's confidence came across as strong as the Starbucks coffee he consumed on a daily basis.

"I'll pretend you didn't just say that. The game isn't played that way. Once you start feeding the beast, you can't stop. It's insatiable. You have my number and I suggest you change your mind by tomorrow. Call me when you do so we can set up a time to meet. I look forward to hearing from you later. Goodbye, John," Joey said, with a tone so flat and monotone that it scared John.

"Fuck you," John said, even though Joey had already hung up.

✳   ✳   ✳   ✳

After work the next day, John was driving home trying to decide how he was going to handle this dilemma with Joey. He was unable to get that *tone* out of his mind that Joey used on the phone yesterday. It was almost inhuman. Maybe he was just using that as a scare tactic that worked to great effect with anyone he was trying to threaten.

He wished he could have told Ray or Vicky about his ace in the hole. Especially how he came about acquiring that ace in the hole.

John got home and changed into some cotton shorts and a plain white tee. He decided he would sit outside on a lounger by the pool and read the latest issue of *GQ*. Perhaps his mind would clear up once he relaxed a bit. While flipping through the latest trends in summer fashion (which pretty much worked most of the year in the desert) he decided that it would be best to meet Joey in person. That way he could see the look on Joey's face if he needed to present his newly acquired evidence as an insurance policy.

He called Joey and set up the meeting. Same place. Joey, fully anticipating John's change of heart, was already on his way to Palm Springs. They decided to meet at eight thirty in the lobby. John made no mention of having anything *new* for Joey, he just said to be there and they would talk.

John changed into some clothes that made him feel slightly more *important* and headed out the door. Turning off of Gene Autry onto Highway 111, he immediately noticed a big black Lincoln Navigator that seemed to be following him. Maybe he was just being paranoid. As he continued down 111 and approached Date Palm drive, John noticed that the Navigator was still keeping up with him. It seemed to follow him as he changed lanes and something about it just didn't seem right. *Could be Joey,* he thought, but there was definitely more than one person in the huge black SUV.

Paranoia getting the best of him, he decided to turn off of 111 onto Frank Sinatra instead of turning directly onto Country Club. The left turn he made was pretty erratic, too—there would be no way the Navigator would be able to follow. He turned onto Bob Hope and found his way back to Country Club. Whew, no Navigator to be found.

Pulling into the Marriott parking lot however, he noticed that same black Navigator parked near the front entrance in the handicap spot. John wasn't sure what to do. Either this was a huge coincidence or he was being followed. *Well, I'm here; I may as well just go meet Joey and see what happens.* He parked the MDX and walked into the resort, passing by the Navigator on his way in. He tried to make out the people inside the behemoth vehicle but the windows were tinted darker than the law allowed.

As soon as John entered the lobby, Joey picked him out and approached him.

"Let's go to the Lobby Bar and have a drink." Joey said.

"Sure, what the hell," John said, thinking that maybe a drink would calm his nerves and give him a better chance to see what Joey's game was.

They found a nice quiet table near some beautiful plants. Joey moved the table as far away from the other patrons as possible.

"So what do you have for me, Sir John? I'm glad you decided to come to your senses," Joey said, in an overly friendly tone now.

"Joey. Listen to me. I don't have anything for you now, later, or ever. This is over. I appreciated doing business with you before but it can't happen anymore. I thought I would do the right thing and tell you in person. Let's just go our separate ways." John said, having stirred up as much confidence as possible.

"Aren't you the gentlemanly type? You know, I kinda like you and this is going to be really hard. Truly it is—"

"Before you go on," John interrupted, "just tell me this: were you having me followed here? If so, why? What good does it do you?" John asked.

"Sir John. Sir John. Whether or not you were followed is a question I cannot address, even if I wanted to. So don't ask again. As for not giving me any more *goods*, that's a decision that I'm afraid you will need to reconsider. It would greatly behoove you to do so." Joey's tone was as cool as always.

"I told you. No. Never. So play your next card, Joey. Here I am. Go for it!" John sounded almost threatening. This was a John even John himself did not know.

"Like I said before, I like you. And I don't want to go there with you. Okay? Are you fucking listening to me?" Joey stared at John and grabbed him at the shoulders for effect.

"Don't touch me, Joey. Let's just have this out. What are you going to do if I don't give you any more of your precious gossip?"

"Let's just say you'll change your mind. Don't worry about the how or when, but believe me it will happen. And soon. Sorry you feel this way. I'm giving you one last chance to reconsider right now before I have to go to Plan B."

"No Plan B, Joey. Just tell me what you're going to do."

"Fuck. You are one stubborn motherfucker. All for what? Your morals? Dedication to your job? Your professional ethics? What happened to all that shit last month when you were feeding me like there was no tomorrow, huh? All of a sudden you rediscovered them? Like a born-again Mr. Ethics?"

"Exactly. I realized the error of my ways. Now tell me what you're up to."

"Stubborn!!! What is with you? Just watch your step over the next few days, that's all I can tell you."

"Uh, no. Not gonna happen." John realized he was going to have to play his trump card. "Have you ever heard of a thing called phishing, with a *ph*?"

"The fuck does that have to do with anything?" Joey asked, his calm, cool demeanor somewhat rattled.

"Oh. A lot. Seems like someone we know who happens to be sitting across me in the Lobby Bar is involved in a major phishing scam. Stealing customer's credit information, those who purchased some abs exerciser. Know anything about that?"

The look on Joey's face said it all. "I don't know what you're talking about."

"The true words of the guilty. I have proof, Joey." He pulled out an envelope from the pocket of his Zegna sports jacket. "The contents of this envelope prove your involvement in this scam. Your liability is implicated all over the place. Don't try to be a smart-ass and deny it, either. This isn't the only copy. If you, or anyone you're involved with, lays a finger on me, I turn this evidence into the proper authorities."

"How the fuck …? How did you get that? You're bluffing. You have nothing," Joey said, clearly flustered now.

"Never mind. I'm good at what I do, Joey. Don't fuck with me. Here, this is for you. All the evidence I have. Like I said, I have copies. Have it!" John threw it across the table at Joey. "Have a good night, Joey."

John stood up to leave. Joey grabbed him by the arm and dragged him forcefully back down to his chair.

"Don't fuck with *you?* Don't make me laugh. Okay, maybe you have something. Either way, it doesn't matter to me. How can a dead man take any action?"

"What did you just say?" John asked, stunned.

"I won't repeat it. You heard it, and I know you did. You've made a big mistake. It's been nice knowing you. You're in more trouble than you ever thought. Your *evidence* only pisses me off more. You're done, John. That's it. Adios."

Joey stood up and left. John remained seated at the table. Alone, stunned, and more frightened for his life than ever before.

CHAPTER 15

▼

Joey Styles left the meeting with John feeling incredibly uneasy. How did John get that information? Joey was sure he kept his tracks covered really well. Obviously not. Something bothered him about that. Was John smarter than he was giving him credit for?

He had a lot of thinking to do. The evidence that John uncovered revealed more than his involvement in an illegal phishing scam. He looked through the contents of the envelope that John had presented him with just to make sure. As he read it again, a sense of dread came over him. There was proof that the scam was a collaboration between himself and a mystery partner, unnamed in the evidence. Emails showed details of what percentage Joey was to receive from the proceeds.

Joey's problem was that the numbers in the email show Joey taking a bigger cut than what he had previously agreed to with the mystery partner. Before he could even take the time to think of ways out of this mess, his cell phone rang.

"So how did it go with your man? What good shit did he bring us?" It was Harlan Daley, Vice President of Production at Heavyweight Studios. Harlan also happened to be Joey's mystery partner in the email scam.

"Ummm, well Harlan, we kind of find ourselves in a bit of a—"

Harlan cut Joey off before he had a chance to explain. "We need to raise the stakes with all the gossip about PopeyDopey. The movie opens soon and we need to get people talkin'. Even if you have to start makin' shit up, I don't give a fuck. Do what you need to do."

"I'll do what I can. We can't afford to get sued again—lawsuits cost us a fuckin' fortune last year. One more biggie could put us under. But don't worry, Harlan, I'll make something happen."

"Whatever it takes. Just do it!"

Harlan hung up abruptly. Joey had no clue what his next move should be. Truth was, he kind of liked this John guy and admired his spunk. As much as Joey hated the fact that John had all this new shit on him, it was certain that he had underestimated John. He had the means to get rid of him permanently, but that wasn't the right move at this stage of the game. He would have to come up with something better. Regardless, he would have to make sure that John was on edge at all times.

*   *   *   *

John hadn't heard from Joey in just over a month. Outside of being tailed once in a while by that damn black Navigator, there had been no sign of danger whatsoever. John could only take a certain amount of comfort from this; his paranoia never faded and the more he thought of it the more he wondered when something was going to happen.

He would have never been able to get by lately without the support of Vicky, and to a lesser extent, Jennifer. He would chat with Jen online several times a week, and would talk with her whenever she was home when he visited Vicky. Otherwise, things had pretty much settled down with Jen. Vicky would never know about their adventure to Century City.

Things at work were pretty much BAU—business as usual. For some strange reason, life for the Nasty folder had been picking up lately. John and Ray would spend many a lunchtime discussing the latest *entries* and how to best handle them. John found he was spending far too much time in the office of Victor Nunez going over how these emails were affecting the reputation of the company, and strategizing over how to curb the problem.

It was an unusually slow day in early May when John received a strange item in his mailbox (the physical, old-fashioned mailbox—as opposed to the email box). Mixed in with the latest issue of *SC Magazine* he subscribed to for security news, was an interdepartmental mail folder. It was addressed to him but there was no sender information.

He opened the envelope to find a single sheet of plain white paper that at first glance appeared to be just a blank paper. He lifted it out of the envelope and laid the sheet on his desk. Across the middle of the paper a message was laid out to spell 'I AM WATCHING YOU'. The message was comprised of letters that were cut out of various newspapers, in an assortment of fonts. Very much like those menacing threat messages that you'd find in those silly movies of times gone by. *What ever happened to those movies, by the way?* John thought, likely in a feeble attempt to lighten the mood.

Ray approached behind him and when he spoke, it frightened John so much he literally jumped out of his chair. "What the hell is that, John? Whoa, whoa, take it easy there man, I didn't mean to scare ya. You seem about as nervous as a long-tailed cat in a small room full of people in rocking chairs. So, who sent that?"

"I have no clue. No sender." John couldn't think of anything else to say.

"Do you think that the message is meant for someone else? Maybe it was placed in your mailbox by mistake," Ray said optimistically.

"Ray, come on, look who we're dealing with here. Me. John. Just when I thought my life was almost, like actually, settling down."

"Good point. So what are you going to do about it?"

"Not sure. I think I'll tell Dan and see if he has any idea."

"Are you sure you wanna bring anyone else into this? Maybe we should just keep it to ourselves for now and wait it out," Ray suggested.

"Nah, what do I have to lose?"

"Your job? What about that shit a few months ago that you gave to our mutual friend there. Think it has anything to do with that?"

"Maybe. How would anyone find out? Hmmm, let me think about it."

John thought about it. *Could Joey be behind this somehow? Does he have another insider at DesertFinancial, someone who he could get to send a message from the inside like this?* Likely not, but he wouldn't put anything past Joey.

"You're right, Ray. We'll just keep a lid on it for now. I'm locking it up in my desk drawer for the time being."

If John had been paranoid before, he was doubly so now. This just took the cake. This message meant one of two things: either Joey had another insider here, or someone at work may know something about John that they shouldn't, and that knowledge can mean serious trouble. Both scenarios freaked him out.

Several minutes later, John once again jumped out of his chair with someone sneaking up behind him.

"Oh my God, John, are you okay? You seem so *jumpy* today! What's up? I haven't seen you in a while. Email just isn't the same as good ol' face time, hey?" Tara said, while swinging John's chair towards her so that he was now facing her instead of his computer screen.

"Tara!! What are you doing here? It's been forever! What up, girl?" John was excited to see her. She looked really good, too.

"Guess who just had an interview with Patrick Bowman?" Tara asked rhetorically.

"You, obviously, but the real question is for what, and more importantly, *why?*"

"I know all about him, don't worry. Didn't you see the job posting on the Intranet? Seems he's so busy he needs an admin assistant."

"Are you kidding? I guess he's busy, but does he really need an assistant? Holy shit." John settled into his chair, sat back straight, and let his shoulders relax a bit. Tara's visit came at a good time and would take his mind off things. "Well, there'd be nobody better for the job. I'd put in a good word for you, but I don't really know him enough to say anything. The guy is hot and cold, man. Some days it seems like he loves me and then the next day it seems like he wants me outta here."

"Well, the interview went well, and I hope to find out by the end of the week! Hey, let's do lunch today? Are you up for it?"

John looked at Ray. Ray gave him a wink that pretty much said, *yeah, go ahead stud.*

"Sure, let's take some extra time today, we'll get our burger fix too. We haven't done lunch for way too long."

✳   ✳   ✳   ✳

They decided to eat at Tyler's, a place famous for their burgers. As soon as they were seated, John looked at Tara lustfully, then, in his mind, gave himself a slap for going there. *You're a taken man, John.* Vicky Vicky Vicky Vicky.

"So your boyfriend Ray allowed you to go with me, yes?" Tara said, teasing. "I saw that look you guys gave each other. Is there something you're not telling me, John? They say that being a metrosexual is just the first step in crossing over to the other team."

"Hardy frickin' har har, Tara. Ray and I have just become good friends."

"Uh *Huh.* Whatever. So yeah, what do you think of me working for Patrick Bowman? I really gotta do whatever I can to get away from where I'm at. Paula hasn't changed. Anything would be a change for the better."

Because they were starving, they ordered a plate of French fries first, so they could chow down on something quickly. As soon as the fries were brought to the table, they each lunged for one at the same time. Tara slapped his hand and took the first one for herself.

"Ouch. Bitch! Just kidding. I hear ya about the job, though. It sure would be interesting if you got it, then you can give me the lowdown on him. He's not your typical IT Director, that's for sure. I'm really hopin' for ya!"

They caught up on each other's lives for the next hour. Time flew by. They had so much to chat about: John's relationship with Vicky (he didn't mention anything about Jennifer at all) and Tara's newfound freedom as a single woman. It didn't take long for John to realize that Tara's comfort level with him was stepped up a notch now that he was the one in the committed relationship. He had always worried that she saw him as a good friend that just wanted to get into her pants. Okay, he still wouldn't mind doing just that but now it simply *couldn't* happen.

John enjoyed this new, at-ease, more-open-than-before Tara though. He enjoyed listening to her recent dating experiences. They sat there laughing hysterically as Tara recounted the gruesome details of the blind date she went on last weekend. John considered whether to bring up how she seemed so much more at ease with him, then thought better of it as he didn't want to rock the boat.

If their new friendship was always going to be like this, who was he to mess with it? John decided that he would let things be and see how it went. He wasn't sure how often was too often to see Tara; now that he was tight with Vicky he didn't want to behave in a way which could be deemed inappropriate. He would have to keep his lustful thoughts in check and try his best to keep his mind on what appeared to be a renewed friendship on solid ground.

*   *   *   *

Jennifer couldn't believe that her time at Cathedral City High was about to come to an end. Prom was coming up and school would be done in just over a month. The situation with Shawn seemed to be improving, the bitches at school were still staying away, and her mom was really happy with John.

She decided that there was no better time to bring up an issue with her mom that had been on her mind for months. Jen's use of her mom's Prozac had been tapering off gradually, almost to the point where she didn't need them anymore. Apparently her mom was still addicted to them though.

They were sitting down to dinner: a delicious home made pizza that the two of them had made together. Jen loved helping her mom cook.

"Mom, I think I need to talk to you about something. Can we have a serious discussion?"

"I'm not sure, you sound so, well, *serious*. I hope it's nothing terrible. Should we finish eating first or do you want to talk about it now while we eat?" Vicky asked, undoubtedly worried given the tone in her daughter's voice.

"We can talk about it while we eat. Don't worry; it's not about me. I'm not in trouble or anything like that. In fact, for the first time in a very long time my life is going pretty good. I hope you've been able to tell."

"Of course, I'm so happy that things are working out for you. I was just worried that maybe you were doing a good job of hiding things from me. You've proven yourself to be quite good at that. But sorry, that's getting off topic. So obviously it's about me—Go ahead. I'm all ears."

Jen took a deep breath. She had been anticipating this conversation for quite some time.

"Mom. I don't know how to start this. I'm ... well ..." Jen stopped in mid-sentence.

"You can tell me or ask me anything. I love you so much, Jennifer. Whatever we need to discuss we can discuss. Having an open and honest relationship with my daughter is so important to me—"

"Okay, okay," Jen interrupted. *Might as well get right to the point.* "I know you're taking Prozac. I've known for a long time. I can't believe you would just have it out in the open like that in the medicine cabinet. I have a confession as well ... I ... I've been taking some of your pills. I'm so sorry. Not as often as before, but I did. I thought I was addicted but I find I don't need them much anymore." Jen paused for a second as she noticed Vicky about to say something but continued on because she wanted to get everything out before her mom responded. "My main reason for bringing this up, other than confessing to using some of your pills, is to ask you why you're still taking the pills."

"Wow. I figured you probably knew about the Prozac. Maybe in some strange way I wanted it to be discovered. Why else would I just leave them out like that? But ... wow. Okay. I'm a bit flustered—forgive me." Vicky was sweating, and it wasn't because of the spicy pizza sauce. She took her napkin and gently wiped her forehead before resuming the conversation. Vicky was relieved and panicked at the same time. At least they were having *the conversation* that she'd been avoiding. She tried to continue without demonstrating signs of panic. "Prozac is not your friend, Jennifer. It is incredibly addicting and very hard to stop. Before your father and I got divorced, I was having difficulty coping with just about everything. When the divorce went through, and my life started falling back into place, I thought I would stop using it. I went cold turkey with devastating results. Remember that time that seemed like forever when I was just super mega bitchy? That was me without the Prozac. I had to start taking them again."

"I don't really know much about it, just that it's supposed to put you in a *happy place*. I'm sorry I took them, but I really needed something. So are you saying that you think that once you start using it you can't stop?" Jen asked.

"Almost. It's something I struggle with every day. There are so many side effects that really suck, and they come and go as they please, wreaking havoc on your body. I'm so glad that you're not dependent on them now. If you can stop, you should just stop. You don't need them, Jennifer." Vicky took a huge bite of her pizza slice, the cheese dripping down her chin, creating a 'cheese beard' as they would call it.

"Mom. Cheese beard! Ha ha," Jen said, grabbing the strand of cheese with her thumb and forefinger and eating it for herself. "I know. I started researching it a bit on the Internet, found some weird stuff and then just stopped. I figured what I didn't know wouldn't hurt me." Jen paused to take a few giant bites of her pizza. All this talk was making her hungry. "So what are you going to do to stop using them? I mean, your life is going pretty good. John seems like a great guy, and you seem so happy together. Not that happiness is tied to a *man*, but I don't hear you complaining about anything at work or anything else. And you're not the kind of mom to hold things in either. When you're unhappy, believe me, I know it!"

"I know I know. I'm sorry. I'm glad we're having this discussion though. Let's promise each other to keep the lines of communication open from now on. Okay???"

"Promise. Promise. So is there anything I can do to help as far as trying to get off the Prozac?"

"I wish there was, honey. Actually, just talking about it will probably help me more than you know. I'm really glad we had this talk. I think I'll make another appointment with my doctor and see what I can do to wean myself off this stuff. Now that I think of it, there is something you may be able to do. You know that I'm not the greatest at finding stuff on the Internet. Would you be able to look up information on how to best decrease dosages? I wouldn't even know where to begin to look. I can do the basics online, but you seem to be the Internet *queen*. Whatever you can find would be awesome. You don't have to do it today or anything. Whenever you have time." Vicky felt wonderful to have someone to share this part of her life with, but more importantly, to have reached the first step in achieving the type of mother-daughter friendship that had eluded them for all this time.

"For sure, mom, for sure. I'll bookmark the sites and we can go over them together. Then maybe I can teach you how to get better in searching for things. Sound good?"

"More than good. Thanks for being so understanding. I love you, Jennifer."

"I love you too, mom."

Vicky and Jennifer hugged like they used to when Jennifer was a little girl. They both fought to hold back the tears, but this time, unlike many times before, the salty drops flowing down their faces were tears of joy.

*   *   *   *

John and Aaron were sipping their Venti Caramel Frappucinos as they stared across at the travel store. Today was abnormally hot for May, it was ten a.m. and the temperature was already well into the nineties. They knew that their cold Frappucinos weren't the best way to quench their thirst and beat the heat, but the drinks were damn cold and full of caffeine and sugar—a surefire winning combination.

What was Ray doing talking to Travelchick for so long? Ray had told them he would be about five minutes behind and would meet up with them. Travelchick sure was smiling a lot.

Ray walked across, ordered a regular coffee and joined them at the table.

"Hey, Ray. Did you notice it was slightly warm outside? Why the fuck are you getting a hot coffee?" Aaron asked incredulously.

"You know I hate those sugar and fat filled drinks. Hello? When have you ever seen me order one of those overpriced concoctions? I'm a simple coffee guy all the way," Ray said.

"Okay, okay, maybe we were too preoccupied with you making time with Travelchick over there. What's up with that???" John asked.

"Oh nothing. Nothing at all. There's nothing to tell," Ray calmly replied, with a *huge* smile on his face.

"Bull shit," Aaron said, stretching out the words to form two distinct syllables.

"We were just talking. I felt like chatting with her."

"Dude. That just isn't you. I haven't known you for *that* long, but that was just totally out of character for Ray. So give it up man. Spill 'em," John said, getting fed up with Ray's evasiveness.

"What? *What?*" Ray paused for a moment for effect. "Okay. You guys really wanna know what we were talking about?"

"No. Forget it. We're not interested anymore. Let's go back to work," Aaron said, in a tone mixed with equal parts sarcasm and seriousness.

"Okay, Okay. This is what went down."

Ray went on to explain his visit with Samantha at the travel office. He was going there to book a trip for September to take with his wife. Ray was the consummate traveler and took at least three vacations per year. While discussing the possibilities for where to go and what to do, Samantha revealed that she had a free travel agent pass for two to Vegas this weekend: air, hotel and food included. Ray explained that he loved going to Vegas and revealed that he was a frequent visitor and a self-professed high roller at Bellagio. *You don't know nothin' about being a high roller,* John thought.

Apparently Samantha's boyfriend did not want to join her. He hated Vegas. Ray jokingly suggested that he should go instead, and the next thing you know she agreed. Ray promised that they would sleep in separate beds and that the trip would be purely professional. Somehow she concurred and plans were set.

"Simple as that." Ray concluded.

"Get the fuck out of here. You're making this shit up, right? Aaron, let's go across and confirm this." John said.

"No need. It's a done deal. Why would I lie about something like this? Why would I make this shit up? I was joking when I said I should come along and a few minutes later, we're going."

"But how? What is Darlene going to say? She's gonna fuckin' kill you if she finds out ... isn't she?" Aaron asked, trying his best to conceal his jealousy.

"I don't even know if I'm going to tell her yet. Maybe I'll just say I'm taking a drive down there with you guys. And if I do, you guys will cover for me in the future, right?"

"Yeah, of course. But it's just a *professional* trip, right?" John asked.

"Not if I can change the rules in the middle of the game," Ray said.

"Say what? I thought you were totally and completely happy with Darlene," John said.

"I am. But at this stage of my life, when will I ever get another opportunity like this? Alone with a hot chick in Vegas of all places? What happens in Vegas ..."

"Yeah, I know. I know. But won't you feel guilty?" Aaron asked.

"Look. It hasn't even happened yet. Plus for all I know she could change her mind, or perhaps she was kidding. I got her card and I'm supposed to call her

Thursday to confirm. And even if we do go, what are the chances of anything happening? Give a guy a break here. I'll let you guys know what happens if we even go. But c'mon though, let a guy bask in the glory for once, okay?" Ray said, almost offended.

"Good point. Boys, a toast to Ray Douglas. My hero. You got more game than you lead on. L'chaim!" Aaron said.

"I second that. Ray, you rock! Mac Daddy Ray is here to stay," John said.

They clicked their coffees together and quickly headed out so they could rush back to work even though it was already twenty minutes to eleven. They were going to have to try to cut back on these extended coffee breaks.

John enjoyed seeing Ray in such high spirits from his experience with Travelchick. All that caffeine from the Frappucino helped too—they were able to tackle their daily tasks at least twice as quickly and efficiently as usual.

John still couldn't understand what, or who, was behind the mysterious 'I'm watching you' messages. What were they watching anyway? His paranoia was really taking its toll. The more he thought about it, the more it got to him and everyone around him became a suspect: even Ray, Aaron, and Dan. This wasn't right. Couldn't he rule these three out? They were his friends. They weren't capable of this.

That night when he was on his computer he broke the promise he made himself not long ago. He saw no way around it. He was going to have to do some *research* by going into some mailboxes.

This was his sanity at stake. Well worth breaking his promise for.

John hated himself for opening Dan's mailbox. This was something he never thought he would ever do. Not in a million years. Dan was a great guy, a good boss, and surely wasn't capable of being behind those messages.

Thankfully, Dan's mailbox didn't reveal anything. John wasn't looking terribly hard, but he could just sense that he wouldn't find anything incriminating there. A sigh of relief passed over him. Of all people, John would have been most upset if he were to discover that Dan was behind this.

John spent the next hour going through many mailboxes in an attempt to unearth anything that would lead him to an answer. Unfortunately, there was no evidence to be found. He saw many things that he wished he had never seen; often about people he would have never guessed would be up to the activities he discovered. *What is with these people?* John wondered, for the millionth time.

John decided he needed to tell Vicky about the threatening message. He called her up and asked if she would come over for a swim.

Vicky showed up wearing only a bikini. *Awesome. That'll keep my mind off things for a while.* They swam and lounged around in the water and even gave each other neck massages. They entered into a long discussion about which was better: massages or sex. Either way, you can't lose, they decided.

Oooh yeah, this was the life.

After taking a sensual shower together, John found a pair of boxers, shorts and a shirt that Vicky had left in his room for occasions just like this. They went to the living room and sat down on the couch, each with an ice-cold beer in hand.

John told Vicky about the messages. He omitted anything to do with his suspicions of Joey for fear of slipping up about his detective outing with Jennifer.

Vicky listened and offered whatever support she could give. She didn't exactly understand why anyone would do something like this to John.

They laid together on the bed, taking turns massaging each other's feet.

Half-hour into the foot massages, both of them fell asleep. John woke up at five, looked over at the alarm clock, then at Vicky, and freaked out.

"Shit shit shit, Vicky, it's five a.m. Is Jennifer going to worry about you?"

Vicky slowly sat up, wiping the sleep out of her eyes. "No. Don't worry. She knows where I am and that I am with you. She's really happy for us. I think she'll understand."

"Are you sure? She's not going to freak?" John sat up.

"No. She'll be okay."

"Do you want to go back to sleep?"

"Nahhh … I'll just head home and I'll be there when she wakes up. That okay with you?"

"Of course. Thanks for everything, Vicky. What would I do without you? Honestly."

"I'm always there for you. Now kiss me with that lovely morning breath of yours and let me get home!"

CHAPTER 16

▼

After getting a few more hours of well-needed rest, John came to work the next day relaxed and slightly less paranoid. He thanked the God of Loving Girlfriends that Vicky was always able to keep him centered and balanced, regardless of whatever shit he was going through in other aspects of his life.

Right before coffee break, Dan was returning from a meeting and was carrying a stack of mail with his notebook. He delivered Jill's, then Ray's, then stopped at John's desk. He dropped a yellow envelope in front of John and noticed John's face go slightly white. "What's wrong, John? Are you feeling okay today? Lookin' a little pale there, fella."

"Oh, nothing. I think I need more sleep," John lied.

"Ya sure? Almost looks like a fever or something. You're sweating a bit, too. If you're feeling like shit, may as well go home before getting all of us sick."

"Nonono, I'll be okay Dan, thanks."

"All righty. Just let me know if you don't feel up to staying."

"Thanks, Dan. Will do."

John waited until Dan returned to his own desk before opening the envelope. He took a brief glance over his shoulder to make sure everyone was busy working. John found an envelope opener and with a quick flick of the wrist opened it up.

'I AM STILL WATCHING YOU', the message said.

The word *still* was in a huge font that took up almost half the page. The effect was not lost on John's nerves. Goosebumps ran through his body and he shivered almost violently.

Who in the royal fucking hell is sending these messages? John was beside himself.

That's it, John decided. He realized it was time to tell Dan about it. After doing some unethical detective work, he was confident in ruling Dan out as a suspect.

He sent Dan an email requesting his presence in one of the meeting rooms nearby. Dan quickly responded asking if now was a good time. John emailed back saying yes, right now. They often got a kick out of the inefficiency of using email, when they sat only a few feet away from each other.

John placed both the menacing messages into an envelope and followed Dan to the meeting room.

"Thanks for meeting with me, Dan. This won't take long."

"Do we have a really serious security breach? Anything really good and juicy?"

"Unfortunately nothing like that. This has to do with me." John slid the envelope across the table for Dan to look at.

"What the hell is this?" Dan asked in a curious tone.

"Someone here is sending me these. I have no clue why." That's all John said. He didn't mention anything about Joey or anything else that may provide any clues. At that moment, John regretted bringing Dan into this. What if somehow Dan were to become suspicious of him?

"Hmmm … I don't know what to tell you, Johnny Boy. Is there anyone that you suspect would be behind this?" Dan asked. It was apparent that he had no clue what to do about this, and where to even start.

"Not a frickin' clue. I just wanted to bring it to your attention. Plus, this explains my ghost-like face when you handed me the envelope earlier."

"Ahhh. Now it makes sense. Glad you're not sick anyway. But what can I do for you here? Start a covert investigation?"

John could tell that the wheels in Dan's brain were turning now.

"Sure, whatever you can do. Maybe see what you can come up with from whoever is handling the mail. Anything would help. It's kinda freaking me out."

"I can see that. Leave it to me. I can't make any promises, but if I can find anything I'll let you know. So has there been anyone you busted recently that may be trying to just get your goat?"

"I thought of that. It's possible, but unlikely. I'll just keep doing my job and hopefully these damn things will just stop. Anyway, thanks for listening, Dan."

"De nada. No problemo, etc. etc. So what else is up with you? We haven't chatted much lately," Dan said, wheeling his chair closer to the table.

They spent the next half hour in the meeting room just shooting the breeze, catching up on each other's lives. John held a lot back, but gave him the lowdown on everything with Vicky. Dan was surprised, and didn't really know that things had got serious. He expressed concern about Vicky's famous email, but John was able to pretty much explain everything away. John was worried that Dan may think he was using his position to exploit the female population at work, but Dan really didn't go there. It was a good chat, and it made John feel better.

*   *   *   *

Vicky called him in the afternoon to check up on him. John told her about the new message and how it freaked him out. He told her about his talk with Dan and how it generally lifted his spirits. She offered to make him feel even better by taking him to the Cheesecake Factory for dinner. That would hit the spot for sure. He was looking forward to it.

They met up at the Cheesecake Factory and had a great meal, great conversation and great cheesecake, in no particular order of importance. They took a walk around the shops at the River, and allowed themselves to enjoy the beautiful evening. It had cooled down to a much more comfortable eighty-five degrees.

"What a lovely evening. Have I told you I loved you lately?" Vicky asked.

"Not enough. Tell me again," John said.

"Love you love you love you!" Vicky said, the volume of her voice increasing with each mention of the word love.

"Ditto ditto ditto!" John said jokingly. "Ha ha ha, you know I wuv you, Vicky. Now gimme some sugar, baby," John puckered up and waited for his kiss.

Vicky kissed him and they hugged. She let go and told him that she would have to get back home to Jennifer, as she had promised her that they would spend some quality mother-daughter time tonight. They kissed once more and made their way to the parking lot, where they parted ways.

*   *   *   *

It was eight thirty and John didn't really feel like going home, but he understood that Vicky needed time with Jennifer. He wondered how Jennifer was doing; he really hadn't talked to her much lately. He made a mental note to catch up with her online either tonight or tomorrow.

John drove around aimlessly then ended up at the video store to get a movie. A special edition of *American Psycho* had been released on DVD, and even though he had seen the movie twice, he wanted to see what the special edition was all about. Christian Bale was awesome in this movie, perhaps his best role. John felt that this was one of the rare occasions where the movie actually captured the true essence of the book, much like *Silence of the Lambs*. He couldn't wait to see the extras for this DVD. He always felt that *American Psycho* was perhaps the most misunderstood piece of modern literature. *Why did people have so much trouble grasping the subtle humor in the book?* John always laughed at the extreme irony in the fact that Gloria Steinem, the most vocal in her opposition to the release of the *American Psycho* film, ended up getting married to Christian Bale's father.

John rented the DVD and headed home. He parked the MDX and took a brief walk around the meticulously landscaped grounds on the winding paths. It was now dark (Palm Springs gets very dark at night) and a perfect time to watch a movie. John hated watching movies at home when it wasn't dark outside.

John entered his house, set the DVD down on the kitchen table and turned on the light that hovered above the kitchen counters, providing just enough brightness for him to see his way around. John hated wasting energy and used the lighting in his place sparingly.

He made his way into his room and threw off his shirt onto the bed. Ahhh, now he felt comfortable. It was still hot outside and John was still sweating. John imagined his grandparents in the kitchen telling him how he looked like he was *schvitzing*, the Yiddish word for sweating profusely. The refreshing, yet artificially generated air conditioning would work its wonders in no time. By the time he popped the movie into the DVD player he would be all cooled off.

John went back to the kitchen to get a Coke and make some popcorn in the microwave. He poured the popcorn into a large bowl without spilling a single kernel, grabbed the can of Coke and dropped it in the bowl with the popcorn, picked up the DVD with the other hand and made his way to the den. He was a master at this.

As he entered the dark den, a voice stopped him dead in his tracks.

"Don't *you* look comfortable and relaxed?" The voice came from a chair in a dark corner of the room.

"What the fuck?" John was stunned. The voice scared him enough to drop the popcorn bowl, spilling many kernels across the floor.

The Voice turned on a light.

"Joey? The fuck are you doing here and how did you get in?" John was seething mad now.

"Never you mind, Sir John. Let's just say I'm not the only one who knows how to break into places. Did you and your hot little stepdaughter think you could just break into our offices without any consequences?"

"What??? I don't know what you're talking about!" John was so startled by Joey's invasion of his privacy he found nothing better to say.

"Oh, John, John ... I thought I knew you better than that. Don't deny it. Jennifer was pretty good with that security guard, but eventually he sang like a fuckin' canary. Giving him a fake phone number and MSN? Did you guys actually think that was gonna work?" Joey laughed in mock hysterics for a moment before continuing. "John. I'm disappointed in you."

"I don't know what to say, Joey. Other than, oh, I don't know ... *Get the fuck out of my house now!*"

Joey remained silent. His silence was like a shrill scream drilling into John's ears.

"Seriously, Joey, if you don't leave now I'm going to call the cops. Or better yet, I'll make sure that evidence I have hits every paper in LA. You'll be in jail so quickly your head will spin ten times faster than Linda Blair in the *Exorcist*. You asswipe."

"Oooh, what a threat. Sorry, John, but I have the upper hand here."

"From where I stand, I don't see how that can be."

"Ahhh, that's where you are so very wrong, John. Did you forget who you were dealing with? That night we met at the Marriott, did you notice a black Navigator following you?"

"Duh. But what does that have to do with it?"

Joey stood up and faced John. He glanced at John with an intimidating glare, stared him in the eye and then sat back down. "You probably didn't notice that specific truck after that night. That would be because my guys change vehicles often. I've been doing a lot of research on you, John. I know all about you and your lovely girlfriend Vicky, and that hot daughter of hers. I admire you, John. Just think: if you marry Vicky, Jennifer will be your stepdaughter. What a family you guys would make. I think I'd give my left nut for a stepdaughter like that!"

"You sick fuck, Joey. Do I have to say it one more time? Get *out. Now!*" John screamed it, and was ready to knock this guy's lights out.

Joey ignored him again.

"Oh come on, John. Humor me here. Just for a second. Tell me you haven't thought about sticking it to Jen as well. Keep it in the family, right?"

John approached Joey with a clenched fist and took a fake swing, stopping a few inches before Joey's nose. He grabbed Joey by the collar and lifted him with a strength he didn't know he had in him. Joey rose in the air as if he was as light as a feather. They were standing face to face again.

"Joey. Asshole. Leave my house. Now. I'll rip your filthy limbs off if you don't get out of here. And I'm just pissed off enough to do it." John couldn't believe these words were coming out of his mouth. He underestimated Joey for sure. He knew it was just a threat but he wanted to scare Joey as much as he could.

"Enough with the idle threats, John. It's time to get to the business at hand. Now let go of me and I'll bring up the one and only order of business. Then, I promise you, I will leave your place and leave you alone. Deal?" Joey stuck out his hand.

"I'm not shaking your fucking hand, asshole. But if you'll get outta here, then fine, be my guest. Enlighten me. What's your *order of business*?" John said with as much sarcasm as he could muster.

Joey helped himself to the chair again.

"Here it is, John. The reason I'm here. You know what I need from you. I'm sure you have more than enough info on Pope. I'm being honest with you when I tell you that if I could get this stuff any other way, I wouldn't be here. I actually kind of like you, John. But business is business. If I don't get what I want, I will seriously fuck you up. I have the means to do it. Don't question my abilities. Do the right thing, John."

"What in the world are you talking about? You're sounding like a babbling idiot." To make his point, and more so to piss Joey off, John took his index finger and placed it between his lips and flicked it up and down, making the *bmbmb-mbmb* sound.

"Don't be so fucking *glib*, John. This is a serious matter we're dealing with here. Now listen to me. Give me what I want. Or else. It's that simple."

"You're lying. Fuck you, Joey."

"Not lying. Sorry."

"Idle threats, that's all this is. I don't believe you for a second," John said, hoping with all hope that what he was saying was true.

"No threats. All real. It is what it is. Give me what I want. Failing that, you're in deep shit. Have a good evening, John."

With that, Joey stood up and handed John a card with his cell phone number written on it. He smiled a satanic smile and walked out of the room and towards the door.

"You're lying, Joey. You're an asshole, but you're a better person than this. You won't go through with it. You won't hurt me," John called out to him, in a last ditch attempt at *something*. At what, he didn't know.

Joey said nothing and walked out the door. John stood motionless in the middle of the spilled popcorn and had no idea what to do next.

CHAPTER 17

▼

It was another sleepless night for John consisting of far too much tossing and turning in bed. He could not believe the predicament he found himself in. He would drift off for several minutes at a time; each instance waking up and wishing the events that transpired in his den were nothing more than a David Lynch inspired nightmare.

He arrived at work in no mood to be the least bit productive. He needed to tell someone about everything just to get it off his chest. Vicky was obviously out of the question; she would worry too much.

After completing some menial tasks, he grabbed Ray and told him he needed a major caffeine fix. They walked over to Starbucks, and commented on how happy they were to actually see a cloudy sky. The weather over the last few days had been just too damn hot, and the heat was the last thing John needed in this mood he was in.

They took their regular seat and ordered their drinks. Ray commented on how John looked like shit today, so John recounted the story of everything that happened with Joey.

"Holy shit, I'm sorry that he's being such a prick," Ray said, in a deadpan tone that didn't impress John all that much.

"Being such a prick? A prick? That's more than a prick, dude. This guy is the biggest fucktard that I have ever met. He's making serious threats! *You* know the guy. What should I do???"

"I don't really know him that well. We talked a few times and that's about it. I wish I had never brought up his name. I wish I had some advice for you, but what do I know about shit like this?"

"I don't expect you to know *anything* about this. I just need your advice, Ray. What would *you* do?"

"If it were me, I'd wait him out. See if he's bluffing. My guess is that he's just blowing smoke out his ass. And if not, at the last minute, kill his operation by giving him what he wants. You have no choice."

"But If I give up more stuff, then I'm risking my job. Big time. And who knows who's sending those fucking messages through the snail mail?" John had a thought. "Since you seem to consort with some shady characters, what about any hackers? Do you know any serious computer hackers with no morals and nothing to lose?"

"What do you think I am? A gangster? Just cause I know Joey Styles. I wish I knew a real serious hacker. But no dice. Hey, what about you? You're the guy with all the security credentials. You must know a big time hacker or two," Ray said.

"I wish. But I wouldn't want to lose my professional designation by hanging out with any of the black hats. Ya never know what kind of trouble I would get in."

"What kind of trouble do you think you're in now, John? I'd say pretty fuckin' bad. What would a hacker do for you anyway?"

"I don't know. Something. Anything to get me out of this mess." Somehow, something was nagging at him that Joey was for real, and that it really *was* a threat. Ray confirmed it. Either way, he finally resolved to just give in and hand over the goods.

"I hope everything works out for you. I really do," Ray said.

"I guess that's all I can do. Anyway, here's Aaron."

Aaron sat with them and made a comment about Travelchick, thankfully steering the conversation away from John's troubles.

"Yeah, that low-cut top is rockin' today, man. Hey Ray, isn't tonight the night you call her to make the plans for the weekend?" John asked, completely switching gears in his brain.

Aaron piped in before Ray could answer: "Why don't you just go across and ask her now? Why wait for tonight? I'm sure you're dying to know anyway."

"I guess I could. I just don't want to come across as too eager."

"Eager Beaver. That's you, Ray. Or more appropriately, eager *for* the beaver. Ha ha. Man I crack me up sometimes," John said, happy that his problems were no longer the focus of their conversation.

"You're such a card, John. You need to be *dealt with* and have your Ace kicked," Ray quipped. "But okay, I'm going over there right now."

"Bueno Suerte," Aaron said.

"Yeah, good luck, bro." John added.

*   *   *   *

Ray Douglas was nervous. He had never done anything like this before. It wasn't as if he was shy with women, but since getting married he had remained faithful to Darlene and didn't really think about cheating. He always enjoyed looking at women, and flirting back when they flirted with him, but something about Samantha the Travelchick told him that there was a good chance of something happening in Vegas.

As he approached Samantha he noticed she was on the phone. She held up her index finger to indicate that she would be with him in a minute. He looked across at John and Aaron who were watching his every move. They both gave him the thumbs up.

Samantha hung up the phone and looked up at Ray.

"How's it going, Ray?" She asked.

"Really good. Just hangin' with the boys, as usual."

"You guys are a bunch of horndogs sometimes. I see you ogling all these women that come in to get their coffee. I honestly don't know if I can trust you on a weekend in Vegas. Even a strictly platonic one," Samantha said.

"Oh, we're just a bunch of regular guys. And I'm just a chickenshit anyway. I think if you came on to me I just wouldn't know what to do," Ray said disarmingly. He was only half-serious.

"You're a strange guy, Ray. But my instincts tell me that you're harmless and nice. So I guess you want to know if the weekend is still on, right?"

"Yeah, why not? I just came to say hi though. But sure."

"It's on. I'll meet you at PSP at five thirty tomorrow for an evening flight to Vegas. Is that good?"

"Most definitely. I'll see you there, Samantha. Looking forward to it. Get ready to win a whole lotta money and eat a whole lotta food!"

"Yippee! More money is a great thing. See ya tomorrow, Ray."

Ray returned to the table to join the boys.

"It looked good to me. Is it a go?" Aaron asked.

"All systems go. I'm kind of in shock. Does it show in my face?" Ray asked.

"Not at all, ya dawg. Lucky fucker—Ray and Travelchick. So what are you telling Darlene?" John asked.

"I think for now I'll tell her that I'm heading to Vegas with you two. That okay with you boys?"

"Yeah. No problem. Is everything okay with Darlene though? I hate to put a damper on things here, but I just wanna know," Aaron said.

"Everything is okay. No big problems. We've been married for eighteen years, guys. We're happy. But I'm just in the mood to do this. Maybe I just want a bit of adventure in my life," Ray said.

"Cool. Just watch it. Don't fall in love with her or anything while you're there," Aaron suggested.

"Fuck! Lighten up, Aaron," Ray barked.

"All right. I'm just being silly. You know you're our dawg, Ray. Seriously, big props to you!" Aaron said.

"Yeah, props to Ray!" John echoed.

✳   ✳   ✳   ✳

The rest of the day just dragged for John. He spent about an hour going through Heather Sweeney's email box to see if there was any new evidence on Pope. Thankfully, there was more than enough evidence. John sent a few of the emails to print on a secluded printer that was sitting in a corner of the IT department floor. Nobody even remembered that the printer was there—it was perfect for printing any secretive stuff.

When he came home after work, a part of him expected to find Joey once again waiting for him in his place. Thankfully that wasn't the case. No Joey. As uneasy as John felt, he desperately needed sleep. After throwing a frozen pizza in the oven and ripping through it in several minutes, he decided to watch some of the extras from the *American Psycho* DVD before going to bed early.

He recalled Vicky saying she would likely be taking advantage of some Jennifer Time tonight, because with prom coming up soon, Jen would be really busy and hanging out with her friends a lot.

✳   ✳   ✳   ✳

The phone woke him up at seven on Friday morning. His mumbled speech became much clearer as soon as he heard the fear in Jen's voice after telling her that Vicky was not with him.

"Mom went out for some groceries last night and didn't come back. She left at ten thirty, and I was really tired so I just went to bed. I was up for a bit, and wondered why she hadn't come home but figured she stopped by your place. I fell asleep, woke up this morning, and she's not here. Where could she be?" Jen spoke quickly as if everything she just said was one long word.

"Say what?" John asked, immediately jolting upright from his supine position. "What do you mean she's not with you? Are you sure?"

"I'm sure. I was positive she'd be with you. Now I'm worried." There was a fear in Jen's voice that hadn't revealed itself to John before.

John's mind raced around aimlessly, unable to come up with any answers. He told Jen to sit tight and hopefully she would be show up at work, and there would be a reasonable explanation for her absence.

John called her number at work and hoped Vicky would be there. The call went right to voicemail. She could still be at work, and not answering her phone. He rushed towards the den, turned on his PC and logged on to the network server at work to check if she had logged on this morning. No such luck. Vicky was officially missing.

That is until his cell phone rang several minutes later. It was Vicky, and her voice was as shaky as the leaves of a palm tree in a ninety-mile per hour windstorm.

"John? What's going on? I'm in some strange house somewhere and I've been handcuffed. I don't know where we are and I don't know why this is happening. I was coming home with my groceries last night and these goons pop out of a big black SUV and just grab me. The guy who was driving told me that this is all about you somehow. Please, John. I've been here for what seems to be forever. Help me!" Vicky's tone was still screechy.

John continually circled the perimeter of his den. "Don't listen to anything they say. I'm so sorry about everything. Trust me, Vicky. I will make sure that you are safe. Please. Trust me. And Vicky … I love you."

"I'm scared. Do what you need to do. I love you too." Vicky rushed the words out, as the phone was yanked away from her.

John was miserable. He was sure that Joey would only inflict harm upon himself; he hadn't at all figured that he would do something as terrible as to kidnap Vicky. Was he that poor a judge of character? John always prided himself on being a pretty good judge of character, even in the worst of times.

Now what to do? His first thought was of Jen. What is she thinking right now? Without wasting a beat, he whipped out of the house and jumped in the car so he could run to Vicky's house to make sure Jen was all right.

He arrived at Vicky's in record time. He ran towards the door and rang the doorbell. No answer. *Shit!* He knocked on the door a few times; turning his head every few seconds towards the street to make sure Joey's goons weren't still in the area for some reason. Jen still wasn't answering. It was possible she had gone out.

He decided to try calling the house. He knew Vicky had call display—hopefully Jen would see it was he, and would answer. Jennifer answered after the first ring.

"Is that you out there?" Jen asked.

"Yes. It's me. Open up."

"What is going on? Where is mom?"

"I'll explain. Open the door. Nobody is here. We're safe."

Jen opened the door and let John in. They sat down on the couch. John recounted everything, not leaving anything out. He was very jittery and visibly shaken up.

"Oh my God, oh my God oh my God!" Jen said, unable to think of anything else to say.

"I'm at a loss, Jen. This guy is more of a prick than we thought."

"I'm so sorry. If it weren't for me, you wouldn't be in this mess. I was the one who convinced you to break into his office. That obviously pissed him off big time. What can I do to help?" Jen asked as she stood up to pace around the room. John gazed at her pacing back and forth and it just made him even more on edge. *You're making me dizzy, Jen!*

"I don't know. I really don't. I'm just going to call him and give him what he wants and hopefully he'll just let her go," John said.

They sat there together in silence. Nothing was said for what seemed like an eternity. Jen broke the silence by offering a hug. John obliged. Human touch was just what he needed right now. He asked her if she wanted to stay with him until this ordeal was over. She thanked him for offering, and explained that she would just stay at home for at least the next while. And anyway, they both hoped that Vicky would be back safe shortly.

John thanked her for understanding and told her he was going to go home, get the envelope of goods for Joey, then call him and put an end to this for once and for all. He couldn't do this to Vicky. He would have to put his career at risk; there was no other way. He promised her that he would call as soon as he knows anything, and she promised the same.

He left Jen and drove home. He would have to review the emails he printed out earlier about Pope and make sure they were salacious enough to make Joey happy. He made it home, got himself a Coke and went to the den to go over the emails, half expecting Joey to be sitting there waiting for him. This was going to be the case for quite some time. The violation John felt from having someone break into his place like that and be so nonchalant about it was something he would struggle with to get over.

John peered over the emails and read them more intently than when he initially discovered them. Fortunately for him, there were a few emails there that contained enough to keep the gossip machine rolling for quite some time.

John took a deep breath and exhaled heavily. His career with DesertFinancial would likely come to an end, but at least he'd have Vicky back.

Time to call Joey.

He picked up the phone and dialed Joey's number. No answer. Right to voicemail. *Shit! Where the hell are you when I need you?* He tried again with the same result. John didn't know what to do with himself. For what seemed like the millionth time lately, he wondered how the hell he ever got into such a mess. If what he was doing were to be discovered at work, what would happen to him? Would they press charges? Was his career the only thing that was to be ruined? These questions were too much for him to deal with right now. He popped a few extra strength Tylenols, hoping it would relieve the throbbing in his head. Maybe he would even sleep a bit before trying Joey again.

CHAPTER 18

▼

What started out as a pretty good night yesterday for Joey Styles, turned out to be rather unpleasant by the time the night was over. He was successful in getting to Vicky and bringing her to his second home in Riverside. He knew that once John realized that he was really serious, he would come around and would get what he wanted. Taking Vicky was a huge risk for him, but he had done it before to get results and it worked wonders. But everything changed when he got an unexpected call from Harlan Daley.

Somehow Harlan had been made aware of the fact that Joey was screwing him out of quite a bit of money on the email phishing scam. Harlan was now raising the stakes on Joey. Not only did he expect to get all the gossip on Pope, he was now demanding half a million dollars in cash to compensate for what Joey was skimming off the top.

Joey wondered how Harlan became informed of Joey's plan. Could this John guy be *that* good? Impossible. There had to be another explanation. Either way, John was going to be the one that ultimately paid. John broke into his office and got that info, and for that Joey would forever hold a grudge.

Still, there was something about John he really respected. But there was no room for admiration here; he was going to make John pay. He even turned his phone off earlier just to piss John off and make him sweat. Joey bet that John would keep trying to make amends, but little did he know that the stakes were about to be raised.

Well speak of the devil, Joey thought, as his phone rang, the display showing John's number.

"Sir John. How's things? What's new and exciting in your life? Missing anything?" Joey said with a chuckle.

"I'm not even going to reply to that. You know why I'm calling. You win, Joey. That's it. I'm giving in. Wherever you want to meet, we'll meet, and I'll give you your shit. And it's really good shit. Believe me."

"Really? No way! Awesome! It feels so good to hear you say that," Joey said sarcastically. "But not so fast. Don't get me wrong; I'm happy to take the stuff off your hands. But now there's more I want from you. Remember when you broke into my office?"

John cut him off before he could continue. "Remember when you broke into my fucking *house*? I think we're even on that one."

"Anyway, like I was saying, remember when you broke into my office?" Joey paused a few beats for added effect. "Seems you uncovered some interesting stuff, which didn't exactly sit well with someone. Now you're going to fucking pay for that little lapse of judgment."

"What are you talking about? I'm giving you what you want, Joey. That's that. Game over. You get what you want, then I get Vicky back. Fair is fair," John said. That last nerve John must have possessed was practically a goner, Joey figured.

"Not so fast. Your little B&E expedition that you pulled on me with your hot little *friend* there cost me a bundle. And I'm not in a financial position to make it up. So if you want Vicky back, you're going to have to come up with five hundred K, over and above the stuff you got on Pope. That's the new deal. Non fucking negotiable by the way."

"I can't be responsible for your shady dealings, asshole. How am I going to come up with that kind of money, anyway? Not going to happen. I called you, in good faith, with full intention to play by *your* rules and give you what you want. Now you're changing things on me again? You're a piece of work. More like a piece of shit, actually," John spat the words out. Joey was getting to him.

"Non negotiable. That's the deal. When you have what I want, call me and Vicky will be set free."

"Where is she by the way? How do I know you and your goombahs aren't going to torture her?"

"Oh, Vicky is fine. What do you think I am? A creep? Far from it. Vicky is being treated well while we have her. Take my word for it. She's fine. You should know that though, my boys just had her call you."

"Why should I take your *word* for anything? Your word is shit to me. I asked you where she was."

"You must be joking. Why would I tell you where she is? Just don't call me until you have what I want. Bye!" Joey hung up prematurely, wanting to leave the conversation with the upper hand.

Joey had no plans to hurt Vicky—that was true. But he didn't really know what he would do if John didn't come up with the money. That would be something he'd have to think about later.

*   *   *   *

After Joey hung up on him, John screamed out loud and almost threw out his voice in doing so. How was he ever going to come up with that kind of money? John was in shock. For the first time since he was fifteen years old, he began crying and couldn't stop the tears. He was in so deep now. John felt helpless. Instinctively, his thoughts were consumed with an imminent trip to Casino Morongo to start winning some money. The logical part of his brain stopped those thoughts in their tracks, telling him that he couldn't go down that road again. He had finally paid his mother back, and the line of credit at the bank was almost down to zero. He was almost debt free for the first time in many years. Gambling was certainly *not* the answer.

Wiping away the tears, John went to the bathroom and looked in the mirror. You look like shit warmed over twice, John said aloud. He decided that if he were able to make himself look semi-presentable, he would actually go back to work so that he could keep his mind occupied. He pulled out the Clarins Moisturizer and Fatigue Fighter, and applied them to his face. Within a few minutes he looked much better. *Never underestimate the power of good product.* Yep, the words of a true metrosexual.

*   *   *   *

Arriving at his desk, John was greeted by a smiling Ray. "You look like shit, man. What's going on?"

"Long story. I'll tell you at break. What about you though? Today is the day, huh? Ray and Travelchick. By the smile on your face I don't have to ask if you're excited.

"One part excited, one part shit-scared. I'm even having second thoughts. What if the opportunity actually comes up to get some action? I have no idea what I would do. Honestly."

"Holy, man, take it easy. Chill out, my brother. Don't think about all that stuff. Just go and have fun. Don't think about stuff like that happening. Just think of it as a fun time with a hot chick and go from there."

"Thanks, man. Good advice from a guy who looks like crap."

John tried to fill the next ninety minutes of the day with mundane tasks. Tara came by to tell him that she got the job working for Patrick Bowman. John was happy for her, but she could tell that his mind was somewhere else. They promised to get together for lunch next week.

As coffee break approached, John emailed Aaron to tell him that he and Ray had a meeting and would not be able to join him. They grabbed an empty meeting room nearby so John could keep Ray up to date with the new developments. Ray shook his head in disgust over Joey's antics and again apologized for ever bringing up Joey's name. Together they were unable to come up with a good plan of attack for John. Ray promised to call John if he thought of anything that may help.

John called Jen's cell phone to ask how she was doing, and to tell her about the latest developments.

"Five hundred thousand?? Holy shit!! What are you going to do?" Jen asked, in a tone mixed with equal parts anger and worry.

"I don't know. I don't think I could come up with that kind of money fast enough, so I think I'm going to have to fight back. I don't know how, but I gotta do something."

"Can I help? I'll do anything. I wanna get this fucker. More than anything. He's goin' down. When you're done work, call me and we can figure something out."

"Thanks, Jen. I'll call ya. You sure you're holding up okay?"

"Uh huh. I'm still in a bit of shock, but I feel partially responsible for this. So I wanna help. Don't worry about me. Let's just figure out what we're gonna do."

"You rock, Jen. You really do. Thanks."

John tried his best to keep his mind on his daily routine at work. Just after lunch Dan approached and pretty much ordered John to go home and get some rest. John was in no position to argue, so he closed off all the running windows on his computer and shut down for the weekend. He wished Ray luck on his trip, in more ways than one, and went home.

John was exhausted. He was pretty much on autopilot for the drive home, which was quicker than usual because of the early time, even for a Friday afternoon. He got home and jumped right into bed, and slept until five. He woke up feeling somewhat refreshed, but still angry that the current state of affairs in his life was in fact a reality, and not a recurring nightmare.

Now with a clearer head, he hoped to come up with some sort of insight into how to handle Joey. He wished that he had a way to come up with the money, but was sure that the only way to get Vicky out of this mess was to fight fire with fire. *But how?*

John thought of what Ray said yesterday about knowing any hackers. If he were able to hack into Joey's life, surely there would be something there to provide enough ammo to fight back. At a time like this, John really wished he knew more about the highly technical aspects of information security so that he would be able to do the hacking himself. He made a mental note to take more SANS courses—if for some reason he were to get out of this mess professionally unscathed.

His thoughts kept coming back to the same person: Lee. Lee was the only guy that John knew that had the skills to help him out. Two things stood in the way of asking for Lee's assistance. One, Lee was as straight-laced as they come. Two, John wasn't quite sure that Lee wasn't behind the 'I'm watching you' messages. He highly doubted the latter, but knew that the chance of Lee actually doing anything that wasn't on the up and up was pretty slim.

Still, it was worth a shot. He had no better ideas.

He found Lee's on-call cell phone number in his own cell's address book, and hit the green button to dial.

Lee picked up and answered in his regular, professional-sounding tone. "Lee speaking."

John skipped the pleasantries and got right to the point. "Lee. This is John. I need your help. Desperately. Can you meet me? Coffee, or whatever you want, is on me."

"Umm, yeah, I guess so … It sounds serious … Sure, what the hell. If you're buying, the least I can do is listen. Where and when?"

"I don't care. Pick a place in your area. Have you had dinner yet? I'll buy you dinner if you haven't eaten yet."

"Dinner? Oooh. Far be it from me to pass up a free dinner. My girlfriend will have to understand my ditching her."

They made plans to meet at a small Italian place that just opened up near Lee in Palm Desert.

*   *   *   *

They both arrived at the restaurant at the same time. "Good timing," they both said, practically in unison.

They sat down to a table in the corner of the restaurant that hadn't yet filled up.

"This place gets really busy by seven o'clock. Good we're here early," Lee said.

John made a mental note to bring Vicky here, assuming he a) gets out of this mess and b) that the food is good.

After spending about two minutes discussing work, John went right into why he called Lee to this meeting. He kept the story focused on the Heather/Pope/Joey situation. He didn't reveal any other information about his wrongdoings at work. John did his best to read Lee's reaction, if only to rule him out as the perpetrator of the 'I'm watching you' messages. If Lee was behind them, he was a great liar, or actor, or both. John felt confident in his assessment that Lee was genuine.

"Wow. John. I don't know what to say. I can't believe you're in this much trouble. My only question is: what do you need me for? I know I don't have half a mil lying around, so in that respect you're outta luck."

"I don't want you for your money, honey." He touched Lee on the knee for effect. John wanted to make Lee slightly uncomfortable. Take the home-court advantage away, so to speak. "Hehehehe ... seriously though. I want you for your brain, Lee. You know a lot about ethical hacking, and I need to use your skills to get back at this guy."

"Whoa, whoa ... hold on there. What are you asking me to do?" Lee asked, ripping into a fresh-out-of-the-oven breadstick that tasted even better than the famous breadsticks at Olive Garden.

"I need to find all I can about this Joey guy. The more I know, the more I can use against him in my fight. I need Vicky back. You're my only hope."

"Only hope? I feel like Luke Skywalker, and you're Han Solo, and only *I* can save the world," Lee said, his face becoming more animated than John had ever seen from his *Star Wars* loving coworker. "Sorry, I just had to. I want to help, but I can't afford to risk my reputation."

"Sorry Lee, but what about *my* reputation? I'm pretty much fucked at DF, even if I do get out of this. Eventually things will get out. I'm lost. I'm not asking you to compromise your status at work, and we'll even do all the hacking from my PC at home. That way none of the hacking we do can be traced to you. I'll take full responsibility for everything. It will all be tied to my IP address anyway." John shoveled half of a breadstick in his mouth.

"You really are in a bad way, aren't ya? You're forgetting that there's always a way of re-routing internet traffic so that it doesn't look like it's originating from your IP. But I digress. Still. I've never really used my skills for the dark side, I've pretty much been a Jedi all the way." Normally this *Star Wars* talk would put John off, big time, but from Lee it was still somehow cool.

Their dinner arrived and they both went at their plates with equal ferocity. John was starving; he hadn't eaten much today, and it was obvious Lee was just as hungry. John would take a bite of his food, sip his wine, and then make another attempt to convince Lee to help.

After an hour of constant pestering, John eventually got through to him. It was probably the pity card that did the trick. *Whatever it took,* John thought, *as long as Lee was going to help.*

"Okay. Enough pestering me already. I'll help you. If only because I can't stand people like this Joey guy. Everything he stands for just pisses me off. Plus I feel bad for you. My opinion, for what it's worth, is that you don't seem like the kind of guy who is the slightest bit malicious in his intentions. I don't know how you ended up in a state of affairs like you're in, but I don't think you deserve it. So, when should we start?"

John was elated. "Tonight, if you can. I owe you big time, Lee. Anything you want, just name it!"

"I haven't done anything yet, but if I can help you, then we'll talk then. Maybe I'll think of something. Until then, let's get to work."

They finished their meals and John paid the bill. John told Lee to follow him home so they could get to work.

*   *   *   *

Ray Douglas was extremely anxious. He had just told his wife Darlene that he was off to Vegas with his two friends from work. The only lies he ever told her were of the white variety. Rarely, if ever, did he lay a whopper like this on her. He would have some serious *'splainin'* to do if he ever got caught.

He drove to the airport and parked in the long-term parking. He paused for a moment to give himself one last chance to bow out, and head back home. *C'mon Ray,* he said to himself, *you need some adventure in your life, and this is it. No excuses.* There's always a chance that Samantha was going to chicken out too. He almost expected her to not show up.

Ray grabbed his carry-on out of the trunk and walked inside and approached the United counter, hoping to find Samantha in the line. No luck. Maybe she *did* chicken out. Before he could finish the thought, he felt a poke in his side. He quickly turned around and found Samantha right behind him.

"Betcha thought I wouldn't show," Samantha said.

"I figured that might be a possibility. Glad you're here, though. Ready to win some major dough?"

"Hell, yeah. Let's get this party started!"

While boarding the plane, Ray started panicking. Was he really here, with this woman he rarely knew, to head to Las Vegas of all places? Where what happens there, stays there? There was no getting out of it now. He would have to deal with whatever consequences arose from whatever happened, *if* anything happened.

The fifty-eight minute flight passed incredibly quickly. Ray and Samantha made small talk for the first part and progressed to more personal issues like how they both met their respective partners. By the time the plane made its descent onto the runway at McCarran, Ray was feeling much more comfortable with his choice and was even beginning to appreciate Samantha's company.

"So are we really staying at the Bellagio?" Ray asked, having only stayed there once, even though he always gambled there. He was a big blackjack player, and knew the odds were the same no matter where you played. Ray knew that if the slots were your main game, Bellagio was definitely not the place to play.

"Oh hell yes, that's where we're going. We've both just got our carry-ons, so we don't have to pick up any luggage. Let's grab a cab and check in and chill out a bit before we hit the casino. Sound good?"

"Sounds great."

After checking in and arriving at their luxuriously decorated and meticulously clean room with two double beds, Samantha went to the bathroom to freshen up while Ray lay down on his bed. He looked up at the ceiling and again wondered what he was doing here.

Samantha came out of the bathroom looking more refreshed, and approached Ray. The first words out of her mouth shocked Ray, who prided himself as someone rarely shocked: "So I think you should just kiss me now to get it out of the way. Then we could go on with our platonic trip and have fun. If we get this over with first then you won't spend the rest of the weekend getting all worked up about what it's like to kiss me."

"Aren't you being rather presumptuous, Travelchick? Think we're hot now, don't we," was all Ray could come back with.

"Presumptuous or not. Am I right?"

"That's not the point."

"It's *exactly* the point." Samantha walked up to Ray and kissed him. It was a pretty innocent kiss.

After the initial shock wore off, reality set in and Ray realized that he might never again get an opportunity like this. So he opened his mouth and turned the kiss into something slightly less innocent. They kissed for a minute longer before Samantha pulled away. "Well, that was nice. Very nice. You're a good kisser, Ray. But you're married and I'm happily involved, so that's it. Now let's go make some serious money!"

Ray couldn't believe how this girl could turn her feelings on and off like that at the drop of a hat. *Travelchick was wired just like a guy.* He didn't know whether to respect her more for it, or to hold it against her. Whatever. He got to kiss a hot woman. And now it was time to gamble. Bring on the weekend!

CHAPTER 19

▼

John and Lee were sitting at John's computer preparing for their night of hacking. For the first time in a few days, John felt a sense of hope and optimism.

Lee opened up a DOS window and was about to begin. "Okay, so we're basically on a fact finding mission about this guy, right? Before I get to work, do you want to watch me or would you rather just not know. Time is obviously of the essence, so I won't be able to explain as I go. If you watch, I think you know enough to learn a lot. But given your, er, situation, did you really want to know this stuff? I'm just saying ... I don't want you to have more ammunition to get you in more trouble in the future. Okay?"

Lee's words stung. "Ouch! Harsh. What do you think I am??? Brutal! But okay, I can see where you're coming from. I don't know, I'll watch you at first but may go turn on the tube in the kitchen after a while."

"Up to you. Well, first we gotta do some *nslookups* on tattleinc.com so we can find out some more info. Then we'll search the ARIN database for the technical contact info in case we need to make some calls and put our social engineering skills to use. But that's a last resort. I hope to be able to hack in to their network pretty easily. If what you told me about the physical security of the place is true, they probably place the same amount of importance on *network* security. I'll have a rootkit on their network server and have full control of it in no time. I'm not putting you down here, John, but I'm pretty confident that once I get onto his PC I'll be able to gather a lot more information on this guy than you did. Plus I have the luxury of time on my side, where you guys were in a huge time crunch. So now's the time where we both shut up and I do my work. Sit back and enjoy the ride."

Lee began and John sat there in admiration and awe, coming to the realization that he was witnessing a master at work. Lee typed like a madman and worked with an intensity he had never seen before—even in the movies. Wow. John knew he was in good hands.

As much as John tried, he was unable to keep up with Lee and get a good grasp of what he was doing. John just sat back and prayed to the God of Semi-Ethical Hacking that Lee would succeed.

It wasn't long before Lee stopped what he was doing and turned toward John to explain his progress so far. He told John that he was able to initially compromise the network server, and eventually the mail server. Having gained control of the mail server, he now hoped to find any log information residing on the server that would show correspondence from Joey's home PC to the work network. All they needed was the IP address of Joey's home PC and then he could begin hacking that, which would probably get them the information they need.

Lee went back to it and John headed to the kitchen to get himself a drink. He offered him a Coke but Lee preferred coffee. John brewed a pot and poured himself a coffee instead, and brought a large mug to Lee. "Just don't spill it all over my PC," John warned.

"Oops," Lee pretended to spill the drink. "Okay, I found Joey's home IP. I'm just doing a portscan on that IP address right now to see if there's any open ports. If not we can always try some stuff on port 80, but … oh hell, no need. He's got a few open ports. Sweet. This is going to be easy. I'll be on his home system in a few minutes."

Lee kept his frantic pace. John sipped his coffee and continued to stare, dumbfounded, at how good this guy was.

"Sorry to interrupt you, Lee, but tell me something. Why don't you work in the security department? You'd be a huge asset." John always wanted to ask Lee to join them.

"I don't think so. Not for me. I pretty much do a lot of security stuff for the networking group. All those firewalls and perimeter hardware keep me pretty busy. If you ever need anything, just come ask and I'll help out. But right now I gotta concentrate on more pressing issues. Like your *life,* dude!"

John shut up. Once Lee had control of Joey's home PC, they sat there and started their fact-finding mission. They went through everything: his emails, his tax info, and pretty much anything they could get their hands on. It was almost eleven o'clock before they felt they had sufficient information.

There would be a lot that John would have to sift through later, but the biggest piece of information they could use immediately was the fact that Joey owned another house, in Riverside, which was almost halfway between Palm Springs and LA. The house was rarely used, and after reading a few emails residing on his hard drive, John had reason to believe that this is where they were keeping Vicky.

John literally jumped up and down, unable to contain his excitement. "I can't thank you enough, Lee. I've told you several times before, I know. But dude, seriously, you *are* the man. If I get Vicky back, I owe you my life." John stuck his hand out. Lee stood up and shook it. "I would hug you right now, but something tells me that you're not the hugging type."

"You'd be right about that one. Hey, remember, this never happened. I was never here. You and my girlfriend are the only ones who know. I'm glad to have helped. I hope you get what you need, and that Vicky is safe. You don't need to let me know what happens … I just hope to see you at work with a smile on your face on Monday."

John smiled. "You're a *mensch*, Lee. It's a Yiddish word. If you don't know what it means, look it up when you get home. Thanks, man," John said, almost gushing.

"No problem. Glad I could help. Good luck with everything." Lee just walked out of the den and walked towards the door. John followed and showed him out. Now the real work was about to begin.

*   *   *   *

The first thing John had to do was to call Jen and get her up to date. He called her and let her in on everything that he and Lee were able to dig up. Jen thanked him and let out an audible sigh of relief. Then: "Holy shit! Who is this guy? Can I use his services in the future?"

"This was a one time deal. I wish I could use him all the time myself. I was so lucky to get him to help me with this. He's as straight-laced as they come, man. No diggity."

"So what should we do? Should we take a drive to Riverside and check out that house?" Jen asked, excited now, ready to take action.

"We should, but I don't really know what to prepare for. I just want to get her back safe. She promised me she was okay, and they weren't hurting her, but I have no idea what these guys are capable of. I think it's safe to assume that Joey is not with them, and that they're doing whatever they're told. I don't know what we should do. This is going to sound really weird … but, should I be packin'?"

"Packin'? As in *heat*? Cool, Johnny is serious, yo! If you have *heat,* then I say why the fuck not? A guy's gotta do what a guy's gotta do. I say go for it. How many guys did mom say were holding her?"

"She thinks there are two, but there could be more. I highly doubt it, though. These people need to be paid, and I can't see Joey springing for more than two goons. Plus, he seriously underestimates me. He doesn't think I will fight fire with fire. So I would say two guys is the likely scenario."

"Hmmm. Whaddya think? When would be the best time to storm the place?" Jen asked.

"Hold your horses there, cowboy. I gotta say—you are acting incredibly strange for a girl whose mother has essentially been kidnapped."

"Totally. Like yeah, I know what you mean! I guess 'cause I think we're gonna get her out of it. And now that you tell me all the shit you drummed up about that Joey fuck, I just have a good feeling, yo!

"But we gotta be calm. So whaddya say we catch them in the middle of the night? Lets both have a mini-sleep, then I'll come get you about 2:30 a.m. We'll drive to Riverside and if everything goes smooth, your mom'll be with us on the way back."

"2:30 it is. See ya then!"

John hung up and headed straight for the top shelf of the storage room closet. His grandfather had always kept a Colt 45 Single Action Army gun there, and although he didn't ever use it, he liked to have it around just in case. John's current situation qualified as *a just in case.* His grandfather kept it mostly as a collector's item, and although it didn't qualify as an antique, it was still worth significant coin.

John recalled spending time with his grandfather as a child, just the two of them together in the desert with all the cacti: it seemed that there wasn't a living thing anywhere for miles. His grandfather would remove a few empty cans of tomato sauce from the trunk of his red Cadillac, and place one on top of a cactus. Grandpa took the gun from the front seat, and in one quick motion, would proceed to blow the can full of holes, just like Clint Eastwood. After grandpa got the chance to show off, he would then patiently and methodically demonstrate to little John how to load, hold, and fire the gun.

These memories reminded John how much his grandfather resembled Clint Eastwood, even in his final year of living. John once again thought of how hard it was for him to watch the end of *Million Dollar Baby*, as his grandfather reminded him more of the current Clint than the gun-slingin' Clint.

John handled the gun, grabbed the box of bullets sitting next to it, and loaded it as if it was second nature to him. He felt uncomfortable, yet somehow at ease regarding the potential use of the gun. The Colt resembled a toy gun at first glance, but as soon as you get it in your hands you knew it was the real deal. John was generally against the use of guns; though tonight, at this point in his life, he would even join the NRA if it meant getting Vicky back.

He made himself a chamomile tea, sat down with today's Desert Sun newspaper, and relaxed on the couch. After finishing his tea and reading a few news stories, he turned out all of the lights and went to bed, setting the alarm for two a.m.

*   *   *   *

Ray and Samantha were doing well at the blackjack tables. Ray sat down first while Samantha watched. He was up $2,500 rather quickly. Samantha looked on, impressed at Ray's skill. She wasn't used to these high stakes—normally she wouldn't gamble with more than a hundred dollars on a given night. This was a thrill for her.

As an act of generosity, Ray handed Samantha five hundred dollars worth of chips to gamble with. She initially resisted accepting Ray's gift. Ray persisted, and eventually Samantha gave in.

"You really don't have to do that, Ray!" Samantha said, playfully punching him in the ribs.

"It's found money! No big deal. You're taking me with you on this trip, it's the least I can do. Just have a seat and play."

They sat and played together as time flew by. By the time their backs started getting sore from all that sitting, they noticed that it was almost one a.m. After starting really well, Ray had almost lost all of his chips during a brutal dry spell. His luck changed back after doubling down and hitting *21* on a big hand. Ray was up over four grand, and Samantha had turned her five hundred into seven fifty.

"Well … that sure went pretty good for the first night. Not exactly high-roller money, but I take it it's more than you're used to playing for. So what do you think, Travelchick? I don't know about you, but I'm starving! Go for a bite?"

"I'm all over it! Let's go get some Chinese food and bring it back to the room and chill out watching TV. Plan?"

"You read my mind."

They found a good Chinese restaurant and ordered Cantonese chow mein, kung pao chicken and ginger beef. The smell was driving them crazy as they traveled with it on the lengthy excursion through the hotel to their room. They set the food on the work desk in the corner of the room, and both took turns going to the bathroom to change into more comfortable clothes.

Changed and relaxed, they both dug into the food. The makeshift kitchen table was situated right by a large window that overlooked the dancing fountains. Ray had seen the *water show* at the Bellagio many times, but he never grew tired of it. Seeing it through the window of an actual hotel room made it extra special. They laughed and shared more stories about growing up. Ray was enjoying himself immensely; it even seemed like Samantha was having just as good a time. He was too shy to ask her though. He just assumed she was, and went with it. Thoughts of Darlene popped in and out of his head, but for now he put them aside until the weekend was over. Now was the time to just enjoy. *Live in the now,* he told himself.

Having finished every bite of their food, Samantha gathered up the food containers and threw them out. She jumped on her bed and found the remote to the TV and turned it on.

"What should we watch?" she asked.

"I don't care. I'm actually pretty tired. Pick something and we'll watch it," Ray replied, pulling back the covers and settling into the ultra-comfortable bed.

"Are you really going to sleep?" Samantha asked, somewhat puzzled.

"Yeah, it's pretty late. *Way* past my bedtime. I'm no spring chicken, remember?"

"Ha ha. You don't act your age, though. So hey … what do you say we pick up where we left off when we first got up to the room?"

"Say what?" Ray asked, lifting his head to rest against the headboard.

"You heard me. I think we should finish what we started. I need a release. You kind of got me going earlier," Samantha said, rather convincingly.

"I thought you said—"

"Will you just shut up? Come here. Now," she interrupted, with a tone so authoritative it took Ray by surprise.

"Samantha. Sweetie. I don't know … what about all the stuff you said about the kiss being all I'm getting? I'm confused."

"Look. Ray. I'm a chick, a *travel* chick if you will, who is apt to change her mind. I'm a pretty impulsive person. I brought you here, didn't I? Isn't that pretty damn impulsive? Well, to be frank, I'm really frickin' horny right now. Let's just have some fun. It will never leave this room. Our secret forever. Now get your little ass in my bed and fuck my brains out!"

Never being one to back down from an offer quite as audacious as that, Ray dropped all inhibitions and joined Samantha. He had spent so many mornings staring down her top from afar, and now here he was, unbuttoning her shirt and cupping her breasts. Ray was as hard as a rock and could barely hold it in.

Samantha was quick to notice and tugged down on his boxers, pushing them down towards his ankles. She took Ray in her mouth and went to work on him. Ray grabbed her hair and pulled it back, grabbing on for dear life, trying not to come too quickly. He was past the point of no return here—he would need to hold off so that he could finish the deal, so to speak.

He couldn't stand it anymore, if she didn't stop sucking he was going to lose it. He pulled back, held her by the hand and lifted her up to face him. They fell onto the bed together, and within a second he entered her.

Samantha was a screamer. The more she screamed the more it turned Ray on. Then she started the dirty talk. This freaked Ray out, but turned him into a total animal. He pumped intensely until he couldn't hold back anymore. He told her he was about to come—and just as he was about to—she squeezed her legs together in a way that guaranteed to delay his orgasm.

"I'm almost there too, but I want my release first, so keep pumping like you were and grab my ass while you're doing it … yeah … that's it … fuck … fuck … fuck … ohmyGodohmyGodyesyesyeeeeesssssss!" she screamed.

Every muscle in Samantha's body relaxed. After a brief moment she gave him a wink that suggested she was ready for him to continue and have his fun too. It only took him about thirty seconds before he was able to share in her joy.

"Wowee fucking wow. You're amazing," Ray gushed.

"Mmmm. You ain't such a bad one, yourself. That was pretty damn hot. I would normally wanna cuddle now, but that would make it even more wrong than it already is. I'm all about minimizing the guilt," Samantha said, again in a tone so deadpan that Ray wondered how this chick can turn on and off her feelings so quickly.

"Good point, I guess. We'll just wash up and then go to sleep. Separate beds I take it, though that seems rather odd given what we've just been through," Ray said.

"It's the only way. I hope you understand."

"I do," Ray lied.

They both limped towards the bathroom and cleaned up before climbing into their own beds and very quickly falling asleep.

CHAPTER 20

───────────── ▼ ─────────────

John was on his way to Vicky's house to pick up Jennifer when a sudden rush of panic overcame him. His life was never supposed to be like this. He had been through more in the last few months than many would ever experience in a lifetime. What would he do whenever his life slowed back down to a normal tempo? Would he be able to handle the leisurely pace that he had become so accustomed to before all this started? Or had he become addicted to all of the drama that was beginning to define him?

These thoughts paralyzed him. The city was incredibly quiet and there was almost no traffic on Highway 111 at 2:20 a.m. With no cars in sight ahead or behind him in the MDX, John just stopped the car and put it in park, then lowered his head against the steering wheel. He sat there, alone with his thoughts, in the car for several minutes before being scared out of his pseudo-reverie by a honking horn behind him.

He realized there was no time for contemplation of any sort right now. He had a serious job to do: he needed Vicky back before anything else was going to happen. *Snap out of it boy,* he said to himself. John quickly turned the ignition key, jammed the MDX into Drive, and put his foot on the gas pedal and high-tailed it towards Vicky's house to fetch Jen.

"So what's the plan?" Jen asked right away.

"I have no clue. I guess we'll figure it out on the way. We have about an hour, so I'm sure we'll think of something."

"Did joo bring jor leettle friend?" Jen asked, in her best *Scarface* impression.

"Aha. Yes I did. Not a bad *Tony Montana,* actually. What the hell do you know about *Scarface,* anyway?"

"I love *Scarface*. Great flick. I think you should go *Tony Montana* on their asses when we get there."

"Don't think so … I'm only bringing it as a last resort. Now let's go over our plan of attack."

John and Jen discussed the plan. Not ever having to deal with a situation even remotely resembling something like this before, all that either of them were to come up with was whatever they had seen in movies and cop shows.

"Shit. This is brutal. We're so lame when it comes to this stuff, aren't we? Okay. Let's take a step back, and try to analyze the situation. Start from when we pull up to the house. We'll take it step by step and go from there," John said, as they approached the turn-off for 60W.

They were counting on at least one of the two *goons* to be asleep when they arrived at the house. They figured they would park a few houses away, then advance toward the house quietly. That's about all they could come up with.

Before they knew it, they were already in Riverside and only several minutes away from the house. They hadn't even discussed the possibility that Vicky wasn't even in the house. "Let's not even go there," John said. "We're going to assume, and pray, that your mom is there."

John followed the directions he had printed out from Mapquest, and drove towards the street where they hoped Vicky was being held. They first drove right down the street and passed by the house before doing a U-turn so they could park on the proper side of the road.

John parked the MDX and grabbed the gun from the glove compartment and placed it in the front of his pants. He pulled his black t-shirt down to hide the bulge of the gun.

"Got your trusty lock picking kit?" John asked, before they left the car.

"Sure do. As long as there's nothing too whack with the locks on the door, we should be in quick. Let's do this. I want my mom back," Jen said.

"Showtime. Let's do it," John said, with as much conviction as he could muster.

The street was eerily quiet. This was probably a good thing. The sky would probably begin to lighten up shortly, despite being 3:40 a.m. The sun rose awfully early here. There was a slight humidity in the air that wasn't present in Palm Springs. John was sweating already.

"I'm going to go around the back and try to work on the back door. It looks more secluded there. You might as well come along, I don't think we should split up, not yet anyway," Jen whispered. She sounded amazingly confident given the circumstances.

"Whatever you say. I'm with ya."

They walked stealthily towards the back yard of the house, searching for any signs of life inside the house. All the lights were off in this two-story residence, which blended in with all the other homes surrounding it. This street was the epitome of suburbia, not at all the type of place you would assume to be the site of kidnappers and their victim.

Jen quietly climbed the steps toward the back door and removed a small flashlight from her pocket so she could examine the lock. She only needed about five seconds to determine that this one was going to be easy. She nodded towards John with a smile on her face to signal that she shouldn't have any problem.

Just as John was glancing toward the neighboring houses to ensure they weren't being watched, he heard a slight clicking sound resembling a lock being opened. He turned his head towards the back door and saw Jennifer's hand on the doorknob, ready to open it. He sidled beside her in front of the door and gave her a mini-thumbs-up.

"Ready to go in?" She asked.

"We've come this far. Open the door," John said, terrified about what might be waiting for them on the other side of the door.

*   *   *   *

Jen opened the door and they walked in to the back hall of the house. They could barely see in front of them, so Jen pulled out her flashlight again and flipped it on. She shone it ahead of them to reveal an empty kitchen: a table and a few chairs but not much more. It was obvious nobody spent much time here. They stopped at the end of the kitchen before the main hallway. Now that they were inside they had no idea what to do next.

"Doesn't even seem like anyone is here," John whispered.

"I know. Maybe they're upstairs. Don't give up. She's here. I can feel it. Call it mother-daughter intuition. Obviously nobody is on this floor, so we have to decide if it's upstairs or downstairs. I say upstairs. Follow me."

John followed, feeling somewhat emasculated by putting his fate in the hands of a seventeen-year-old high school girl.

They found the staircase leading upstairs. Both did their best to make as little sound as possible, literally walking on their tiptoes. John couldn't help be reminded of the joke about the proverbial farmer's daughter where several farmhands each tried to climb the stairway above the ranch to reach her; each time the farmer would hear a noise he would yell *who's that?* The farmhands would make a *meow* sound to pretend it was the cat. The punch line had the dumb farmhand saying *it's me, the cat* instead of meowing. It was always much funnier when someone told it. He tried to laugh—even in his head—but his nerves wouldn't allow it.

Jennifer reached the top of the stairs first, with John two steps behind. There was enough moonlight emitting from a window on the side of the house that allowed them to maneuver around. There was no need for a flashlight.

The top floor of the house consisted of three rooms: one directly in front of them, one towards the end of the hall near the window and another slightly to their right. The room near the window appeared to have several locks on it. The room in front of them had a closed door with no locks and the room to the right was open. They both looked at each other and swung their heads toward the locked door to demonstrate their collective agreement as to the next move.

Just as they were stealthily making their way towards the locked door, each felt a tap on their shoulder. Initially, both John and Jen believed the tap was coming from the other. The deep, aggressive voice behind them quickly revealed that this was unfortunately not the case.

"What the fuck do you two think you're doing?" the voice said.

Jen turned to face John and in true Hollywood style told him: "It looks like we've got company."

The bulky figure behind them was not amused. "This isn't the movies, honey. You two are in serious shit."

John turned around to notice that Deepvoice had a partner. *Shit.* Both men were tall and bulky.

Jen winked at him and instinctively John knew he had to make his move now.

With a swiftness and velocity he didn't even know he had in him, in one quick move John reached into his pants, grabbed the handle of the gun, and swung the barrel directly onto the bridge of Deepvoice's nose. Hard. There was a loud *crack* as the barrel of the gun made contact between Deepvoice's nose and eyes. Deepvoice reeled backward and intuitively brought his hand to his nose to check for blood. Yup. And lots of it.

As John did his thing to Deepvoice, Jen took her cue, and, with every bit of strength she could muster, used her steel-towed boot and hoofed Goon#2 right in the groin. Goon#2 keeled over, writhing in pain. Jen noticed Deepvoice still reeling from the blow from the gun, and right away decided that what was good for one, was good for the other. She wound up and kicked Deepvoice even harder than she did Goon#2, and with more precision. Both men were now keeled over.

John was really getting into this now. Adrenaline was surging through him intensely. This was like the flight-or-flight mechanism intensified to the power of ten. Heroin junkies could only *wish* for a rush like this.

John saw this as their sole opportunity to take advantage and guarantee victory over these goons. With the gun still in his hand, he began pistol-whipping both men as they were both trying to get over being hoofed in the nuts. He struck Deepvoice one more time on the head, and Goon #2 twice.

It all seemed to transpire so quickly. Seemingly in a matter of a minute, both men were practically unconscious.

John and Jen looked at each other with disbelief, as if to say "Did this really happen?"

"Holy fuck. Look at what we did! I guess we caught them by surprise, huh?" John asked, somewhat rhetorically.

"Never underestimate the power of surprise and the potential from being underestimated. They obviously saw a skinny guy like you and a short, cute, girlie like me and didn't figure we had it in us. Fuck, that felt totally awesome. I feel so *alive!*" Jen said, her voice full of unbridled enthusiasm.

"Now that we have these guys incapacitated, I think we should go find some rope, or tape, and tie them up. What do you say?" John asked.

"Good plan, man. You go look for something to use and I'll start working on those locks on that door down the hall, where I bet they have mom. Which reminds me … Mom! Mom? Are you there? Can you hear us?" Jen screamed.

"Jennifer? John? Is that you?" Vicky's voice came from down the hall, slightly muffled.

"Holy shit. She's here, Jen. She's *here*. You go work on the locks and I'll get stuff to tie these goons up with."

John, feeling comfortable enough now to turn on the hallway light, ran down the stairs to the kitchen to search for anything that could be used to confine the goons. He rummaged through all of the drawers and cupboards and finally found some duct tape. That would have to do.

By the time he joined Jen upstairs, she had already worked through the first two locks and was attempting to crack the last one. "This lock giving you trouble?" John asked.

"Yep, I can't seem to get this one," Jen said in frustration.

"I'm so happy to hear you guys. You two are amazing. How did you find me?" Vicky asked from the other side of the locked door.

"We'll explain everything on the way home. I can't wait to see you, Vicky. Now sit tight while Jen works on the locks, and I take care of your two captors. There were only two, right?"

"Yes. Only two," Vicky confirmed.

"Thank God. Whew," John said. He left Jen to finish work on the last lock, and revisited the two goons still lying on the floor in extreme pain. He had never had to tie anyone up before (though he hoped to someday soon with Vicky as they became more adventurous in the bedroom, but after this, it was unlikely Vicky would comply), but necessity being the mother of invention, John devised a way to restrain the goons. He dragged both men towards the middle of the hallway, which overlooked the main area of the house. Wooden stairway banister-type poles were spread out evenly across the hallway, making up a railing that would prevent someone from falling over onto the main floor. He wrapped the tape tightly around each man's wrist; then with the same piece of tape, wound it securely around the wooden banister. He repeated for each limb for both goons. When he was done, both men were essentially attached to the railing, and not going anywhere.

Jen was not having the same kind of luck with the third lock. As soon as John finished making the goons a part of the railing, Jen called to John to help her with the lock.

"How am *I* going to help you with it? You're the expert lock picker here," John said, instantly regretting it as he realized that Vicky was on the other side of the door.

"The gun, silly," Jen said. "Just shoot the frickin' thing already. I want to get mom outta here!"

John pulled out the Colt and fired at the lock, which shattered upon impact.

Jen swung the door open and Vicky emerged, looking frightened, tired, excited and elated all at once. She and Jennifer hugged, each not wanting to let go. Vicky gazed at John, standing beside them, as she hugged her daughter.

When she finished hugging her daughter, Vicky rushed into John's arms and hugged him with the same intensity as she had Jennifer. "Thank you so much for saving me, John. I don't know what happened that led to this, and I don't know how you did it, but thank you. Now let's get out of here and put an end to this nightmare."

"My sentiments exactly. I love you, Vicky. Now let's get the hell out of this place."

Passing by the goons, Vicky stopped, and—in a move that stunned both John and Jen—unraveled a few extra pieces of tape and tightened the restraints on the goons. "There, how do you like that, you assholes? I know you probably can't hear me, and I know you didn't really hurt me, but still. I hope this hurts like hell when you come to!"

"Mom, look at you! You rock!" Jen exclaimed.

They descended the stairs and headed towards the front door.

"Anything else we should do before we leave?" John asked.

"I don't think so. The guys will come to, and eventually someone will find them. If they're strong enough, sooner or later they'll break out of the tape. Maybe. If not, oh well. No sympathy from me," Vicky said.

"Okay. We're outta here," Jen said.

The three of them opened the door and walked out of the house. John shut the front door behind them, and in doing so, hoped and prayed that he was shutting the door to this chapter in his life that has caused him so much grief.

"Where's your car?" Vicky asked.

"It's just down the street. I don't know about you guys, but I'm frickin' starving over here. IHOP?"

"I could use some comfort food. Let's all have some pancakes! I think we should stop and change clothes first. Walking into the IHOP with bloodstains on our clothes probably isn't the greatest idea," Jen pointed out, surveying the splatter from Deepvoice's nose that made it's way onto their attire.

"No doubt. Home first to freshen up, then pancakes for everyone," John said.

They walked across the lawn and started towards the sidewalk. The sky was turning a beautiful teal blue, that perfect color that revealed itself only at this time of the morning just before the sun was about to rise. John always loved this early part of the day. He made a promise to himself that he would get up early once in a while so he could revel in the splendor of the dawning sky. He would always be reminded of the blissful feeling rushing through him at this very moment, having finally rescued Vicky and getting her back into his life.

As John realized that his daydreaming about the sky was leaving him about twenty steps behind, he felt something cold press against his cheek.

"Not so fast, *Sir John*," Joey Styles threatened.

"Oh, you gotta be kidding me," John muttered.

CHAPTER 21

▼

Joey Styles still had a gun pointed at John's head, while Vicky and Jennifer were now only a few feet away from the MDX.

"Um, yeah. Vicky, Jennifer, you may want to turn around now if you don't want to see your lover boy blown apart," Joey called out.

Vicky and Jennifer turned around to see Joey standing behind John with a gun pointed at his head.

"Oh my God. Oh my God!" Vicky cried out. Jennifer just stood there, dumbfounded.

"I would get your pretty little asses away from the car and join this little party John and I have here," Joey ordered. "Seems we have some stuff to settle here. Now *move!*" Joey yelled, loud enough to wake the neighborhood.

Jennifer and Vicky ran towards them. Joey told them not to make any sudden moves or John would be a goner. He instructed them to walk ahead and go back into his house. As they all traveled back to the house of horrors, Joey insisted that John remove the gun he was holding and hand it to him—slowly. With a gun pointed at his head, John figured he had no choice but to oblige.

Joey took the gun from John with his left hand while maintaining his grasp on his own gun, still pointed at John's head. "Okay, all of you, we're all going to head into the living room," Joey said as the four of them entered the house.

"Don't you think Vicky has been through enough? What are you trying to prove here, Joey? Just let us go. We'll call it even," John attempted. He was grasping at straws here. He had no clue how they would get out of this one.

Vicky and Jennifer walked into the living room and turned on the light so they could find their way around. They both picked up chairs and sat themselves down, as Joey had instructed. Joey followed, with his gun still pointed at John's head.

"Bobby? Harold? Where the hell are you guys?" Joey screamed toward upstairs, wondering where his goons were.

"Uh, Joey? I don't think they're going anywhere for a while. Take a look upstairs and you'll find them, er, rather incapacitated," John explained.

"Are you fuckin' with me, John? Vicky, is he telling the truth?" Joey said.

"Yes. Go and check for yourself," Vicky answered.

"I don't trust you guys, but I'll have to take your word for it," Joey said, kicking a chair in front of him and pushing John towards it so he would take a seat. "Now, no funny stuff or I start shooting. And I'm not kidding, either. Now I'm pretty pissed off. I made sure my boys didn't hurt you, Vicky, and I kept my word. Right?"

Vicky remained silent.

"Are you deaf *and* dumb, Vicky? I asked you a fuckin' question!" Joey shouted.

"Yes. You kept your word. Very gallant of you. Now be a *real* gentleman and let us go. Please," Vicky begged.

"You can't be the *least* bit serious," Joey said, laughing heartily. "Now. To tell you all the truth, I have no idea what do with you all. I just know I can't let you leave. So where do we go from here? Hmm. I could just kill you all, but that's not really my style. But, if either of you makes any funny moves I *will* start shooting." Joey began pacing the room, enjoying this puppet master role. "Hey, I know. Let's play a game. The rules go like this: Vicky, Jen, you two make such a wicked mother-daughter team. Now, if I'm going to change my mind and play nice, I'm going to need you guys to do something for me. Vicky, I want you to remove your daughter's top. And Jenny honey, when you're down to your nice little bra there, I want you to do the same to your momma. Then, if everybody's following the rules, I'll revisit my plans about what to do with you. Vicky? I'm waiting."

Vicky remained in her seat, motionless. "Sorry, but that's not about to happen," Vicky spat.

"Lippy little bitch, I should have had my boys have their fun with you."

Just as Joey finished speaking the words, a very loud slamming sound came from the front of the house. Not a second later, a new houseguest emerged into the living room. "Freeze! Everyone! Riverside Police Department. Nobody make a move. Mr. Joey Styles? You are under arrest for kidnapping. Drop your gun, Mr. Styles. *Now!*" The police officer ordered.

John, Vicky, and Jennifer each looked at each other in disbelief.

"Thank you, officer. You came just in time," Vicky said happily.

As the second officer was placing the handcuffs on Joey and mirandizing him, John asked the officer how they knew what was going on. "Did the neighbors hear us?" he asked.

"No. Funny you should mention it. It was actually an anonymous tip from Palm Springs County, of all places. The caller appeared to possess enough information to lead us to believe that he was telling the truth. We had to follow up."

John knew immediately who the anonymous caller was. He made a mental note to thank Lee as soon as he got the chance.

The officers took their statements and made sure that everything was covered. It turns out that this was not the first time that Joey had resorted to kidnapping to further his agenda, whatever it was. Neither the Riverside County Police Department or LA county PD were aware of Joey's second house in Riverside, and the anonymous tip was just the catalyst they were looking for to catch him.

When the police officer was confident that all the pieces of the puzzle were in place, he allowed John, Vicky and Jennifer to leave the house, along with all of the terrible feelings that went along with it, behind. The three of them walked quietly toward the car, and each couldn't wait to get back to Palm Springs.

✳   ✳   ✳   ✳

They sat in silence for the first part of the drive back. The ordeal had taken so much out of them.

Vicky broke the silence: "Again, guys, thank you so much for rescuing me. I was so scared. I didn't, in my wildest nightmares, ever think that I would be a part of such a horrific situation. I didn't think I would make it out alive. Even though the guys didn't hurt me, or hardly touch me, I just had a bad feeling. I'm just so delighted to be with the two people I love again. I know that you guys have a lot of explaining to do, but let's not talk about it yet. I can't deal with it right now. I just want to get home and sleep. All day. We can talk about it tomorrow, as in Sunday."

"Good plan. I'm sorry about everything, Vicky. It's all my fault," John said, as he turned to the right and looked her right in the eyes. He removed his right hand from the steering wheel and lightly brushed his fingers across her cheek. Touching her this way seemed to have an amazing healing affect on him. He hoped it worked the same way for her. "I'll explain tomorrow, but for now, let's get home. Are we still in the mood for pancakes? I'm buying. I'm absolutely starving."

"I am. Let's get changed, then eat. Then we can go home and sleep all day on full stomachs! Mom?" Jen asked, hoping her mom was still in the mood to at least eat breakfast with them.

"Uh huh. But no talk of anything that lead to what happened. I want my life to get back to normal," Vicky said.

"Deal," John said.

"Ditto," Jen agreed.

*   *   *   *

Ray woke up on Saturday morning with feelings of confusion, and to a certain extent, regret. He thoroughly enjoyed his time with Samantha last night, and not just the sex. He enjoyed her company. He felt so *young* in her presence. He hadn't felt like that in a long time. Still, he had no delusions that this was any more than a one-night stand, or one-weekend stand. He would have to deal with whatever lingering repercussions when he got home.

It was only Saturday though, and the weekend wasn't even half over. *What would Samantha have in store for him today?* She had got to be the most unpredictable person he had ever met.

He looked over at the other bed and noticed Samantha was already up and having a shower. He couldn't wait to see how she was going to act today. This was certainly an adventure that was much more than he bargained for.

Samantha opened the door to the bathroom and entered the room wrapped in a towel. "Good mornin' sunshine," she purred. "What's on the agenda today?"

"I don't know. You tell me. You seem to enjoy making most of the decisions. What would you like to do?"

"Oh, man. I'm not *that* transparent, am I? I'll admit I like taking charge of things, but I want you to have *fun* though. What do you feel like getting up to?" Samantha asked.

"I know I'm frickin' hungry. That's all I can think about right now. One step at a time. Food first. Then we'll go from there," Ray said.

"I see a buffet breakfast in our immediate future. I've actually never eaten at the Bellagio Buffet here, have you?"

"No, we've always found it to be too pricey. We usually go somewhere else. But if it's all part of the deal, I'm in."

"It is. So go have a shower, and we'll go oink out."

Ray stood up in his boxers, and moved towards the bathroom. He would normally be somewhat shy in this situation, but given the circumstances he was way past the need to be shy.

Ray entered the shower, turned the levers toward *H* to make it really hot, and let the water cascade down his body. He washed away any reminders of last night and told himself that today was a new day, and opened himself up to whatever Samantha had planned.

*   *   *   *

John was driving home after dropping off the girls. They had just finished eating more than enough food to last them the weekend. Each of them had a large stack of pancakes, sausages, eggs, toast and hash browns. No need to eat for the rest of the day, that's for sure.

He was exhausted and desperately needed rest. He decided he would sleep first, then call Lee when he woke up. He really wasn't sure what to with himself today, other than sleep. John wasn't looking forward to tomorrow; as much as he loved and trusted Vicky, he couldn't be sure that she would fully understand everything, especially Jen's involvement.

Finally arriving at home, John parked the car. Just as he was closing the car door, his cell phone rang. Unknown number. He wasn't sure whether to answer, but decided he should just in case.

"Yeah?"

"John, it's Joey Styles."

John had to kick himself to ensure he was not dreaming and this was in fact really happening. Joey again. This guy was *Freddy* and *Jason* rolled into one.

"What the fuck are you doing calling me?"

"I'm at the jailhouse making my *one phone call.* You're it. Don't you feel *honored?*"

"I don't understand. We're done, Joey. I don't ever want to hear from you. Ever, you fuckin' Freddy Jason Kruegger Voorhees, or whoever the hell you are."

"Don't hang up. Please. Just listen to me, okay? I need to ask you a few important questions, which I didn't get to before the cops came." Joey was practically begging. John could sense a pure desperation in his voice.

"You have got to be joking. Really. If the cops came, you were going to have your sick-fuck fun with the girls. You really are a true asshole, in every sense of the word. Why would I answer anything for *you?* Leave me alone."

"Don't hang up. I may be able to help you," Joey said, in a last ditch attempt to prevent John from hanging up.

"Say what???"

"I may be able to help you. You heard me. But first, please just answer my question."

"Maybe I'm just too tired, but sure, go ahead. Let's have some fun. Your ass is in jail and will likely stay there for a while. So fine. Go." John was dead tired, and really wasn't in the mood, but stayed on the line nonetheless. He was aimlessly walking around the pool, taking turns staring into the clear water below and the day breaking sky above.

"I need to know what you have on me. You obviously found the house, and who knows what else. I *did* underestimate you. I admit it. I'm going to be in jail for a while I'm sure, but I just have to know what you have on me and what you're going to use. And, if I can help you, I'd like to take some comfort in knowing that you'll go easy on me."

"I'm really in no mood to help you at all right now." John was second-guessing his decision to stay on the line.

"Look. I apologize for everything. I know that sounds like just empty words, but it's true. Please. Answer my question and then I may have some information for you," Joey pleaded.

"It doesn't work that way," John replied. "I call the shots now. And before I answer your question, *you* are going to tell me how you can help me. Then, and only then, will I think about answering your question." John's head became dizzy walking aimlessly around the pool. He took a seat on a lounger beside the pool and laid back.

"I guess I have no choice. Here goes then … tell me something, and be honest, were you the one responsible for giving me up to Harlan Daley about the email scam?"

"Harlan who?"

"Do you mean to tell me you've never heard his name before?" Joey asked.

"Never. I don't know where you're going with this. My patience is really wearing thin here, no thanks to you. You've fucked up my life lately. So get to the point," John growled, trying not to betray the curiosity he was feeling.

"You didn't have anything to do with Harlan finding out I was trying to scam him, then?"

"No!" John yelled at the phone.

"Well … that makes things interesting. It turns out I *can* help you. When Harlan found out, he came after me to make up the difference, and that's why I came after you. You *were* responsible for uncovering it, but now I know it wasn't you who told him about it. Someone else did though. I don't know who that person is, but I *do* know that they also work for DesertFinancial."

"What??? How do you know that?" John was interested now, and sat up.

"Let's just say I know someone at the phone company, and I got them to peruse Harlan's phone records and see if there were calls to your head office. See, when I did that, I fully expected that you were the one. But I had a hunch that it wasn't you behind telling him. And if what you're saying is true, then guess what? There's someone else at your company that is doing a lot of talking to Harlan Daley."

"How can I trust that what you're telling me is true and that you're not trying to worm your way out of something?" John paused for a moment, his head spinning. His first thought was that Harlan was just communicating with Heather, who was having her fling with Pope. But Heather didn't work at head office, so she was likely out. "So are you telling me that you have no links whatsoever to DesertFinancial, other than knowing me?"

"That's what I'm telling you. Someone else there is doing a lot of talking to Harlan Daley. I don't know what that means to you, but I thought it would help," Joey said, finally believing that he had got through to John.

"I'll have to see about that. I still don't trust you, but I'll definitely follow up on that." For some reason, John trusted that what Joey was telling him was true. It was now apparent that Joey was not behind the '*I'm watching you*' messages. Someone else, an employee of the company, was not only behind those messages but was likely the same person that had dealings with this Harlan Daley guy. *Great,* John thought, *just when I thought my life was on it's way back to normal.*

"Now tell me what you have on me. I need to know what I'm facing here," Joey said.

"I have a lot. Worst of which is the income tax stuff. The IRS doesn't quite care about how I went about getting the information, so the illegal search defense won't work for that one. I won't use it, if what you're telling me is true. The kidnapping charge may keep you in jail long enough, along with whatever else they have on you. That's it, Joey. I'm done with you. Thanks for the info, and goodbye."

John hung up and began walking zombie-like towards his front door. He wasn't quite sure what to make of the conversation with Joey, but he somehow deemed Joey to be genuine in this instance. Regardless, right now all he could think about was sleeping. He would deal with everything later. As soon as he walked in his place he went right to bed. *Sleep, glorious sleep.* Despite having just taken part in an adventure worthy of a movie script, John fell asleep quickly.

∗   ∗   ∗   ∗

Ray and Samantha's second day in Vegas was spent doing all the typical tourist activities: walking the strip, strolling through the canals of the Venetian Hotel, heading up to the top of the Eiffel Tower at the Paris Hotel, cooling off while shopping the shops in the MGM Grand and generally walking so much that blisters were guaranteed. He really enjoyed Samantha's company, and almost wished that this trip were more than just a weekend.

Ray wasn't much into shopping, but he enjoyed accompanying Samantha into the clothing shops. He especially enjoyed watching her try on the various outfits she was looking to purchase. All those months staring at her from across the way at Starbucks, and here he was shopping with her, carefully observing her body, studying every glorious curve.

Before they knew it, it was almost time for dinner. "What should we do for dinner? I'm still a little full from our huge brunch, but I guess either way we should probably head back toward the hotel," Samantha suggested, as they were passing by the various shops underground the MGM Grand.

"I don't care. I'm having a good time, and not very picky about what I eat. So whatever you like is good with me," Ray said.

They decided to take the monorail from the MGM to Bally's to save some time in getting back to their room. They agreed to have a little siesta before dinner to catch up on some sleep before another night of eating, drinking and gambling.

It was 6:30 when Samantha woke up from her nap. She quietly paced around the room, trying to decide what to wear for tonight. She would have to ask Ray where he wanted to dine, and that would give her a better idea of the proper evening attire.

She leaned over a sleeping Ray and tapped him on the shoulder to wake him up.

"Wake up, sleepyhead," She whispered.

"Whoa, whoa … I was having a really strange dream," Ray mumbled, groggy from having been woken up suddenly from a deep sleep.

"Did it involve me?" Samantha asked suggestively.

"No, no, nothing like that."

"Awww, that's too bad. Nothing better than the real thing though. What do you say? Before we eat how 'bout you fuck my brains out again?"

"Samantha! What is with you? I can't keep up with you. One time only, right? You're gonna give me a heart attack here. I like you, I really do. I just can't turn things on and off like you. Let's put everything sexual in the past, and just enjoy ourselves. I think it's better that way," Ray said, taking the leadership role for the first time with her.

"Suit yourself, honey. I'm horny and I'm getting myself off no matter what. I'm not offended, don't worry. I'm just gonna do a little something myself here while you can either go get ready, or watch if you like."

Samantha reached inside her purse and pulled out a vibrator. Ray had actually never seen one in use before, other than in the odd porn movie he'd seen. With reckless abandon, Samantha ripped off her shorts and panties, and quickly went to work with it. Ray was instantly aroused.

He watched for several minutes, before finally giving in and reaching into his own pants to touch himself. Samantha looked over at him and ordered him towards her.

"Enough of this self pleasuring stuff, we may as well finish each other off. I'll keep my friend here going, while you can enter me from the back. There should still be a few condoms left over from last night, so put one on and get your dick over here," Samantha said, with a forcefulness that almost frightened Ray.

Ray took her orders and did as he was told. He had only tried it that way once, but never like this. He looked at her long, dirty-blonde hair flowing down her back and couldn't believe how sexy this woman was. He only lasted thirty seconds. She then made him take control of the vibrator so she could orgasm as well.

She grabbed a hand towel that she had conveniently placed nearby and cleaned herself up. "Wow, that was hot," she said.

"Umm. *Yeah.* I'll say. Shit, you're killing me here. Who are you, Samantha Travelchick?" Ray said, somehow exhausted again despite waking from a great nap only several minutes ago.

"I'm a *chick* who knows what she wants and goes for it. I try not to think too much about what-ifs. I live my life day to day and whatever happens, happens. What else can I say? Let's get ready to eat. I'm starving now!"

"What do we do when we get back to Palm Springs? Do we just pretend all this didn't take place?" Ray asked, still rather confused.

"We just resume our lives. You can look at me across the way and watch me work from your table at Starbucks, and we can visit and maybe have coffee once in a while or something. But what else *can* we do? You're married, I'm in a serious relationship, and that's the way things are. We're having a wicked time, aren't we? Let's just not think about the future and live for today. We have good food to eat and good money to be made. So let's get on with the weekend of fun, shall we?"

"Yes, ma'am," Ray said. Samantha was unlike anyone he had ever met, and was someone he would never forget. Mystified, he decided that she was probably right and walked right into the lavishly appointed bathroom for his second shower of the day.

CHAPTER 22

▼

The time was 5:27 p.m. when John woke up. He felt refreshed, but as soon as he got out of bed he realized that although the horrible ordeal with Joey and Vicky was over, there were still issues left unresolved.

Most important of which was Vicky. How would he and Jennifer explain everything that led up to Vicky's kidnapping? He recalled Vicky saying that she wanted to have the day to rest and spend time with Jen, and that they would discuss it tomorrow.

He needed to check up on her though, so he picked up the phone and called her. She had also just woken up and was relaxing with Jennifer, making up for the few lost days. She promised that she was feeling okay and that she would call him tomorrow to make plans. They were both tired, and the conversation was rather stilted, but each was comforted by the phone call.

John hung up and decided to call Lee. Lee answered and was very humble about making the call to the Riverside Police. He said that it was no big deal and that any one would have done it. Lee wondered whether John would be in at work on Monday, and John couldn't answer. He said it all depended on how the discussion with Vicky went tomorrow. Lee understood and wished him luck. John smiled as he hung up the phone, realizing that there was much more to Lee than just your average computer geek.

*　　　*　　　*　　　*

Vicky and Jen both slept in rather late, taking advantage of the much-needed catch-up slumber. Neither was in much of a mood to rehash the events of the past few days, so the dialogue was kept light. They lounged on the couch and idly watched television. Jen was feeling uncomfortable not being able to share anything about the whole ordeal with her mom, so instead she brought up another subject that would hopefully get Vicky talking. "So how did you cope without having your pills with you?" she asked her mom, worrying about Vicky's dependence on the Prozac.

"I honestly don't know. That first night I almost launched into a full-fledged panic attack. I hadn't yet taken my pill for the day, and I had just last week cut my dose in half, just like we talked about. The side effects from reducing the prescribed amount are bad enough *without* missing my daily intake. By the next day I didn't know what I was going to do. My brain was acting very strangely. I just thank God that you and John saved me. I still don't want to talk about it yet, but I'm so happy. I'm not sure my system could have handled another day." Vicky was getting tired just talking about it. The truth was, Vicky experienced one of the worst panic attacks of her life during the first night of captivity. She was thankfully able to talk herself out of it, and was breathing regularly within one hour. "I don't want you to ever have to worry about getting hooked on these psychological medications, Jen. Promise me that you'll come to me if you ever feel tempted."

"I promise. I just don't understand why the medical profession doesn't seem to care so much about handing these pills out like they're candy. And all that research I did about the pharmaceutical industry … it's enough to make a girl jaded. But whatever. I know I'm not going to be taking up a career in pharmaceutical sales." Jen wasn't in the mood to continue with this topic so she changed the subject. "So anyway, once we order a pizza, should we just rent a girlie movie and eat some popcorn?"

"Yeah. Sounds like a perfect evening. I'd invite John but we'll see him tomorrow. Plus nothing in life is more important to me than my time with you. If you ever decide to go away for college, I don't know what I'd do without you. But that's something I've been working on for a long time now. But while I have you here, I gotta capitalize." Vicky's eyes were tearing up. Jen reached towards the Kleenex box on the end table, yanked a tissue out, and gently wiped the tears from her mom's face. Vicky kissed Jen on the cheek, and told her to pick whatever pizza toppings she wanted, and to choose whatever movie she wanted. Jennifer was the boss tonight.

*   *   *   *

Ray and Samantha were all dressed up with nowhere to go. They both were dressed in the seamless mix of formal and casual—perfect for a night out in Vegas. Neither felt like walking, so Samantha called down to the Le Cirque restaurant and made a reservation. Ray was astounded that they were able to get in right away. Normally, Le Cirque was very busy, and required reservations much in advance. "One of the perks of being a travel chick," Samantha explained.

Sweet, Ray thought. He had always wanted to eat there but could never get in.

They were savoring every bite of their Noix de St Jacques Rôties appetizer—which was basically roasted scallops in an applesauce—when they finally got around to talking about their jobs.

Samantha described all the perks of being in the travel industry, not the least of which was being able to stay for free at the Bellagio and dining at their one-hundred-and-five-dollars-a-person-without-drinks Le Cirque. She didn't like having to sit at a desk all day and deal with some of the rude customers that came in.

"Or the three guys that sit across at the Starbucks and ogle you in the morning," Ray added.

"Yeah, and that too. So what about you? Tell me about *your* job."

Ray told her all about his new position in security. He didn't get into too much detail, and generally gave the impression that he was content there.

"So what's that weirdo IT Director really like?" Samantha asked.

"Who? Patrick Bowman?"

"Yeah, I guess. You know, the really short guy, the one that has his hair in that gay ponytail sometimes?"

"That's him. How do you know him?"

Samantha downed a mega-sip of her wine. "He stops by sometimes to talk to me after getting his coffee. He's kinda creepy. Get this: a few weeks ago, I was working really late finishing some paperwork, and I look across and there he is all by himself reading the paper. Then, he starts cutting up the paper into all these little pieces. Like a madman. I had no idea what he was doing. He looked like such a *dick*. He must have caught me looking at him, cause the next thing I know he rushed out of there like the *Tasmanian Devil*."

"He was cutting up newspaper? As in, cutting out specific letters?" Ray asked.

"How the hell do I know what he was doing? I just thought it was weird. Whatever. He's a creeper. I don't know how that guy ends up running the whole

IT department there. He's either really smart, or a great ass-kisser. Isn't that how most people get ahead in big companies these days? Brown nosing?"

"Pretty much." Ray answered. Ray became silent for the next few minutes, keeping his head down and concentrating on the delicious food.

"What's wrong, Ray? You haven't said a word since the waiter removed our appetizers."

"Nothing. Well, yeah, something. I think my friend John, the tall, skinny one that's in our coffee group, is in a bit of trouble. I can't really explain it, but I've gotta call him. Right now. Will you excuse me for a second? I'm just going to the lobby and phone him. I promise I won't be long."

"Sure. Sounds like it's serious. I'll be here … I'm not going anywhere."

✳   ✳   ✳   ✳

John was surprised to see Ray's cell phone number show up on his call display. "Ray?"

"Yeah. I have some news for you."

"Why are you calling from Vegas? You *are* still in Vegas, right?" John was just chilling on the couch, more or less meditating.

"Uh huh. I'm still in Vegas."

"So? What's going on? You gettin' it on with Travelchick or what?" John interrupted.

"Maybe. Maybe not. I'll tell you later. But right now I'm more concerned about you. Everything go okay with Vicky?"

"Yeah, it did. Thanks to Lee. *Very* long story though. We'll talk about it Monday. But what's so important?"

Ray told John about Patrick Bowman cutting up the newspaper. John wasn't sure what to say at first, but it kind of made sense, even though it didn't exactly *prove* anything.

"I know it doesn't mean for sure that he's our guy, but it sure wouldn't surprise me," Ray said.

"Me neither. Thanks, buddy. I'll work with it, and we'll talk more when you get back. Enjoy the rest of your trip, and again, thanks. Don't do anything I wouldn't do!"

"Ha ha ha. Good luck, man. Glad to hear Vicky is alright." Ray hung up.

Now John had something to go on. Patrick Bowman may very well be the one responsible for sending those threatening messages. There was too much to think about, and much more to *worry* about right now. Nevertheless, John decided that meditation was still the best plan of action right now. He threw in a mellow new age disc in the CD player, hit play and tried to calm his mind.

CHAPTER 23

▼

The loud ringing of the phone woke John from a very deep sleep. He was so groggy it took him seven rings to realize that the sound of the phone was not coming from his deep reverie.

He finally picked it up and answered unintelligibly. The words came out sounding like *Scooby-Doo* saying hello. "Rarhro?"

"John? Is that you?" Vicky asked.

"Yeah, yeah … sorry … I was sleeping. What time is it?"

"Sorry for waking you. It's after ten. I should have waited till noon, but I know you wanted to get together and I thought we'd make a full day of it."

"Definitely, yes," John said, trying to hold back a big yawn. It didn't work.

"Nice yawn there, Chewbacca. You must have been having quite a sleep. Why don't you just come over when you're all bright-eyed and bushy-tailed?"

"Will do. I'm sure I'll be there before noon so we can all have lunch. I'll see ya then!"

＊   ＊   ＊   ＊

John arrived at Vicky's well before noon, as promised. He couldn't help but look around the block for any strange vehicles. The whole real-life nightmare was still fresh in his mind, and although he knew that Joey was behind bars and shouldn't worry, he really couldn't help but hold on to a touch of paranoia.

Vicky invited him in and he noticed that Jen must have been upstairs. Vicky threw her arms around his neck and kissed him passionately. John missed this. A lot.

"Mmm, I *so* missed this," he growled.

"Me too. Jen's just upstairs getting ready, so maybe we can chat a bit before she gets down." Vicky led John toward the couch. They sat down, hand in hand.

"So how much did Jen tell you?" John asked, not at all wanting to hear the answer.

"Not much. But I would be lying if I told you I wasn't worried about everything that led up to what happened. I care about you so much John, and I can tell that you went above and beyond to make sure no harm came to me. I don't know what happened, and I think Jen should be here when you guys explain it, but regardless, I will forever be grateful to you for putting yourself on the line for me."

"I love you, Vick. I'd do anything for you. I hope you understand everything when we explain. I'm kind of worried, and I hope this doesn't come between you and Jen. She's a great girl. You've done a tremendous job of raising her." He looked right into her eyes to further validate his words, and wouldn't stop looking at her. Vicky's eyes started to swell up. "Don't cry, Vick." He kissed her right underneath the right eye, capturing the tears with his lips.

"You're a real sweetheart," Vicky said, just as Jen was descending the stairs to join them.

Trying to hold back the tears, Vicky asked Jen to join them. Jen sat on the dark leather lounger beside them on the couch.

"Now that we're all rested, I guess you can tell me how the situation escalated to the part where I got kidnapped," Vicky said, wasting no time in getting right to the point.

John and Jennifer looked at each other, not sure whether they should start from the very beginning and tell Vicky the truth about them meeting on MSN well before they were *officially* introduced. John interpreted Jen's look as a *no*, so with that, he began.

John started with the account of them breaking into Joey's office in LA, although he moved the timeline up a little bit so that it didn't look like they went *right* after meeting. He figured he would start with the bad news first, and go from there. Jen intervened occasionally as both of them enlightened Vicky with the account of what went down and why. As they were telling their story, both John and Jen attempted to read Vicky's expression for signs of anger or disappointment. John wasn't sure what Jen could read from her, but John was having difficulty deciphering anything from Vicky's expressions. He was freaked out about it; he thought he was able to read Vicky better and wished she had been more vocal as their story was told. Finally, they finished and waited for Vicky to speak.

"Whoa. I don't know what to say. Give me a moment here." Vicky looked somewhat upset, but not too bad, John thought. "That's a lot to process. I guess I just don't get why you chose my daughter to bring with you to break into that asshole's office."

John was uncomfortable with Vicky's use of the phrase *my daughter*. *Uh oh. How do I explain this?* John wondered.

Jen stepped in. "It was *my* idea. All mine. I knew he was in trouble and thought I would totally be able to help him. It wasn't his fault. He actually turned me down several times. I insisted." Jen was confident and forceful when speaking.

"Why would you do that, Jennifer? And how did you become a professional break and enter person? This is sure news to me. But that's not a discussion I want to have right now. That's between you and I, Jen. John, you don't have to be a part of *that*." Vicky *did* seem somewhat irritated now.

"Mom. Please don't be mad at me. That was another time in my life. When you and dad were fighting all the time. I wasn't a *criminal* or anything!" Jen exclaimed, trying to defend herself.

Vicky was visibly agitated and was tapping her foot wildly. "We'll talk about it later. I'm just disappointed that even though she suggested it, *you* went along with her," Vicky said, pointing at John. "In doing so you were putting my daughter in harm's way. And you had only just met her not too long ago. I don't know what to say about that. I love you, John, but I gotta say that I don't think that doing that was the smartest decision." Vicky stopped, unable to think of anything more to say.

"It was my fault!" Jen pointed out again.

"Jen! Please. That's not the point!" Vicky screamed.

Shit. This was exactly what John feared. "I apologize, Vick. It was a lapse in judgment. I don't know of any other way to put it. I was going through a lot. And didn't know what to do. Please try to understand," John begged, in a last ditch appeal.

"I'll think about it. Actually, I really don't want to talk about this anymore. I *am* grateful that you worked together and saved me. So we'll end it at that for now. I think we should eat now."

The three of them ate together, making attempts in vain at light conversation. John and Jen could sense that Vicky was still rather angry, and wasn't quite in the mood for talking. Taking the last bites of his sandwich, John made a decision to let Vicky and Jennifer have some time to themselves.

"Look, Vick, I think maybe it would be a good idea for you two to have some time together, now that you know the whole story. I've said all I can. I apologize for bringing Jennifer into this. Whenever you feel like discussing it more, or if you just have more questions, just call me. I'll go home and try to plan out my next move after hearing the new information from Joey and Ray. I'll call you later to see how you're doing. Is that okay?"

"Maybe that's best. Thanks for understanding. I'll see you to the door," Vicky said, leading him towards the door. She gave him a hug and a squeezed his hand before he left.

John left Vicky's not feeling too great about his future with her. Hopefully she would come around, but either way John realized that there was nothing he could do to help her understand. Either she would come around, or she wouldn't. All he could do was hope.

∗   ∗   ∗   ∗

Ray and Samantha's flight was about to land in Palm Springs. Their Las Vegas weekend, filled with everything Vegas is all about, was about to come to an end. Both of them continued their love affair with Lady Luck last night, collectively winning a few more thousand dollars. Ray hadn't experienced this much excitement and adventure in Vegas, ever. He was sad that it was over, and now found himself practically speechless.

"You're pretty quiet now, which is pretty uncharacteristic of you now that I've got to know you pretty well. What is it?" Samantha asked, studying Ray's face and trying to read his thoughts.

"Does it matter? As soon as this plane lands in a few minutes, we both part ways and go on with our lives. Don't you find it the least bit strange?"

"What did you expect when we decided to go on this little trip together? Didn't you know that no matter what happened in Vegas, was, like the saying goes, going to *stay* in Vegas? I can't think of a more appropriate situation to apply that overused phrase to. Ours fits it to a *T*."

"Good point. I guess I just didn't expect to have as much fun as I did. I'm glad we didn't get freaky again after Saturday afternoon. One more time and I'd be hooked. I'm not saying I'm falling in love with you or anything—don't worry about that. I know we both have separate lives, but I'm just … I don't know … I've never been in a situation like this before. It's gonna be weird seeing you sitting across from us every morning again," Ray said, returning his seat to the most uncomfortable upright position and made a motion to straighten his back.

"True. It will. But that's life, right? Let's just be happy we had a great time and leave it at that. Maybe we'll do it again sometime even. Until then, we just have to go back to life before the trip," Samantha replied.

Ray wondered whether there were other guys that she shared experiences like this. He shouldn't care, and had no right to be jealous, but the thought of her doing this with other guys drove him crazy. He couldn't help himself to bring it up.

"So am I the only lucky guy, other than your boyfriend, that's had the privilege of having this experience with you?" As soon as the words came out of his mouth, Ray hated himself for saying it and wished he could rewind time by five seconds.

"Oh my goodness, is Ray jealous? I'm surprised. Jealousy doesn't become you. You're a married man! What's with you? Relax. We had a great time. Just be happy with that. And to answer your question: no, believe it or not, this has never happened. You can choose to believe me, or not. One thing you should know about me by now though—I'm pretty much an open book. I say what I mean and mean what I say."

Ray was sheepish now. "I hope I didn't offend you," he said, embarrassed.

"Not at all. Go home to your wife and be the great guy that you are. Let's not talk about it anymore, all right?"

"Alright. Promise."

They said their goodbyes just outside the airport and went their separate ways. Ray watched her walk away and had to pinch himself almost to the point of drawing blood in order to realize that what occurred over the last forty-eight hours was not a dream. What would he tell the boys at coffee? He wasn't sure. The more pressing issue was what he was going to tell Darlene, and how was he going to pretend that he was just there with the guys?

✳   ✳   ✳   ✳

"Damn, you two look like shit!" Aaron said to John and Ray, as he sat down to meet them for their Monday coffee. As usual, he was running late and didn't walk over with them.

John had just finished keeping Ray up to date with the whole Vicky/Jen/Joey situation. Both didn't sleep well last night.

"I guess you could say that we both had quite the weekend," John said.

"Well, well. Very nice! Let's start with Ray. Dude, you and Travelchick—how did it go, man?" Aaron was excited to hear the details.

"I don't fuck and tell," Ray said, a huge smile coming across his face.

"If the smile on your face is any indication, you got yourself some Travelchick action, you bastard," Aaron said, taking a long sip of his Frappucino.

"I really shouldn't say much. But it was a great weekend though. She's awesome. And I mean *awesome*. That's all I'm saying," Ray said, the smile still plastered on his face.

"No gory details?" John asked, throwing his hands in the air as if to say *what gives*.

"Maybe later. I feel weird with her sitting right across from us," Ray said, shooting a sideways glance at her as she was on the phone with a client.

"Understood. But you better give it up, you fucker. So what about you?" Aaron asked, looking right at John.

"My weekend was, shall we say, eventful. I'm going to let you in on a long story, dude, and you're not going to believe it. Are you ready? And by the way, before I begin, how much time do you have?"

"I can take a little longer," Aaron said, looking at his Oakley watch.

"Good. This is going to take awhile. Ray and I already told Dan we were going to take a supersize coffee break, so he's cool with it. So anyway."

John began to tell his story. He recounted all of the details, leaving nothing out, ending with their suspicion of Patrick Bowman.

*   *   *   *

Patrick Bowman was sitting in his office admiring Tara, who sat in a cubicle just outside his office. It was a normal Monday afternoon for him—still catching up on all the emails and voicemails that accumulated over the weekend. It bothered him that so much of the executive staff spent far too much time on the weekend at work. Patrick wasn't the workaholic type.

The phone rang and brought him out of his mid-afternoon zone-out time.

"Patrick Bowman here."

"Hey man, it's Harlan."

"What's shakin', Mr. Daley?"

"Did you hear about Joey Styles?"

"No, I haven't." Patrick answered, standing up to shut the door of his office. "What happened to that weasel?"

"Arrested for kidnapping. I guess your boy John there outsmarted him and now he's in jail. That guy is a resilient bastard."

"He's obviously smarter than I gave him credit for. Hmmm. That's funny. Joey in jail, all because of John! I didn't really want Joey in jail, but hey. More importantly though, what are we going to do about Pope? I want the guy to pay," Patrick said, taking a seat in his overpriced executive chair and placing his feet on his equally overpriced executive desk.

"Oh, he'll pay. I can't let him get away with what he did to my old buddy's daughter at that party on Mulholland. You understand how difficult this is for me don't you Patty-o? Even without any new gossip on the guy, focus groups are just lovin' the screenings of the new flick. He's sure to make us a mint at the studio. But it's only money, right?"

"I have a thought for you. I know we just wanted to hurt him, but think about how much money he would be worth to you *dead*. The movie would do even more box office, and think of all the DVD revenues … not to mention overseas dough. If the movie is as good as you say, just imagine all the extra cash he could generate you. You said yourself that after this movie he's free to sign with another studio, and the buzz I read says he's close to inking a deal with Paramount. I follow all the news on that lowlife," Patrick said, violently cracking his knuckles.

"I don't know, Patty-o. Believe me, I've thought about it before. But, now that Joey's in jail I don't know who to rely on to get the *job* done, if you know what I mean."

Patrick was upset that Harlan wasn't as enthusiastic about his idea. Ever since Pope date-raped his daughter, Patrick was hell-bent on revenge, and really wouldn't think twice about seeing him dead. "Just think about it, Mr. Harley Davidson. It drives me nuts every day I read about him. Scum like him don't deserve to live. I'm sorry, I wish I could get over it, but I can't. I've tried. It's been almost two years, and time is healing nothing for me. Susie is getting over it I think, but I just can't get past it," Patrick said, slamming his fist into the desk as if Harlan could see him emphasize his point.

"Hey, I understand. Susie is a great girl, and she didn't deserve that. I've watched her grow up. She's like a niece to me. I want revenge, too. Let me think about it, okay?" Harlan paused, waiting for Patrick to respond. Realizing no response was coming, Harlan broke the silence. "So what are you going to do about your boy, John? You still playing the 'I'm watching you' game with him?"

"Yeah, I probably will. He has no idea I've been watching him since the day he started. I just love fucking with his mind. As soon as he started catching on to Pope, I had to really bump up my spying on him. I thought he may eventually lead me to *something,* I don't know what, but I guess he's smarter than I thought. I don't know what I'm going to do with him, but whatever. All I care about is Pope being dead. Think about it. I gotta go, I have a line up of people at my office wanting to talk to me. Later."

Patrick hung up, hoping Harlan would come up with a plan to rid the world of Pope. He eyed the group of IT drones waiting outside his door and motioned for them to come in.

CHAPTER 24

▼

The week was flying by for John—he couldn't believe it was Friday already. He had been working with Ray and Aaron all week in trying to come up with a way to deal with Patrick Bowman. They couldn't figure out what he had to do with Harlan Daley. As the week went on, John fully expected to be called into the guy's office and be fired on the spot. He found it odd that nothing of the sort had happened yet.

The Riverside Police department luckily did not release the names of anyone involved with the details of Joey Styles' kidnapping charges, probably because Jennifer was still a minor. Other than Vicky, Ray, Lee, and Aaron, nobody at DesertFinancial had any knowledge of what happened to John last weekend. *With the exception of Patrick Bowman of course,* whose knowledge of the details may or may not be extensive.

John's relationship with Vicky was still somewhat strained. They talked daily, spent one evening alone last night, and had lunch together on Tuesday. He couldn't help but notice something missing in the way Vicky interacted with him. It was hard to put a finger on what it was exactly—she was just, well, rather distant. He prayed that in time she would come around. At least she still wanted to see him, and was offering her support in dealing with the Patrick thing.

John was about to get in the shower before heading to work when his cell phone rang. It was Jennifer.

"Hey Jen, what's up?"

"I'm sorry. I'm so totally sorry, John. Last night mom and I had a long talk, and she kept pressing me about us going to LA to Joey's office." Jen was distraught, and she was having difficulty continuing. She sniffled a few times before going on. "She said it didn't make sense. I told her the truth. I told her that we knew each other before we were introduced. I didn't want any lies between us. I couldn't lie to her anymore. And I know what that means to the relationship you have with her, and if it fucks it up, I'm forever sorry. I just had to. I hope you understand my position."

John tried to swallow with the huge lump that had developed in his throat, which seemed to be as difficult as trying to siphon a basketball through a kiddie straw. *Shit, this was all he needed.* He was silent for a good thirty seconds before he could bring himself to speak. "I understand. I'm the adult here. And I made the choice to not tell her about it. It's not your fault, Jen. I need to take responsibility for that decision. I'm not mad at you. At all. I fucked up, Jen. I'll take the heat. Thanks for telling me. So how pissed is she?"

"Very. I don't know what to tell you. She said she'd be *dealing* with you tonight. I'm so sorry. Will you *really* forgive me?"

"Yes. I forgive you. You deserve to have a special relationship with your mom, and that's the most important thing. You didn't do anything wrong, okay?"

"Alright. I'll try to think about that," Jen said, sounding quite relieved.

"Maybe I'll see you later, if I come over. Otherwise I'll talk to you soon. Bye, Jen." John hung up, butterflies swarming around his stomach like starving bees around a honeycomb.

*   *   *   *

John wasn't in the mood to share Jen's news with Ray and Aaron at coffee this morning. He steered the topic of conversation toward Ray and Travelchick. "Dude, you still haven't really told us the gory details about you and Travelchick. What gives, man? Why are you being so damn secretive?"

"I don't know. It was just *weird,*" was all Ray could come up with.

"You've told us all about the gambling, and that you kinda *got busy,*" Aaron said, using the finger quotes for *got busy.* "It's so not like you to hold out on us. Is everything okay? You've been a little quiet this week."

"I guess so. It was a great time—better than I had ever expected. Like I mean *really fucking* good, alright? And the guilt I've been experiencing with Darlene is brutal," Ray explained with a frown.

"Did ya bang her good?" Aaron asked.

"Guys. Take it easy!" Ray ordered.

"Did you, though?" John added.

"Yes. Yes! Okay? Happy now? It was one of the best sexual experiences of my life. There. I said it," Ray shouted.

"Wowww. You *go*, boy. Ray *was* holding out on us. I'm kinda shocked, but impressed. What are you gonna do about Darlene? What did you tell her?" John asked, raising his eyebrow in a feeble attempt to mimic *The Rock* from *WWE.*

"I don't know. I feel bad. I've never cheated on her. Ever. And here I go having this sex-filled weekend with Samantha. What would you do if you were in my situation?" Ray asked, pointing to Aaron.

Aaron took a long sip of his Frappucino before his speech. "To be absolutely honest with you, I would have never gone. Too much temptation. Guys are wired differently than girls. We have a much lower boiling point. How many guys do you know that would turn down a woman like Travelchick there, if she were coming on to them like gangbusters? Not many at all. So the best thing to do is to avoid situations like that. If I had gone, I don't know what I'd do. I'm not blaming you dude, and I'm not judging you either. As for Darlene, if you think that this thing with Travelchick was a one-time thing, just leave it alone. Don't think about it and don't let the guilt eat you up anymore. Put your efforts back into your marriage. You are happy with Darlene, right?"

"I am. Sometimes she doesn't exactly feel like being terribly intimate anymore, but we still have our fun. I think I just needed a little excitement. And I got it. In spades."

"Would you leave her for Travelchick if she asked you to?" John asked.

"No. Why would I? That would be insane. Though she does make me feel pretty good."

"Travelchick?"

"Yeah."

"You can't look outside your marriage for solutions to problems within it, though. If you ever thought of leaving Darlene, you pretty much have to exhaust every option in working things out first. I really think people take marriage too lightly these days," Aaron said, fully comfortable standing on his proverbial soapbox.

"Who ever said I was thinking of leaving her? I appreciate your advice, but I just think what I'm feeling is good old-fashioned guilt. I love Darlene, and have no plans on leaving her. Especially for one weekend of fun, gambling, good food and sex," Ray said. Ray's irritation was subsiding as he realized his friends were merely looking out for him.

"True, but I'm just thinking ahead. Try to forget about the weekend, as hard as that may seem to be. Samantha is one hot chick, but you should try to put her out of your mind. That's all," Aaron said.

"Good point, man. Just go back to being like us and ogle her from across the way," John suggested.

"I'll try. Thanks guys. I appreciate the talk," Ray said. "Now let's get back to work."

✳   ✳   ✳   ✳

John and Vicky were sitting on John's couch (which could probably seat eight, comfortably), having their *big chat*. Vicky came over right after having dinner with Jen before she went out with Shawn, who was finally coming around in overlooking any of the rumors about Jennifer.

John didn't let on that he knew what was coming.

"John, we really need to talk," Vicky said.

"No good conversation ever began with the words *we need to talk*."

"Unfortunately, this one is no exception."

"Great. Go ahead, Vick. I'm all ears," John said, looking at Vicky all doe-eyed and pulling at his ears, trying his best to stir up a sympathy/humor visual cocktail.

Vicky went on to explain how upset she was that he had lied to her about meeting Jennifer online before being formally introduced to her. Her biggest concern was that if he were willing to lie about this, what else would he lie about? She really thought that their relationship was based on complete honestly, and from the very beginning he was being untruthful about Jen.

John understood, and didn't even attempt to defend himself. He just nodded in acceptance and validated what she was saying. He tried his best to be sympathetic to her feelings.

"And, what are you doing chatting up seventeen-year-olds online anyway?" Vicky added.

"She said she was twenty," was the best he could come up with. For some reason he added: "And what were you doing getting involved in twisted S&M games with men you hardly know? I can't exactly forget about that email."

"What the fuck does that have anything to do with this? Take that back. *Now.*" Vicky was turning red now.

Instantly John felt terrible for bringing it up. He apologized and reiterated how Jen first introduced herself as a twenty-year-old.

"Oh, that just makes it *so* much better," Vicky replied sarcastically.

"What do you want me to say?" *John* was getting somewhat annoyed now.

"I don't know. I really don't want to fight with you. Because as much as I don't want to right now, I still really love you. I'm just going to need some time to try and put everything into perspective with us. I think so much of you, John, and I think your heart is in the right place. I just have some doubts right now."

"So what are you saying, Vick?" John was worried where this was leading.

"As much as I hate to say this, I think that we need to take a little break right now."

"A *break?* What are we, in frickin' high school?" *Oops.* "Sorry. Couldn't help it."

"What do *you* suggest then, big shot? I'm telling you that I need time to think. I've been through a lot in my life, and before I fully commit to you, I'm going to need to reflect on things for a while."

John could tell Vicky spoke with conviction, but at the same time he could see how much it pained her to say what she was saying.

"Whatever you need. I accept full responsibility for not being truthful. And please don't blame Jen. I'm the adult," John said.

"I'm trying not to hold it against her, but she's my daughter and a part of me still feels betrayed. But I'll have to deal with it, and it's between her and I." Vicky dropped her head towards her knees, in a gesture of distress.

John lifted her head gently, and kissed her. "I still love you, Vick. I'll give you whatever time you need. I understand how you feel."

Vicky smiled for the first time since their conversation started. "Thanks, John. I still love you too. I don't think there's a point of doing anything now, it would just be too hard." Vicky stood up. "I'm just going to leave, okay?"

"All right. I understand."

Vicky showed herself out, leaving John sitting alone on the couch, wondering whether his life was ever going to get back on track. It seemed like one thing after another.

John woke the next morning filled with regret. All he had to have done is come clean about meeting Jen online. He didn't want to lose the one person he had finally felt a true connection to. He understood Vicky's position and realized that the only thing he could do was to give her time. Hopefully she would come around.

It did him no good to stew over everything and over-analyze. His career was still in jeopardy, and solving the mystery of Patrick Bowman was now his number one priority.

What better way to take his mind off Vicky than to do some much-needed shopping? John showered, shaved, changed and headed outside.

The half hour drive to Cabazon was quiet. He didn't even feel like listening to music. He needed quiet time in order for his thoughts to come through as clear as possible, without any sonic interruption. Unfortunately for him, no resolutions to any of his problems were presenting themselves.

Arriving in Cabazon, he didn't even know where to begin, though Morongo was definitely out of the question. He felt fortunate to live so close to one of the best outlet shopping malls in the United States. Recalling that he needed a new pair of sunglasses, he decided to start at the Oakley Vault store.

Three hours and five hundred dollars later, he elected to head back to the much warmer climate of Palm Springs. He loved how Cabazon not only offered a great shopping experience, but a great reprieve from the temperatures of Palm Springs.

He was half way towards home on the I-10 when the light bulb went on above his head. Tara! How could he have not thought of this before? Tara works directly with Patrick. Perhaps he could convince her to assist him in figuring out what their wonderful leader was up to. He pulled over to the side of the road and dialed Tara's number on his cell. *Pick up, pick up … please be home,* he prayed.

"Hi this is Tara … you know what to do," her voicemail kicked in.

Shit, John swore aloud. About to hang up, he thought he'd try talking to the machine. "Tara, Tara. Pick up. Please, if you're home, pick up the phone. I need to—"

"Geez, dude, take a chill pill, yo," Tara said.

"Thank God you're home. I need a huge favor from you."

"What kind of favor?"

"I'll explain later. What are you doing now?" John wanted to see her right away.

"I'm going out with one of my girlfriends. We were thinking of going to a movie later too. What's so important?" Tara asked, having no clue about John's recent adventures.

"Something important enough for you to change your plans. Don't cancel on your girlfriend on such short notice, but cut the day short and we can do something this evening. Whaddya say?" John asked, not feeling the least bit guilty for being overly assertive.

"Aren't we frickin' bossy today. What's up with you?"

"You'll find out when I see you. What time do you want to meet?" John was *really* persistent now.

"What about eight? Is that too late for you, Mr. Bossypants? Just come over to my place."

"Cool. Give me the address and I'll be there."

Tara gave him directions to her place and tried once more unsuccessfully to get the lowdown before he came over.

✳   ✳   ✳   ✳

John showed up ten minutes early at Tara's. He couldn't wait to talk with her.

"So what's the big fuss? You seem totally focused on making sure I hear you out. I'm curious. I've been wondering about it all day," Tara said, showing John to the couch in her small, one-bedroom apartment.

John sat down, and Tara sat beside him, leaving about five feet between them to give him some personal space. John wiped the sweat off his forehead and wondered why it was so damn hot in her apartment. "What's with the heat in here? Doesn't it seem rather warm to you?"

Tara leaned back and stretched her legs out. "Yeah, the air conditioning is on the fritz. They were supposed to fix it today but no luck. I'm probably moving out of here before summer gets too hot anyway. It's time I get out of this place. There's a new town home I have my eye on."

"Well it's fucking hot in here. But that's not what I'm here for, to talk about the heat. I need to keep you up to date with everything that's been going on in my life. Are you ready? It's a loooong story!"

"Ooooh! I love long stories. I hope everything is still good with you and Vicky, though," Tara said.

John cracked his neck both ways and settled into his spot on the couch and began. He told her everything, not leaving out a single detail. He trusted Tara; plus he figured the more she knew, the better chance there would be of her helping him out. He noticed Tara moving closer to him as his story progressed.

"Holy fuck, dude. That's extreme. You are living the most interesting life of anyone I know. I thought that *I* led a fascinating life, but I got nothing on you, boy. So I take it you need my help in trying to come up with what my boss is up to."

"That's the plan, yes. Are you up for it?"

"Hell, yeah. The guy's a freak, man. He pretty much lets me do my thing, and isn't really that much of a control freak, but something about him just puts me off. So what should we do? What's the plan?" Tara was much more animated now.

"I'd love to get proof that he's spying on me. But I think our main priority is to discover what he has to do with Harlan Daley, the guy from Heavyweight Studios. I always considered Patrick's mailbox rather sacrosanct, and would never under any circumstances go into it—even though I have the proper network rights to check out anyone's Inbox. That was then. Now I gotta take a chance. That will be our first move. I can do that from home later tonight. I doubt he's dumb enough to leave any evidence on his work email, but if he did I'll find it. Otherwise, we're gonna do some spying on him. Whatever we can come up with and by any means necessary. You in?"

"I'm in. This is awesome and exciting! Let's get the fucker!" Tara exclaimed, pushing John in the chest for added effect. She loved the push-in-the-chest gesture, as it always reminded her of *Elaine Benes* on *Seinfeld.*

"Getting feisty, aren't we, Tarawara?" John lightly punched her shoulder in retaliation.

"What are you gonna do about it if I keep getting feistier, huh?" Tara was now sitting right beside him, their knees touching.

Okay, John, now what are you going to do? His inner voice questioned. "I don't know, but for some reason I can't help but feeling that I really wanna kiss you right now, and I hate myself for it. This sucks." John pursed his lips and squinted his eyes, not unlike the look Luke Perry made famous in *Beverly Hills 90210.*

"It does suck, doesn't it? We've been fighting this for a long time, haven't we? I don't think this is the greatest timing, is it?" Tara asked with a slight hint of concern in her voice. She scooched even closer to him on the couch.

"You know what, my life has been so fucked up lately, I don't know what to think anymore. To hell with thinking right now," John said, moving towards Tara to do something he'd wanted to since first laying eyes on her. He pressed his lips against her, hard, and began kissing her. She reciprocated at first then stopped him.

"This can't be good. Remember Vicky?" She said.

"I can't ever forget her, but my gut tells me I've lost her. And right now I'm so vulnerable and unsure of everything, I'm past the point of thinking. Just keep kissing me, Tara." He grabbed her chin and pulled her towards him. They made out like high school kids for almost an hour, without removing any clothes. John didn't mind it that way, and neither did Tara.

When they came up for air, they straightened their clothes and stared at each other before Tara stood up and walked toward the kitchen to get a cold bottle of water for each of them. "Hopefully this will cool us down slightly."

"I hope so. That was awesome, Tara."

"We didn't even do it yet. Just wait until I get you into bed. Then I'll show you awesome," Tara said with an arrogance that surprised John.

"Really now? We'll just have to put that on hold for a while. For now we got some work to do. I don't know about you, but I'm frickin' *schvitzing* over here, and I need to cool off in the pool. Wanna join me in the pool at my complex?"

"I'd love to, but I think that if I come over I would never leave. So I'm gonna pass. You go for a swim and I'll stay here and have a cold shower. Call me tomorrow and we'll work on our plans."

"I guess that's probably a good idea. I hope this doesn't screw up our friendship. Really. Let's just concentrate on getting Patrick, and put this part of things out of our minds for now." *Wishful thinking,* John thought. "Is that even possible?"

"Good question. But we'll work it out. We're good buds, remember? Now get the hell outta here before I jump all over you."

John was out the door before his mind was able to tell his mouth to say goodbye. No point in complicating his life even further.

CHAPTER 25

▼

John felt a lot better after having jumped in the pool, followed by a cold shower. He was ready to go into Patrick's corporate mailbox, an activity he has always wanted to undertake.

He logged onto the corporate firewall and started the Terminal Services program on his PC. He typed in the IP address of the decoy server that sat in the network DMZ to gain access to that server, which would allow him to connect directly to the workstation on his desk. He fired up Outlook on his work PC and typed in Patrick's name in the Open Other User's folder window.

John spent over an hour going over anything he could find. Unfortunately, he was unable to uncover any evidence that he was looking for. Sure, his suspicions of Patrick being an uncaring, son-of-a-bitch manager were certainly validated in some of the emails, but there was nothing proving that this guy was spying on him. And worse, there was no evidence of anything linking him to Harlan Daley.

He resolved to go to bed and work on Plan B with Tara tomorrow.

*   *   *   *

"Did I neglect to mention that my dad is a retired cop?" Tara asked when John called her Sunday afternoon.

"You *did* neglect to mention that. That's a pretty big thing to omit. What does this mean for us though?" John was hoping for anything, *anything* that could help.

"I'm not sure. I'm going over there for dinner tonight and I'll see if there's anything I can snag from him. I'm thinking anything surveillance related will help us."

John was becoming more optimistic now. He brought the phone with him outside so he could talk with her as he lazed in a lounger by the pool.

"Whatever you can get, that would be awesome. You rock, Tara!" He was now fully reclined, facing the early afternoon sun. Thankfully, there was a slight haze in the sky that minimized the heat of the sun's rays.

"I do rock, don't I? So we'll meet for lunch or something tomorrow, okay? Bring a lunch and we'll find a quiet room to chat."

"Perfect. Can't wait!"

Vicky called later in the day to see how he was doing, and to again express her regret for their conversation the other night. John asked her not to worry and told her once more that he understand the way she feels. He told her he loved her and that he hoped she could find it in her heart to see past his mistakes.

When he got off the phone he asked himself what gave him the right to do what he did last night. He was still in a relationship with Vicky, even though it was *on hold. What is wrong with you, Jonathan Davis? Will you ever get your life on the straight and narrow?*

※   ※   ※   ※

John and Tara actually both brought lunches to work—a rare occurrence for each. John booked a meeting room in the insurance area, as far away from the IT people as possible.

Tara was being rather quiet, which John found somewhat unsettling. He wasn't sure if she was uncomfortable with what happened Saturday night, or whether she wasn't quite committed to their plan. He sat quietly in the over-priced office chair and chowed down on his corned beef on rye.

"Are you alright? You haven't said that much since we got in here," John said, washing down the salty corned beef with Coke.

"I'm great. I just wanted to keep quiet for a bit and make you squirm. Did you think I was mad at you?"

"Why would you do that? Are you just a sadistic freak, Tara? You know how shot my nerves are. You are one mean chick." John glared at her angrily.

"I'm just weird. Deal with it. Rock and Roll. Get it? *Rules of Attraction?* Brett Easton Ellis? But I digress. I thought I'd try to put you off a bit before I laid the good news on ya." Tara smiled at him.

"Good news? Do tell." John's mood went from anger to delight in a split second.

"I went to my parent's for dinner last night, and weaseled my way into my dad's office while they were busy upstairs. He was a detective, and spent a lot of time doing surveillance. He owns some really good equipment, some of it still sophisticated, even for today. I managed to abscond with some phone surveillance equipment. A bugging device, to be more specific." Tara was really enthusiastic now, and was grinning like the Cheshire cat on Ecstasy.

"No way! That's incredible!" John couldn't contain his excitement. "So what's our next step?"

"We listen to his conversations," Tara said matter-of-factly.

"What do you mean? Don't we have to find a way to bug his phone first?"

"Already taken care of."

"Fuck you. You're lying, right?"

"Nope. I know where he hides an extra key. I came in to work really early this morning, and did the deed myself. It's so easy, if you know what you're doing. All the years of hearing my dad's cool stories taught me a lot."

"No way!!! I can't believe you did that. Are you sure nobody saw you? I'd hate for you to get in shit." John was elated with Tara's news, but was concerned about coming this far and getting caught.

"Nobody saw. It was 5:30 a.m. I figured we may as well act now. And act fast. We're clear. All we have to do is listen and wait."

"If we weren't at work, I'd kiss you again. But let's save that for later," John said.

"Don't make any promises you're not prepared to keep, dude. Let's finish our lunch and get outta here for a walk."

They finished up, threw their garbage in the trash, locked the door to the meeting room, and quickly made their way outside.

*   *   *   *

Patrick Bowman was going over this year's IT budget when his phone rang.

"Information Technology, this is Patrick."

"Patty-o, how's it goin' this fine Tuesday morning?"

"Not bad, Harlan. How's things with you? Getting' all ready for the big movie opening on Thursday?"

Harlan could sense a heavy dose of sarcasm in Patrick's voice. He likely couldn't care less about the movie opening, especially with Pope being the big star. "Yeah, I am. It's looking good, man. But that's not why I'm calling. I think I've come up with a way to rid you of your problem. Permanently."

"You're shittin' me, right? That would be great. What do you have in mind?" Patrick answered, making sure that his door was closed and that nobody was lurking outside his office.

"Do you really want to know? Isn't it best that you don't?"

"No. I want to know. I want to savor every little fucking detail of Pope's demise." Patrick smiled an evil smile.

"Let's just say the big movie premiere is sure to be a *blast*, especially for Popester."

"Be more specific." Patrick wanted to hear it spelled out for him.

"In true Mafioso style, PopeyDopey is going to get into his nice Bentley after the premiere and it's gonna blow up real good."

"That couldn't be done for free though. I'm not exactly in a position to chip in on this. How are you working it out?" Patrick was always about the details, in every aspect of his life.

"My *friend* will just take a percentage of additional revenues that arise from his death. It's not really a set price. This guy owes me a favor. That's all you need to know," Harlan said.

"Good enough for me. I'm sure this will make huge news. Box office is guaranteed to be monstrous. I can't even imagine the publicity you'll get on this. Wicked. I'm pumped. Thanks man, this helps. A lot."

"De nada. De nada. I gotta go, Patty-o. Hey, that rhymes. Hahaha. Make sure you're watching KTLA late Thursday night. See ya."

"Heh heh. Bye."

A surge of intense pleasure swept through Patrick Bowman. It seemed as if two years of hell was going to come to an end with Pope's upcoming death. He felt slightly guilty in taking pleasure from another's death, but he knew that would subside quickly. His daughter would be psychologically paying the price for the rest of her life. In his mind, Patrick allowed himself to believe that Pope was still getting off easy.

＊　　　＊　　　＊　　　＊

John was in the middle of doing his laps in the pool when he noticed a shapely woman's figure standing at the end of the pool. He could never really see that well when he swam, so he quickly front-crawled it to the other side to see who was standing there.

"Hey, Mr. Thin Man. I've never seen you without your shirt off. You really are a thin guy, John," Tara observed. "Don't worry, you're still beautiful though."

"Thanks a *lot*, chickie," John said, pulling himself out of the pool and grabbing a towel to dry off. "How did you get in here? Usually the security guard is pretty good with not letting anyone in."

"I just told him I was your friend from work and flashed my wicked smile at him. He tried to call you to let you know that I was here. When he told me you had come home and were likely outside, I told him I wanted to surprise you, and he went for it. I think I charmed him good!" Tara bragged.

"Man, just one more bit of proof that people have been and will always be the weakest link when it comes to security. Sorry, I had to say that. Comes with the territory when you're a security professional. So now that you're here, what's up? I didn't expect you at all." John was dried off now, but he kept the towel wrapped around his waist in an effort to hide his thinness. He was always self-conscious about being too thin, but having Tara point it out made it even worse, regardless of having just been labeled as beautiful. *I could certainly handle more of those comments.*

"We're set, dude. Patrick Bowman is toast. Done. Like a thanksgiving turkey."

"Are you shitting me? Already? What did we get?" John asked, excitedly. At this moment, John experienced the most intense feeling of happiness since his first date with Vicky.

"All the evidence we need to bring him down. I have the tape in my hot little hands. Well, not literally. It's in my purse. So are you gonna invite me in to see your place?"

"For sure. Follow me!" John couldn't wait to hear this tape. He led Tara into his place and gave her the quick and dirty tour.

"Nice place! Holy crap! How the hell can you afford this?" Tara asked, her feelings full of envy thinking about how much nicer John's place was than her own.

"It was my grandparents' place. They left it to my mom and she in turn wanted me to have it. I would really love to have a place all to my own, but I love staying here to keep their memory alive. But anyway, let's hear the tape. We can talk more about other stuff later." John couldn't wait to hear what Patrick had to do with this whole thing.

John and Tara sat down on the couch in the living room. John didn't even bother offering her anything to drink—which was totally out of character for him. He prided himself on being the consummate host whenever he had company.

Tara removed the mini tape recorder from her purse and hit Play. They listened to the conversation that took place between Patrick Bowman and Harlan Daley. Tara had already heard it multiple times, so she took major pleasure in observing the expression on John's face as he listened to Patrick and Harley's plan. If his jaw could have physically dropped to the floor, it would have.

"Wow. Intense." John couldn't come up with anything else to say.

"Talk about incriminating. The only thing I wanna know is: what does he have against Pope?" Tara said, as she stood up and started walking toward the kitchen. She asked John if he minded if she helped herself to a drink. John told her to knock herself out, and to open the fridge and pick whatever she wanted.

She returned to the couch and sat beside him.

"I just don't understand why he would want Pope dead. That's pretty brutal. Wonder what Pope did?" John asked, still puzzled.

"Does it matter? We have enough to bring him down. Can you say conspiracy to murder?"

They spent the next half hour discussing what Patrick's motives could be. Neither of them was able to come up with anything remotely resembling the truth.

The next hour was spent debating what their next move would be in dealing with this new evidence. Tara pushed for going right to the cops; John pushed for confronting him with it first, if only to derive sick pleasure from watching the guy squirm. Both John and Tara made their arguments and presented valid reasons to support their positions. As time dragged on, both of them were getting tired of arguing with each other. Neither was willing to budge on how they wanted to proceed.

John couldn't take it anymore. "Look, Tara, I hate to use my trump card, but I gotta do it. This is *my* life. And as much as I appreciate all you've done to help, I want to talk to Patrick first before we go ahead with anything. It's important to me. Tomorrow I'm going to storm right in there and have a good chat with him."

"All right. You win. I guess you've been through enough. Plus I guess you still wanna know what *you* have to do with anything. Why the fuck would he be sending you those weird 'I'm watching you' letters?"

"Exactly. I need to have a face to face with our fearless leader and put him in his place for once and for all. I can't wait to see the bastard squirm. I'm *so* looking forward to this. You have no idea! I feel that all of my troubles are finally going to come to a close with this meeting tomorrow. All I want is to take a deep breath, a sigh of relief, not having to worry about what I'm doing, who's watching me, and what impact my actions are going to have on the ones I love. I'm spent."

John stood up to stretch his legs. They had been sitting for far too long involved in their intense conversation without moving much. John walked aimlessly around the living room, as Tara fed him suggestions on what to say to Patrick tomorrow. They talked only for a few more minutes before John just couldn't talk any more. "I'm all talked out. I just want to fast-forward to tomorrow so I can get this done with. Aren't you tired?"

Tara wasn't tired, but she could tell John was. She could see it in his eyes. However, there was still something telling her not to leave. Not just yet. "I'm not exactly tired, no," Tara said, "but then again I haven't been living a psycho life like you. There are still things I'd like to talk to you about, but I know it's too much to ask of you right now. A part of me wants to go home and let you sleep, but the other part wants you to bring me to your bed and take me like I know you've wanted to since we first started hanging out." She stood up to meet him, standing only inches away from him.

"Why do you want to complicate my life even further right now? Are you trying to take advantage of me in my vulnerable state?" John asked, half seriously.

"You sound like a chick. Man, you're somethin' else, buddy." Tara moved even closer. "Look at me and tell me you don't want me. I dare you."

"You suck."

"See? You can't say it."

"I give up. I'm damned either way. If I let you walk out of here now, I'll probably regret the lost opportunity, and if I take you to bed I'm going to feel guilty for betraying Vicky. Godddamit!" John looked down at the ground.

Tara grabbed John by the head and pulled it back up so he was facing her again.

"I've never done this before in my life, honest I haven't, but you know what? I'm taking a stand. I'm going right for what I want and taking no prisoners. I don't care about what you have with Vicky. I'm sorry, but I don't. I've gone through a lot myself in the last few months. Nothing like the psycho life that you lead, but I've been on lots of dates, blind dates, weird stuff ... the whole gamut of single life shit. When you and Vicky started getting serious I was *seriously* jealous. I had it in my mind that you were the one for me, and just stepped aside. No more stepping aside." Tara had a fierce look in her eye that John had never seen before.

"Okie dokie then." John drew out the words slowly for emphasis. "I don't know what to say. Really, I don't."

"Take me to bed," she insisted.

"Maybe soon. Honestly Tara, I'm just too tired right now. It would just complicate things too much. Let me get tomorrow over with and then we'll revisit this conversation. I do really care about you, Tara. Okay?"

"Yeah, fine," Tara said, looking and feeling dejected. "Come get me as soon as you're done with him tomorrow."

"Of course. I'll see you out."

CHAPTER 26

▼

As soon as John got into work, he walked right past the Security area and headed straight towards Patrick's office. He wasn't going to waste a minute of time waiting.

Tara was sitting in her cubicle outside Patrick's office and gave him a big wink. John winked back at her and flashed a sadistic smile. Tara pointed to the closed door and told him he should probably just interrupt Patrick. Once John was finished with him, it wouldn't matter anyway and there would be no hell to pay.

John took Tara's cue and walked right in, swinging the door open with force. The door made a loud clacking sound as it hit the doorjamb.

"Excuse me, John, what the hell do you think you're doing. Can't you see I'm busy?" Patrick barked out. "Sorry Bill, John will just have to wait until we're done. And perhaps even longer. I'll see him when I'm good and ready."

Bill Noyes was the Director of Software and Application Services, and John had always respected him. John quietly apologized to Bill and said that this was a matter of extreme importance and could not be held off any longer. Bill felt caught in the middle, and half-stood in uncertainty. Patrick tried to sit him down but John insisted that if he didn't speak to Patrick right this minute, the future of the IT Department was in jeopardy. Bill believed it, since John was known for discovering all the negative activities with respect to DesertFinancial employees.

Bill left and Patrick slammed the door. He practically forced John to sit down and took a seat behind his desk. "Now, what the *fuck* is going on here? You better start explaining right now. Your outburst really pissed me off." Patrick glared at John with hate in his eyes.

- 220 -

"Awww, Mr. IT Director is all pissed off. Well boo hoo. I'm so sad for him. Nawwwwt! This isn't about me, Patrick. This meeting is all about *you*," he pointed right at Patrick in an accusatory gesture to accentuate his point. "First, I wanna know why the hell you're sending me those stupid 'I'm watching you' messages. Let's start with the easy stuff."

John felt great. He felt completely in command, and couldn't help himself with getting great pleasure in having this guy in the palm of his hand.

"I have no idea what you're talking about. Get out of my office, or I'll see that you're fired," Patrick answered back.

"What are you, the typical murder suspect from *Columbo*? That's what you sound like. *I have no idea what you're talking about, detective.* You couldn't sound more guilty if you tried," John said in a very patronizing tone, trying really hard to push Patrick's buttons.

"Look, I don't know what your agenda is here, Mr. Davis. But I have no time for it. If you value your position here, you'll let me be."

John figured it was time to show his hand. "I don't think *my* position is in question here, *Mr. Bowman*. I'll just get right to the point. Does the name Harlan Daley mean anything to you?"

Patrick's face briefly showed an ounce of fear, but he was able to recover quickly. "Sure, he's my friend, but what does that have to do with anything?"

"Oh, it has a lot to do with everything. We'll try another question: Does the name Pope Harris mean anything to you?"

John knew from the look on Patrick's face that the upper hand in this meeting had just changed.

"Of course it does. He's that overrated movie star. Why would he mean anything to me though?"

"What do Harlan Daley, Pope Harris and you have in common? That's what I wanna know. Are you gonna tell me or are you going to make me solve the riddle for you." John said, making more of a statement than a question.

"I still don't know what you're talking about, John. Fine, spell it out for me. Tell me what we all have in common, if you're so smart." Patrick's voice was becoming less and less authoritative as the discussion progressed.

"*Fine*. I will. How does conspiracy to murder sound? Seems there was a phone call that took place between a certain Harlan Daley and a certain Patrick Bowman yesterday."

"How the …? What?" Patrick stumbled out the words. He couldn't speak, and his face was whiter than a ghost in a snowstorm.

"You know how you were spying on me? Well, I just decided to turn the tables and spy on *you*. Isn't that pretty much my *job*, anyway? I thought I would step it up a bit, and do some surveillance on your phone conversations. Which, I happen to have a copy of—right in my little pocket here. Don't worry, there's copies." John spoke with authority, watching and getting immense pleasure from seeing Patrick squirm.

He waited for Patrick to reply, but he wasn't getting one. John continued. "So now that I have you by the short hairs, you're going to tell me why you were spying on me. And you're going to tell me *now!*"

Patrick sighed. "To be completely honest with you, all I wanted to do is screw with your head a bit. I pride myself on being a pretty good judge of character, and when I hired you I had a feeling that you were going to be one that needed to be monitored. I installed a keystroke logger on your computer and was pretty much watching everything you typed. You made for interesting viewing, I gotta say." Patrick knew he was knee-deep in shit, and figured honesty was his only hope. "As soon as I saw you get involved with the whole Pope/Heather thing, and especially that rat Joey Styles, I just figured I would send you the messages, to try and keep you off track."

John was even more pissed off now. "You're telling me that you knew everything??? You are more of an asshole than anyone ever gave you credit for. Man! So why didn't you fire me when you had the chance then?" John began circling around Patrick's chair, much like a vulture stalking its prey before the kill.

"I wanted to see how far you would go with everything. For a security guy, you sure did email a lot of your personal life stuff to Vicky and others, even with the use of encryption. Hushmail, and other email encryption schemes, are great to protect the information between point A and point B, but nothing will protect you if you have a keystroke logger on your computer. I guess I kind of outsmarted you with that one," Patrick explained, knowing full well that this was the only thing he could be proud of at this moment, if anything.

"I guess I should have run a scan on my PC. Usually Norton detects them though. Shit." John felt a little stupid for not noticing.

"This one is undetectable. But that's not the point. I guess you probably want to know what I have to do with Harlan and Pope."

John couldn't wait to hear this. This is what has been bothering him the whole time. "I'd love to know. That's what I'm here for. It's the only piece of the puzzle that I'm missing."

Patrick realized that he was in serious trouble and that playing the sympathy card was his last resort. "I wanted Pope dead. I won't deny that. The guy is scum, pure and simple. Do you want to know what the little fucker did? He basically date-raped my daughter. She was at a party out in LA at some big-shot producer's house. Susie, my daughter, is friends with the producer's son. Anyway, Pope was there, he picked her up, and according to her, had his way with her. Pushed himself on her and did things to her that no guy should be able to do to a girl who was only sixteen. Sixteen! The guy is dirt. I needed revenge. She is still emotionally scarred from the whole thing."

John noticed tears forming in Patrick's eyes. He couldn't determine whether they were from true emotion or whether it was all an act. He decided he'd play sympathetic and try to bring out more. "I'm sorry about that. I really am. Nobody deserves to go through that. But still, I gotta know, what gives you the right to play God and decide that the guy should die for it?"

"Nothing. It's natural instinct. What else can I say? I thought it would help me, and help my daughter psychologically if her attacker was no longer in the public eye all the time. And you weren't helping by feeding Joey all that dirt on the guy. It was pissing me off, that's why I started to send those messages."

"You really are one screwed up guy. And now you are literally screwed. I could have you in jail for a long time. You know that, right?"

Patrick bowed his head in defeat. "Uh huh. All I can ask for is your understanding. I was doing it for my daughter. I just wanted her to get better. I thought it would help. I love her so much, John. You don't understand. I'd do anything for her. *Anything.*"

Actually, John did understand. All he could think about right now was Vicky and Jennifer, and the special bond that existed between them. He didn't have kids, and may or may not ever have them. But, one thing he realized was that there were few things more special than the bond between a parent and their child.

For the first time since meeting him, John all of a sudden felt sorry for Patrick. Did his daughter deserve to have a father in jail for the rest of his life, regardless of what an asshole he was? Maybe Patrick was a different guy at home; maybe he was a really good father. John had to make a decision, and he hoped the one he was about to make was the right one. "Alright, Patrick. Here's what's going down: first and foremost, remember that I have this tape with all the evidence to put you away. There are copies, so don't even think about getting Harlan and his cronies after me. *Assuming* I can prevent Pope from getting into his car after the movie premiere, I'm going to let you off the hook and not go to the authorities. But, you're going to resign from DesertFinancial and never come back. Ever. I don't want to see you again. You can come up with any reason you want for leaving, I don't really care. Then you're going to make Dan your immediate successor. He deserves it, and you've never really given him the respect he deserves. You will apologize to Jill for treating her like crap for so many years. And finally, you'll cut your hair and get rid of that stupid fucking ponytail. It's so passé."

Patrick was slightly relieved, but he knew his life was always going to be resting in the hands of this guy that he hired, which he grossly underestimated. Nonetheless, he had to admit he had a new appreciation for John Davis. "I have no choice, do I? When am I supposed to resign?"

"As soon as possible. If you need a day or two, go ahead. This all hinges on my being able to prevent Pope from starting his car, of course. Oh yeah, and tell your buddy Harlan all about the tape. I'll be watching out for him too. Anything smart on his part will put him away as well. I'm fucking serious too. Are we clear?" John said, putting the finishing touch on this meeting that, if he did say so himself, went pretty damn well.

"We're clear. Now leave me to wind things up. Good luck with helping Pope. I don't know how you're going to do it. Harlan's connections are unlikely to budge once the word has been given."

"Nice knowing ya, Patrick. I'll always be watching you." John couldn't help making the gesture with the two fingers pointing to his eyes, and then pointing them at Patrick, just like Robert DeNiro's character in *Meet the Parents*.

John gave the thumbs up sign to Tara and headed to his desk with a huge smile on his face.

"What's with the ear to ear, man?" Ray asked as John entered the security area.

"Patrick's done, dude. Things around here are gonna be much better from today on, I'll tell ya that much," John said, still unable to wipe the smile from his face. "But I have more pressing issues to deal with right now. I need your help getting into the big premiere tonight in Hollywood."

*   *   *   *

John and Tara left around noon to beat the traffic to LA. John had spent the last hour with Ray in the operations room duplicating a media pass to Pope's premiere screening tonight at Grauman's. Ray's friend was attending, and was gracious enough to scan a copy of his pass and email it to them. John and Ray took advantage of the company's excellent scanning and printing equipment and created two very reasonable facsimiles that may just permit them entry to the movie event.

"So tell me why we're going to save a date-rapist again?" Tara asked, as they were just passing the Ontario exits on I-10.

"Hey, I'm no big fan of the guy. But I couldn't live with myself if we didn't at least try to stop this. Murder is murder. Can you imagine all of the bedlam that would ensue if this thing goes off? We've come this far, we may as well try to do prevent it." John was still ecstatic over how well his conversation with Patrick went over. Adrenaline was flowing through his veins non-stop.

Tara was fumbling with the adjustable seat controls with one hand and biting the fingernails on the other. "So who's to say we even make it in with those passes you guys created? What if we come all the way here for nothing? I'm kinda freakin' here, dude."

"Don't worry. This will all work out. The power of positive thinking is awesome," John said in a relaxed tone, which surprised him since he was so very far from being relaxed.

✳   ✳   ✳   ✳

The media passes John and Ray created worked like a charm. John and Tara were in. They hung out and rubbed elbows with other media types before the movie started. As soon as Pope arrived John's heart skipped a few beats as he realized that Pope had an entourage, and that getting to him was going to be much more difficult than he had planned.

The movie, much to John's surprise, was fantastic. Pope wasn't exactly a great actor, but he definitely had that screen presence that you just couldn't learn with even years of training. John knew that the film would do huge box office numbers when it opened wide next week.

The beautiful people were gathered outside discussing the movie, with the largest throng of people surrounding Pope. *This was going to be tricky.*

John had to think fast. He grabbed Tara and dragged her in the vicinity of the swarm of people surrounding Pope. He yelled at the top of his lungs: "Pope Harris! My sister is pregnant with your child. I need to speak with you *now.*"

Everyone turned around simultaneously and looked at him as if he were insane. Tara caught on and did a great job of looking incredibly pissed off, as if she had been the one wronged by Pope. One of Pope's bodyguards approached and looked at them menacingly.

"The fuck are you talkin' about, man? Pope doesn't want to talk to you. He did nothing of the sort. Now leave him the fuck alone," the big bad bodyguard said, turning away from them.

Tara took over. "Look, Pope and I go back a long time. Can you give us two minutes with him? Please?" She flashed him her sad puppy dog look, which somehow erased the scowl on the bodyguard's face and made him think.

"Two minutes. I promise," John confirmed.

Reluctantly, the bodyguard agreed and ushered them toward Pope. He and his equally muscular bodyguard friend moved the crowd away from Pope and left John and Tara alone with the big star of the night, right in front of John Travolta's star on the *Walk of Fame*.

"I didn't knock you up," Pope said, looking at Tara. "I've never even seen you in my life."

"I know. You didn't," John said. "We're actually here to help you, but we didn't want to cause a scene."

"I don't need your help. My life couldn't be any better. So if you guys don't mind, now that I know that you're liars, leave me be." Pope started walking away.

John grabbed him by the arm. "Look, Pope, your life is in danger," he said, as Pope turned around to face them again. "Your car is going to blow up, mafia style."

"Say what? Who the fuck would want to do that to me?" Pope actually looked concerned now. He waved the bodyguard away who was likely approaching them to give them their *two minutes are up* speech.

"Patrick Bowman and Harlan Daley is who."

"I know Harlan, but who the fuck is Patrick Bowman? And why would either of them want to see me dead? Harlan *loves* me, man. This makes no sense. Can you please explain?" Both bodyguards were busy fending off the media who were making their last-ditch attempts to get more camera time with Pope before the night was over. The flashing of the cameras kept up, everyone wanting to capture the moment when Pope Harris was to become Hollywood's biggest star.

John and Tara explained everything. Pope listened intently and although he was skeptical at first, eventually accepted the fact that these two were for real. He even invited them over to his bachelor pad off Laurel Canyon. They rode in John's MDX.

*   *   *   *

He thanked them over and over for saving his life. John and Tara were still in shock that they were at the home of Pope Harris, the biggest star in Hollywood, speaking with him as if they were longtime friends. They enjoyed Pope's company.

Pope's Bentley was towed away and had been confirmed to being wired with an explosive device. This news, while nothing new to either of them, sent a collective chill through all three of them as they sipped on their Patron Resposado.

After an hour of chatting, Tara asked the question that had been on her mind ever since they discovered Patrick and Harlan's scheme. "So I gotta ask, man. What ever happened between you and Patrick's daughter? You're a nice guy and all, and I'm enjoying our time with you, but I have a serious problem with you having date-raped someone."

"Wow. You have balls, Tara," Pope said. "It wasn't date rape. We were at a Hollywood producer's party on Mulholland, and it was incredibly boring. She was staring at me all night, and I knew I could have her. I know, that doesn't sound good, but honestly, I *swear* to you, I have *never* forced myself on a woman. Plus, she told me she was twenty. I know that sounds so cliché, but it's true. And I may not be the cleanest guy around, but one thing I'm *not* is a date-rapist." Pope poured them another shot of Patron, and downed his quickly before going on. "As soon as we were done, she told me that now we had done the deed so to speak, she wanted to start seeing me, like exclusively, right? I told her we could see each other casually, but that would be it. She stormed off back to the party. I had just finished my first movie; not a lot of people knew who I was yet. She got my number from one of the movie's producers and kept calling me. We went out once or twice, and again had some wicked sex, but all of it was consensual. I found out how old she was and stopped it right away. I also didn't want to be tied down. When I let her go, I think she started the date-rape story. Rumors were flying that I was a date-rapist, but those paled in comparison to all the other rumors floating around about me. You should know about that, hey John?"

Ouch. John had explained about Joey and the emails earlier. John stood up and walked towards the window and admired the gorgeous view of the city that he used to fantasize about when playing poker. He told himself he would eventually win enough cash to buy his own bachelor pad, not unlike this one. His bare feet loved brushing against the ultra plush carpeting that must have cost Pope a fortune to put in. "Again, I'm sorry about selling the emails. I regret it. Never again. I don't even know if I could go back to work there. Even though Patrick is gone now, I think I've lost the desire to keep spying on people."

"There sure isn't any privacy left in the world," Pope said.

"It's just going to get worse for you," Tara added. "You're about to be the biggest box office star ever. Your privacy as you knew it is pretty much out the window. What are you going to do?"

"I think I know what I want to do first," Pope began.

EPILOGUE — SIX MONTHS LATER

▼

John and Tara were sitting by the pool, enjoying the sunshine and the beautiful November weather. John was reading the latest issue of *GQ,* and Tara the latest *Vanity Fair.*

Tara leaned over and kissed John. "Hey babe, will you go in and fetch my sunglasses from our room? I thought I'd be able to do without them but this sun is really getting to me."

"Sure, as long as you make it up to me later. Maybe after we get home from the big party you'll give me the Tara special?" John asked eagerly.

"You got it, boy."

Just as John was about to go fetch her sunglasses from their room, he noticed Pope pull up in his new Ferrari.

"Hey man, what are you doing here?" John asked Pope as he sat down beside Tara.

"What, I'm not allowed to visit my favorite manager slash agent and his fiancée?" Pope asked, smiling his winning smile. "I love spending time with you guys. I've said it before and I'll say it again, I owe you guys for turning my life around. If it weren't for you, I would be dead. I still can't believe you guys snuck into the premiere like you did that night. Man, I think about it all the time."

Pope had been doing his best to become a better person ever since that night John and Tara scammed their way into the big movie premiere.

After their evening together that night, Pope realized that John was probably the best people-manipulator he had ever met and asked John to represent him.

John resisted at first, not wanting to have anything to do with a guy who still abused alcohol and drugs.

Pope persisted, continuously insisting that he was a changed man. Realizing that he *was* in fact a great judge of character, John trusted that Pope was serious in wanting to change his ways. And who was John to judge, himself being a recovering addict of another sort? John hadn't gambled in almost three years. He was proud of himself.

John was sick of essentially being Big Brother at DesertFinancial, and had had enough of meddling in people's private lives. There was less and less privacy in the world these days, and John no longer wanted to contribute to that.

John reluctantly accepted Pope's proposal and accepted the position of manager/agent. It was a pretty easy life, and as long as Pope maintained his promise to be a good person and leave his past behind, John would have no problem being the *E* to Pope's *Vinnie Chase*, a la *Entourage*. This was his true dream job.

The first few months following John and Tara's official announcement as a couple were difficult for Vicky, but eventually she came around. Initially, John, Tara, Vicky and Jennifer would actually get together for dinner. It became too much for Vicky, who didn't mind John moving on to someone else but at the same time didn't want to have to witness it right in front of her face. The dinners stopped, but John and Vicky still talk occasionally. There would always be a special part of John's heart for Vicky, and Tara understood.

A month into John and Tara's relationship, something clicked deep within him that conveyed to John that Tara was *the one*, and it was time to embrace true monogamy.

Jennifer is no longer with her boyfriend and is enjoying the single life attending College of the Desert. She and John still chat online, and John does his best to continue his role as a positive male influence in her life. To this day, Pope has been nothing but a gentleman on the few occasions he has met Jen. John told them he'd stop talking to both of them if they ever dated.

Ray and Aaron are still happily married to their wives.

"Ahhh, this is the life, man," Tara said, reaching out to grab John's hand.

"*Ah Mechaiah!*" John shouted out.

"What does that mean?" Pope asked.

"My grandfather used to say it all the time here. It's Yiddish for *this is the life!* Couldn't be more fitting for us right now."

"Right you are," Tara said, repeating another phrase that John's grandfather used often.

The three of them lay there, soaking up the desert sun, fully content and looking forward to living their newly formed lives together.

THE END

978-0-595-46166-
0-595-46166-2

Printed in the United States
95984LV00003B/304-375/A